The Grey Gates - Book 3

Hunted

VANESSA NELSON

HUNTED

The Grey Gates - Book 3

Vanessa Nelson

Copyright © 2023 Vanessa Nelson

All rights reserved. This is a work of fiction.

All characters and events in this publication are fictitious and any resemblance to any real person, living or dead, is purely coincidental.

Reproduction in whole or in part of this publication without express written consent is strictly prohibited.

For more information about Vanessa Nelson and her books, please visit: www.taellaneth.com

For all my fellow caffeine addicts - tea and coffee have got me through more days than I can count.

Here's to many more perfect brews.

Contents

1. CHAPTER ONE — 1
2. CHAPTER TWO — 10
3. CHAPTER THREE — 25
4. CHAPTER FOUR — 29
5. CHAPTER FIVE — 33
6. CHAPTER SIX — 46
7. CHAPTER SEVEN — 60
8. CHAPTER EIGHT — 69
9. CHAPTER NINE — 79
10. CHAPTER TEN — 85
11. CHAPTER ELEVEN — 93
12. CHAPTER TWELVE — 103
13. CHAPTER THIRTEEN — 108
14. CHAPTER FOURTEEN — 119
15. CHAPTER FIFTEEN — 126
16. CHAPTER SIXTEEN — 136
17. CHAPTER SEVENTEEN — 146
18. CHAPTER EIGHTEEN — 153
19. CHAPTER NINETEEN — 159

20.	CHAPTER TWENTY	175
21.	CHAPTER TWENTY-ONE	182
22.	CHAPTER TWENTY-TWO	191
23.	CHAPTER TWENTY-THREE	198
24.	CHAPTER TWENTY-FOUR	212
25.	CHAPTER TWENTY-FIVE	217
	THANK YOU	224
	CHARACTER LIST	225
	ALSO BY THE AUTHOR	228
	ABOUT THE AUTHOR	230

Chapter One

Max saw a pair of startled faces staring out of the apartment window at her. A middle-aged couple, the man holding a mug halfway to his mouth, both of them frozen in surprise at the sight of a Robinsage monkey with a woman hanging on to its back going past outside their upper-level kitchen window. The couple was left behind a moment later, replaced by another window as the monkey continued to climb up the old building. Max could only hope that none of the people she was passing had a camera handy. It was all too easy to imagine the headlines. *Marshal carried up building by giant monkey.* She had had more than enough media exposure to last her a lifetime.

Max wrapped her arms more tightly around the creature's slender torso. The monkey was moving without hesitation, using the gaps and texture of the stones for grip. Her eyes watered from the chill air and the stench of the sandy-brown fur pressed against her face. The stink was almost physical, as though the creature spent its life rolling in the worst-smelling substances it could find and never bathing. Not once.

This had not been her best idea. In fact, it was probably one of the worst ideas she'd ever had, a moment of impulse rather than rational thought. She'd arrived at the address barely half an hour before to find a scene of absolute chaos. The monkey had injured several of the building residents who had been trying to keep it contained. The monkey had been trying to fight its way out into the open. She'd emptied a full magazine of tranquilliser rounds into the creature. The drugs hadn't even slowed the monkey down. She hadn't wanted to risk it getting into one of the apartments in the building or, worse, running through the city. So she'd called for back-up and had hoped that wrapping herself around the creature would keep it on the ground where her dogs could get to it and keep it pinned until the other Marshals arrived. Instead, it had taken off up the side of the building and now she was just hoping that it didn't fall off and take her with it plummeting the three - no, four - storeys to the ground. The surface far below was made of decorative stone slabs. At best, a fall would really hurt. And she didn't want to think about the worst case scenario.

The creature turned its head, baring a pair of long, yellowing fangs at her. The fangs were almost as long as her fingers. Its yellow-green eyes with their vertical black pupils stared at her for a long, heart-stopping moment, as if the creature was wondering what she might taste like. Fortunately, it didn't take a bite out of her, turning away, so she was left staring at the ragged, matted fur on the back of its head again. She couldn't remember ever being this close to one of the Robinsage monkeys before, and it was not an experience she wanted to repeat. They were slightly smaller and far more slender than Seacast monkeys, but, as she was finding out, just as strong. The torso she was clinging to was wiry with muscle. She was tall for a human, weighted down by her equipment, and the monkey was carrying her with no apparent effort.

They had stopped climbing, she realised. They were on the flat roof of the building, the monkey still moving despite the tranquilliser rounds and her extra weight.

It stopped and she risked a glance up, past its shoulder, breathing a sigh of relief as she saw her dogs there, then almost choking as she got an extra-large dose of the creature's stench. Cas and Pol had spread out to block the forward path of the monkey. They had shifted into their attack forms, a mass of long-haired shadows in the sunlight, their fangs descended along with sharp, elongated claws that made no sound on the matte roof material as they stalked forward.

The monkey chattered at her dogs in a series of high-pitched noises that grated on her ears.

Cas barked back, the sound deep and full from his great chest, teeth bared. Pol crept forward another two paces, body lowered, prepared to attack.

Max watched her dogs. They would not want to hurt her, but they were ready to jump onto the monkey and hold it for her. They had never done this before, as she had never been stupid enough to jump onto one of the creatures they were hunting until now, but she had an idea that if she let go, her dogs would pounce.

"Ready?" she asked her dogs, throat constricted from the foul air she was breathing.

The dogs' response was to crouch lower to the ground. They were ready.

Max let go, falling onto the roof surface with a thump rather than the more graceful tuck-and-roll that she had intended, scrambling back to her feet and grabbing for her gun even as her dogs surged forward, grabbing a hairy arm each and pulling the monkey down. Her dogs growled, a savage and unhappy sound, as they took hold of the monkey. Her mouth and nose were still full of the awful stench of the creature and she imagined that it tasted worse than it smelled.

Max kept her gun pointed at the monkey but didn't fire. She just had normal bullets, and even though the creature had caused plenty of injuries in trying to make its escape from the building, she still wanted to catch it rather than kill it.

Rapid footsteps sounded from behind her dogs and she looked up to find a quartet of Marshals arriving on the roof, all of them with shotguns ready. The lead Marshal halted a few paces from her dogs, staring at the scrawny, smelly form of the Robinsage monkey, then looking up at Max.

"Did you really hang on to that creature all the way up the side of the building?" Vanko asked. Ever the comedian, he was wearing a grin even as he held his shotgun level on the monkey. A compact man made of muscle and humour, his tousled blond hair stirred in the breeze.

"I did," Max confirmed, grimacing. She could taste the smell of the monkey's fur in her mouth. "I don't recommend it, but I put a full magazine of tranquillisers into it, and it didn't even blink."

"A full mag?" Vanko asked, brows lifting. "Was it the normal stuff?"

"Yes," Max confirmed. The Marshals' science team supplied Marshals with a variety of equipment for the field. The tranquilliser rounds took down most things. Apart from, it seemed, Robinsage monkeys.

"I've got some of the heavy stuff," Vanko said, lowering his shotgun and switching out the magazine for a spare he had carried next to his own thigh holster. There was a far more formal and technical name for the powerful tranquilliser that the Marshals' science team had just released for use, but all the Marshals just called it the heavy stuff. Max thought that the term might have started with Vanko.

Max moved out of his line of fire. She trusted Vanko's aim, but the monkey was struggling against her dogs' hold and it might escape. She didn't want to find out what a dose of the more powerful tranquilliser could do to her human body.

Vanko fired into the monkey, the bang of the shotgun loud in Max's ears. He paused, watching the creature, then fired again when it kept struggling.

After the second round, its struggles grew weaker and it gradually went limp under Cas and Pol's grip.

Max called her dogs back when it looked like the monkey was unconscious and held her own gun ready as Vanko took a step forward and nudged the creature with his foot. When the monkey simply lay there, its breathing slow and even, he nodded. His nose wrinkled.

"Lady above us, what is that stench?" he asked.

"The monkey," Max said. "I didn't know anything living could smell so bad," she added, reaching into one of her pockets for a cleaning spell. Her eyes were still stinging from the stink. Cas and Pol were making faces as they worked their mouths, confirming her guess that the monkey tasted as bad as it smelled. When she had doused herself with a spell, she threw a couple of pieces of dehydrated chicken to her dogs. The tough chews should clean their mouths, at least. They snatched the treats out of the air and retreated, lying down on the roof surface to eat, taking far more care to chew the food than they normally would.

"Raymund is on his way," Vanko reported. His nose wrinkled again. "Holy light, that smell just gets worse."

"I didn't get a chance to clear the building or check for its nest," Max said reluctantly.

"Nest?" Vanko asked, sharp gaze landing on her.

"There were reports of something living in the building basement. Some of the residents went down to investigate," Max said, nose wrinkling. They should just have called for the Marshals, but they had tried to take care of the creature themselves. "There are about half a dozen people injured. This thing attacked me before I got far," Max added. She had also dropped her shotgun on the ground four storeys below, when she had leapt onto the back of the monkey, not wanting to let it get away. She just hoped that none of the building's residents had picked the weapon up.

"Alright," Vanko said. "Osip, Sofiya, wait here for Raymund and his team." The named Marshals, a pair Max didn't know all that well, nodded in response. "Zoya, you're with me and Max and her dogs. Let's clear the basement."

"I brought your shotgun," Zoya said to Max, holding the weapon out.

"Thank you," Max said, taking it from Zoya, heat rising under her collar. Although she was relieved that the weapon hadn't been stolen, one of the first lessons Marshals learned was to keep hold of their weapons, and she had voluntarily thrown hers down to grab hold of the monkey. She could only imagine what Faddei - her boss - would have to say about that. "I just have ordinary rounds, though, so it's probably more useful as a club."

Zoya grinned. Her head barely reached Max's shoulder, but she was made of muscle, her pink-tinted hair in a thick braid over one shoulder, complementing her warm-toned brown skin. She handed Max a full magazine with a blue stripe down the side. "More of the heavy stuff," the other woman said, and changed out her own magazine while Max did the same.

When they were armed, Vanko waved for Max to go ahead.

Going down the stairs under her own power was a much better experience than being carried up the side of the building on the back of a monkey, Max decided, even if her legs were protesting the effort by the time they had descended four flights and were at the door leading to the basement. It had been weeks since her leg had been torn open by another supernatural creature, and although she was now fully healed, she still hadn't recovered the fitness she had lost. But at least she could move without pain. That was something. She glanced over her shoulder to check that Vanko and Zoya were ready. She need not have worried. They had their pen torches clipped onto their weapons already, waiting for her to open the door.

As Max swung the door back, she recoiled at the smell that rolled up the stairs to meet them. It was pitch dark down below. When she had gone down the stairs the first time, there had been a light switch at the bottom and the lights had been working. She relayed that information to the others.

Zoya cursed, wiping her streaming eyes on the sleeve of her jacket. "We do not get paid enough to deal with this," she said.

Max silently agreed, but they all went into the basement anyway, Cas and Pol with them. It was part of the Marshals' job to go into places most people would run away from. The dogs' ears were flat to their heads, their bodies hunched over as if the smell was painful to them. Max wished she could spare them the experience, but the Marshals needed all the help they could get as she didn't know what was waiting for them. Vanko took the lead down the stairs, the bright light of his torch showing nothing out of the ordinary for the first few paces. He found the light switch Max had referred to and flipped it.

Dull yellow light flooded the space. They had arrived in what looked like a storage room, with a series of lockers against one wall, and an open door at the other side from the stairs.

"I was told that door leads to the boiler and pipes room," Max said. "It's the only other open space in the basement. There's another light just outside the door."

Vanko nodded and headed for the door, flipping the switch and heading on into the boiler room, Cas and Pol moving with him.

The stench grew worse as they moved further into the boiler room. Even with the lights above, it was still a shadowed and dark space, and hot from the boiler and pipes. The building apparently used underfloor heating supplied by water pipes that ran through every level. The boiler also supplied the hot water to the building. Max was sweating under her jacket and could only imagine how unbearable the room got in the height of summer.

As they made their way past a tangle of pipes, she caught sight of a haphazard looking structure against the wall. Vanko and Zoya had seen it, too, the three of them turning as one, Cas and Pol going ahead again.

Robinsage monkeys were generally peaceful, despite the smell, but they liked to nest and birth their young in warm, dark spaces. Like boiler rooms.

As they approached the bundle of what looked like sticks and bits of cloth and cardboard, a flicker of movement caught Max's attention. She turned, shotgun ready, in time to see another monkey drop down from the ceiling, its teeth bared, chattering loudly at her. She fired one round into its chest, the report of the gun loud in the confined space. The monkey dropped to the floor, Cas and Pol swarming over it, checking that it was truly asleep and not faking it.

"It's a nest alright," Zoya said from behind Max, her voice pitched loud after the shot. "There are at least two babies in there."

Vanko sighed and shook his head. "Looks like Raymund will have his work cut out for him. They just work in pairs, don't they?"

"That's what Raymund told us, yes," Max said. Unlike other types of monkeys, Robinsage tended to be solitary unless they were in a mated pair. So they shouldn't find any more monkeys in the basement. Despite that, she also knew that they would all want to thoroughly check every floor just to be sure.

By the time they had cleared the building, making their way up and then back down the flights of stairs, Raymund and his team had arrived. The scientists were all clad in white coveralls with face shields, the outfits similar to the ones used by the police's crime scene techs. Raymund Robart was a tall, thin, intense man whose scientific expertise was almost matched by his lack of social skills. No one complained. He was essential to the Marshals' service, and occasionally even remembered to say thank you. He focused on his work while the scientists around him loudly protested the smell. Max couldn't blame them. Despite the complaints, Raymund and his team were professional and efficient in gathering up the two adult monkeys and transporting them to the truck waiting outside, and also gathering up the two babies that Zoya had spotted. With the animals secure, the team dismantled the nest, making sure there were no other young there and no other unwelcome surprises for the building's residents. The building's owner would need to hire a cleaning company to get rid of the lingering odours, and Max didn't envy the cleaning crew their task.

Cas and Pol made the most of the respite by heading to the ornamental water fountain outside the building and taking long drinks, shaking their heads as if still trying to get rid of the taste and smell of the monkeys. The fountain wasn't big enough for her dogs to use as a bath, otherwise she thought they would have tried to get in. Max caught a few faces at the building windows looking down at the courtyard and her giant dogs using the water feature as a drinking bowl. She thought there were a few frowns, but as she and her dogs had helped rid the building of its unwanted guests, she didn't call her dogs back. They had earned their drink, and the water would be pumped from the city's supply, not some private source paid for by the building.

She found time to use another cleaning spell - just in case - and grab a snack from her pick-up while the scientists were loading the monkeys into their vehicle. There probably wasn't anything else for her and the other Marshals to do, but they stayed anyway. Raymund was concerned that the monkeys hadn't responded at all to the normal tranquilliser and wanted to make sure that the creatures didn't escape. To her surprise, he seemed to think that Max's leap onto the back of the first monkey had been entirely appropriate, making sure that the creature didn't get free and end up roaming the city.

Just as she was thinking she might need to go back to the Marshals' offices and write a report, her phone rang, saving her from the dull prospect of paperwork. She answered.

"Max, honey, can you stop by the mortuary at some point?" the warm voice at the end of the line asked. Audhilde. The city's chief medical examiner, and a vampire.

"Sure. I can be there in about half an hour, if that suits?" Max asked, brows lifting. She wasn't quite sure why Audhilde wanted a Marshal's presence - or Max specifically - but she trusted the vampire enough to know that she would have a good reason.

"See you then," Audhilde said, and cut the call before Max could ask for more information.

Max said her goodbyes to Vanko, Zoya and the other Marshals, and headed off in her pick-up, wondering just what it was that Audhilde wanted to see her about. For many years, Max's only encounters with Audhilde had been in a professional capacity when her work and a dead body intersected. Max had always liked the vampire. Despite her great age and power, Audhilde was full of warmth. Their relationship had shifted about two weeks earlier when the vampire had invited Max to afternoon tea and loaned her a few books on magic, opening up a new world of knowledge that Max had never known existed. Max still wasn't entirely sure why Audhilde was taking an interest in her welfare, but was grateful for the additional knowledge. It was unlikely Audhilde was asking Max to visit the mortuary to continue their discussions on magic, though, which left far less pleasant options for discussion. There was the girl that Max had failed to protect from the Huntsman clan, one of several killed by the clan. And then there was the horrific collection of human remains found in a building on the city's docks, victims of a powerful supernatural creature.

Apprehension slid over Max's skin. There had been a lot of deaths and violence recently, and she had an idea she was about to see at least one more body.

Chapter Two

Max found a parking spot on the street between two vehicles whose owners would doubtless recoil in horror if they found her battered pick-up next to their sleek, perfect cars. Max frowned as she looked at the rows of cars parked on either side of the street. It was a normal sight in the middle of the day in a business district. But the city had been short on fuel not so long ago, with protests in the city streets as the council enforced strict fuel rationing. She had wondered if the shortage might have been a good reminder to the city's residents of the need to conserve resources, but judging from the number of cars around, she had been wrong.

Despite the likely horror of the other vehicles' owners, the Marshals' identification in the window meant that her pick-up shouldn't get towed away, no matter how much the city's residents complained. But she also had additional protection for her vehicle in the form of the two giant hounds in the back.

Cas and Pol raised their heads as she got out of the vehicle, their soft ears lifting, although they didn't get up. They were back in their normal forms, looking for all the world like dark, short-coated giant dogs. There were no creatures in sight that they needed to deal with. They were snuggled together in a pile of blankets that Max had added to the vehicle in preparation for winter. The Marshals' mechanics had promised to add a cover for the back just as soon as they had a gap in their schedule. Max was not hopeful. Marshals, and their vehicles, got into all sorts of trouble which often involved hospital treatment for the Marshals and a visit to the mechanics' workshop for their vehicles. Something routine, like covering the back of her pick-up, was far down the mechanics' list.

She leant over the back and gave each of her dogs a pat, checking to make sure that they were warm enough. They might be shadow-hounds, fearsome predators and supposedly resistant to most weather, but her two had got used to a comfortable life with her and she didn't want them to be cold if it wasn't necessary. Satisfied that they would be comfortable as long as she was inside, and knowing that they would transform from sleepy hounds to fierce protectors if anyone tried to interfere with her pick-up, she headed towards the door of the bland-looking concrete-faced building that housed the city's mortuary.

The main entrance was about a half storey above the city street, the building having a generous basement layer to accommodate the examination rooms. Apparently, the city architects didn't like the idea of dead bodies being examined above ground.

The reception area had stone floors and pale grey walls, Max's footsteps echoing as she strode across the space to the enormous reception desk. She had often wondered if the various city buildings were engaged in some sort of competition to see which one could have the biggest, most intimidating front desk. This one took up almost the entire width of the available space and had a solitary, petite woman sitting behind it, her long hair held up by what looked like a pair of pencils shoved in at haphazard angles.

Max must have been expected because the receptionist glanced up and waved Max past the desk. "Audhilde is in the main examination room downstairs, Marshal," the woman said.

Max thanked her and headed past the desk, going through the door that would take her to the stairwell rather than waiting for the lift. She needed all the exercise she could get to build up her fitness again.

Her phone buzzed with an incoming text just as she reached the top of the stairs and she paused, feeling a stupid flutter in her stomach, wondering if it was Bryce finally getting in touch again. She had only exchanged a few words with the Order warrior when she had been an apprentice, but he seemed to be everywhere she went just now. And he had helped her survive against overwhelming odds in the Wild. They had arranged a date about ten days before, just after they had come back from the Wild, but he had cancelled a few hours before they were due to meet. No real explanation, just a brief text that something had come up and he would be in touch when things calmed down. Since then, she had been alternating between ignoring her phone and jumping at every incoming text, feeling like a silly girl. She had sent him a message back, but hadn't heard anything. It wasn't as if she *needed* a date, she reminded herself. She had a perfectly good life.

She looked at the screen and tried to ignore the disappointment she felt when she saw the notice from Faddei. A routine message to all Marshals, reminding them to return their empty magazines and other spent equipment for recycling. Apparently, if he didn't send the notice out from time to time, the rate of returns dropped off. Personally, Max thought that having Leonda or Raymund send the Marshals back out into the field to retrieve equipment was a far more effective tool. She had only been sent back into the field once, in her very early days as a Marshal, and the memory of hunting through the remains of dead animals to collect all of her spent ammunition ranked among her top five least favourite experiences in the Marshals' service. And, wherever it was possible, she had never forgotten to collect her ammunition since then. Faddei didn't expect or need a reply from her, so Max put her phone away and headed down the stairs.

The basement level was noticeably cooler, the air saturated with competing smells. There was the faint trace of decomposition, but it was almost drowned out by harsh chemical cleaners and a softer scent that Max suspected had been added to the air in order to make the place seem less clinical. It didn't work, as far as Max was concerned, but she was sure that it made a difference for the people who came here to identify their loved ones.

The mortuary's examination rooms were tucked away from easy public view along a corridor accessed by a heavy pair of double doors. The first room had a glass wall showing a large room capable of holding multiple examination tables, with lights and other equipment hung from the ceiling, all the surfaces made of hard-wearing materials that could be hosed down as needed.

The examination room held four tables, two of which were occupied. The body closest to Max was fully covered. At the other end of the room, another body was draped with a sheet up to his waist, his chest open, and a petite woman leaning over him. She was covered from head-to-toe in blue coveralls, a matching blue cap and a plastic face-shield, but Max had no difficulty in recognising Audhilde. There was an assistant standing a few paces behind Audhilde, dressed in similar clothing, with the addition of a medical-grade face mask over his nose and mouth.

Audhilde glanced up as Max came inside.

"There you are, honey. You might want to stay over there. This man died from some kind of poison and I'm not sure if it's airborne or not." Even delivering the stark warning, Audhilde's voice was full of warmth. Whatever the poison was, Audhilde would be breathing it in, but there were few things that could kill a vampire.

"Alright," Max said, staying beside the door. Her nose wrinkled slightly at the tang in the air. Rather than the normal overlay of chemical cleaners and decomposition, there was something heavier and tart in the air. "Rot and oranges?" Max asked.

"That's it," Audhilde said, straightening up. "I've been trying to place that scent. It's alright. It's not airborne, then. If it's orange blossom poison, it has to be ingested." She glanced over her shoulder at her assistant. "You can remove your mask, if you like."

The assistant nodded and took off his mask with evident relief, leaving a vivid red impression over the bridge of his nose. Max didn't blame him. She had worn a medical-grade mask once or twice before, searching through animal remains to make sure that there were no larvae, and had found the masks almost as unpleasant as the task at hand.

"That's a rare poison," Max commented, staying where she was at the door of the room.

"Expensive, and you need to know what you're looking for both to buy it and to identify it as the cause of death," Audhilde said. She covered the body with a sheet and nodded to her assistant. "Let's get another blood draw from him, and run the tests to confirm."

"Ma'am." The assistant headed for the equipment trolley at the side of the room.

"Any word on the Darsin victims?" Max asked, as Audhilde stripped off her gloves and put them into a medical waste bin. Audhilde had been patiently and painstakingly working on the remains of bodies that had recently been found at the city's disused docks. Victims of a powerful creature of dark magic with a horrific taste for human flesh. The last Max had heard, Audhilde had managed to identify four separate sets of remains, but hadn't yet put names or faces to the victims.

"Not yet. We've just had a forensic artist in to look at the skulls and we're hoping to be able to put together some sketches soon," Audhilde said. "It's most likely that the victims all came from the homeless population, and we don't have enough remains of any of them to match them to the missing persons that had been reported. Ruutti Passila is still working on it, though."

Max nodded, absorbing the information. She could only imagine how frustrating Audhilde and her team were finding it to not be able to give the dead people's families some answers. And if Ruutti was on the case, it might actually get solved. Max might find the detective irritating, particularly the way the woman could charm answers out of almost everyone she met, but even Max would not deny that Ruutti had a sharp mind and a ruthless determination.

"Thanks for coming, Max," Audhilde said, changing the subject. She moved across the floor. "It's this one I wanted you to see."

Max followed Audhilde's lead, moving to stand on the other side of the covered body.

"You remember the young woman that the Huntsman clan killed a couple of weeks ago?" Audhilde asked, glancing up at Max.

"Of course," Max said, renewed guilt twisting through her. She had been trying to protect the girl, but the Huntsman clan had killed her anyway. "Is this another victim?"

"Not quite," Audhilde said, and peeled back the cover from the body's head and shoulders.

There was another man lying on the mortuary table. He looked ancient, his face pale, skin drawn back against his bones. There was a faded, intricate tattoo on the right side of his neck and shoulder. The symbol of the Huntsman clan.

"Do you know him?" Audhilde asked.

"Should I?" Max asked, frowning. She moved slightly, to get a better look. The man had short, dark hair at odds with the age suggested by his paper-thin skin and prominent bones. Then her breath caught. "It looks a bit like Ivor Costen. He was one of the Huntsman clan who attacked me."

"It is Ivor Costen," Audhilde said. "Dental records and blood work confirm it."

Max's brows lifted. "But he was a young man. Younger than me, I think. How did he get to look so old?"

"I'm not sure. Not yet. I can't find a clear cause of death for this one," Audhilde said.

"Was magic involved?" Max asked. She didn't know of any spells or magic that would make a person age so quickly, but that didn't mean much. As she was learning, there was a lot about magic that she didn't know.

"One of the police department magicians was here and said he couldn't sense any residual magic on the body," Audhilde said, her normally warm manner cooling a little. "But then he didn't believe that this man was barely thirty years old in life."

"And not just that, but he wasn't entirely human," Max said, staring at the hollowed-out face. It was almost impossible to believe that this ancient-looking corpse had been Ivor Costen. The man had been surly and half-drunk when Max had last seen him, furious and bitter that his girlfriend had left him and taken their daughter with her. "I'll need to let Nati know," she said, the words out before she could check them. "Nati Ortis," she said, in response to Audhilde's raised eyebrows. "She was Ivor's girlfriend. She ran away with their daughter, Ynes. They're with Nati's parents now." A good memory rose. Alonso and Elicia had insisted Max join them for their evening meal about a week before. Their small house had been full of love and laughter, Ynes relaxed and happy, and Nati looking far less strained than she had when Max had seen her last, in the Wild. All that warmth and life was a sharp contrast to the bully Ivor Costen had been and the still, wrinkled corpse he now was.

"Ah," Audhilde nodded. "That's good. We notified the Huntsman clan, but they didn't give us details of any next of kin." She hesitated. "Any possibility that the ex-girlfriend could have done this?"

"No," Max said, not needing to think about it. "No one in the family has any magic. And if Nati had been capable of doing this to Ivor, I don't think she would have put up with him beating her."

"That's true." Audhilde blew out a breath, a frown gathering as she looked down at the body.

"Do you know when he died?" Max asked.

"It's really difficult to tell, as I don't know what's been done to him," Audhilde said, sounding frustrated. "In normal circumstances, I'd say a few days, but honestly, I can't be sure. He could have been killed moments before he was found."

"And how was he found?" Max asked, curious. She hadn't formed the impression that Ivor Costen had a close circle of family and friends. And he had been a member of the Huntsman clan. Like all of the Five Families, the clan tended to take care of their own business and be extremely resentful of what they called interference from the city. It was highly unlikely that any one of the Huntsman clan would have summoned the city's medical examiner to Ivor's corpse.

"Ruutti found him in his house," Audhilde said, an unexpected smile appearing. "Apparently she was following up the report of a Marshal being assaulted, and Ivor had missed his appointment for interview."

"Oh," Max said. She wasn't sure how to feel about that as she was the Marshal who had been assaulted by Ivor and other members of the clan, when Max had tried to come to the aid of a girl being chased by the Huntsmans. On the one hand, it was good to know that Ruutti had taken her information seriously. On the other hand, the assault had happened about two weeks ago, and Ruutti was only now getting around to doing follow up interviews, suggesting that the detective had not seen it as high priority. Of course, there were plenty of other crimes to keep the detective busy. Max shook her head. She hadn't actually expected Ruutti to follow up on the assault at all, so she supposed she owed the detective some credit for doing her job.

She looked back down at the body. "It's possible it's dark magic," Max suggested. "In which case-"

"I know," Audhilde said, before Max could finish the thought. "I've already sent a message."

"But you also asked for me?" Max asked, curious. If Audhilde was already consulting with the city's foremost expert on dark magic, she didn't also need a Marshal.

"I did. I wanted you to see this," Audhilde said, looking up. There was something in her face that made Max's stomach tighten. She had rarely seen the vampire look so serious. Then the doors behind Max opened and Audhilde's attention went past her. "Lord Kolbyr," Audhilde said, her voice distinctly cooler than it had been when she greeted Max. "It's an honour to host you."

"My dear Audhilde, you promised me a mystery. That was more than enough. But I also get the pleasure of the company of Marshal Max Ortis. My day is fortunate indeed."

Max was glad she had her back to the ancient, powerful vampire as she was sure her eyes rolled. She got control over her expression and turned to face the newcomer.

Lord Kolbyr was surrounded by the chill sensation of dark magic, his aura creeping out into the air around him, making him seem far larger than the slender, short man he was. He was wearing his dark hair in a carelessly ruffled style that Max was sure would have taken an age to achieve, and dressed in a beautifully tailored dark suit, a blood red rose at his lapel. The rose caught Max's attention. He had sent similar roses to her during her hospital stay a few weeks before, after she had been attacked by a Strump. She had left the flowers in the hospital for the nurses to enjoy, not wanting anything from the vampire in her own home.

She had last seen him in the Wild, wearing another handmade suit that had been peppered with bullets. He had carried himself with the same dignity. He inclined his head to her, which surprised her as it seemed a mark of respect, and she had the impression that Kolbyr did not respect many people.

"Will you take a look?" Audhilde asked, taking a step away from the body. Max copied the other woman, not wanting to be too close to Kolbyr. She had been very close to him once before, when she had freed him from a magical collar that had been holding him captive, and once was more than enough as far as she was concerned. With him back to full health, the chill of dark magic around him was making her skin crawl.

Kolbyr stepped up to the head of the table without comment, looking down at the dead body. His expression went from politely interested to intensely focused as he stared, face tightening.

"Who is this?" he asked, a trace of power in his voice that made Max's fingers twitch, wanting to reach for her gun. She held herself still. Kolbyr had told her once that shooting him wouldn't do any good, and she had seen the evidence of that for herself in the Wild.

"Ivor Costen," Max answered, her voice surprisingly steady. "A member of the Huntsman clan. He was Nati Ortis' ex-boyfriend, and Ynes' father."

"Ah, yes. Charming girls, both of them," Kolbyr said, the words at odds with his tight, focused expression. He didn't look away from the body. "He's had the life force drained out of him," the vampire said, voice clipped. "It's a very old, very difficult ritual. I didn't think anyone else alive knew it."

Max's brows lifted. She wasn't sure if Kolbyr was aware that he had said that last part out loud until he looked up and met her eyes, his own eyes burning with what looked like rage. She managed to stay where she was, finding that, despite her earlier restraint, her hand was resting on her gun, ready to draw. She stayed still. He wasn't threatening her. Not yet.

"Dark magic, then," Audhilde said.

"Indeed," Kolbyr said, turning away from Max and looking at his fellow vampire. "You were right to call me, my dear Hilda," he said. The rage had faded and he was back to his normal, calm manner. Max didn't trust it and didn't relax. Vampires as old and powerful as both Kolbyr and Audhilde were very good at masking their feelings. It was one of the many things that had kept them alive for so long. And she didn't believe that the intense fury she had seen in his face had simply disappeared, faded into the air.

"I'm so glad," Audhilde murmured, a trace of her normal mischief in her face. Max had no idea what the underlying vampire hierarchy or politics were, but she had the notion that in this particular instance, Audhilde did not owe Kolbyr any particular loyalty or fealty.

"Who could have done this?" Max asked.

"An excellent question, my dear," Kolbyr said. "I didn't know anyone was capable of it. Apart from me, of course."

"Of course," Max murmured. "And you did not do this, clearly," she added.

Kolbyr glanced across at her, a hint of a smile on his face that was somehow more chilling than his earlier focus. "You understand me so very well, my dear," he said.

"You said it was old and complicated. Probably someone skilled in dark magic?" Max guessed. She wanted to know, but also wanted his attention on something else.

"Yes. May I?" Kolbyr asked Audhilde, gesturing to the sheet. Audhilde nodded and he carefully peeled the sheet back from Ivor Costen's shoulders down to his waist.

The dead man's skin had shrunk against his ribs, the bones prominent, his torso covered in black hair at startling odds with the thin, ancient skin.

Kolbyr opened his hand, holding it palm down above Ivor's torso, and murmured a word too quiet for Max to catch. Cold magic slid into the air, icy against her skin, and she forced herself to stay where she was, to not take a step back. As the magic spilled across the dead man's chest, she saw the faintest traces of symbols on his skin. She didn't recognise any of them, but it was clear that Kolbyr did.

"There," Kolbyr said, voice and face tight. "Someone wrote the ritual onto his skin. Probably in blood. I'll wager he had no obvious injuries?" he asked, turning to Audhilde.

"None," Audhilde confirmed. "I've been unable to determine a time or cause of death."

"He probably died a few days ago. It takes a little time for the ritual markings to fade. And I suspect he simply died of old age," Kolbyr said, turning back to the dead man. The markings were fading from view, along with the trace of his magic. "I don't recognise the magic-user here," he said, frustration clear in his voice.

"And you are familiar with all the dark magic users in the city?" Max asked. It was a genuine question. She suspected that Kolbyr kept a close eye on his competition.

Kolbyr's mouth twitched, unexpected humour lighting his eyes. "I thought I was."

"Even the Raghavan twins?" Max couldn't help the question. The joint heads of one of the Five Families, Shivangi and Hemang Raghavan, had managed to capture Kolbyr by taking him unaware, trapping him in a magic collar, and dragging him to the Wild to help them with a dark magic ritual. The vampire had not been pleased with the twins. Shivangi's ambition had led to an awful fate. Max could still hear the woman's screams as she was sucked into the underworld. Max had seen what lived there, and whatever Shivangi had done, she had not deserved that fate.

"I knew of their interest," Kolbyr said, inclining his head as if she had just scored a point in a game she hadn't been aware of playing. "But they had considerable help with their plans. They did not possess the necessary skill themselves."

"The other obvious candidate is the demon Queran," Max said. Queran had been involved with the Raghavan twins, and several others, in the dark magic ritual and its preparations. Unusually for the daylight world, Queran was a full demon. Max had no idea how long he had been walking in this world, or how he had escaped from the underworld, but he was here. And he seemed to have taken a special interest in her, for reasons that she didn't want to speculate about. Certainly not here, with Kolbyr so close.

"That would be my suspicion, yes."

"What are you talking about? A demon? The Raghavan twins?" Audhilde asked, eyes travelling between the two of them.

"My dear Audhilde, it seems you are behind on the news," Kolbyr said, a faint smile crossing his face. "I suggest that you invite Marshal Ortis for afternoon tea again and let her tell you all about it."

Audhilde stared back at Kolbyr, her natural warmth fading, the power and age she normally kept hidden sliding under her skin, closer to the surface than Max had ever seen it.

All at once, Max wanted very badly to be elsewhere. Somewhere far, far away. She was standing in a room with two ancient and powerful vampires and was all-too-aware of her fragile human nature. There was an undercurrent between the pair that had sharp, jagged edges that had not been dulled by their years of acquaintance, and she was right in the middle of whatever long and unpleasant history they had. Somewhere no sane person would want to be. Her heart rate had increased and she wished she had not left her dogs in the pick-up outside.

"I'm glad you noticed," Audhilde said.

"It was hard not to," Kolbyr answered. "But do you know what you have done?"

"Do you?" Audhilde challenged.

"This one is far more than she appears to be. She called down the Lady's light into the middle of a dark magic ritual," Kolbyr said. Max shivered as she remembered the event. She had been trapped, convinced she was going to be dragged into the underworld. Calling the light had been an act of desperation. But it had worked.

To Max's surprise, Audhilde grinned, the danger and power in the air fading. "That must have been unsettling for you, old man," the other woman said.

"It was unexpected," Kolbyr conceded, inclining his head.

The sense of danger had gone completely, and Max still wasn't entirely sure what had just happened. When Audhilde had invited Max for afternoon tea, the invitation had said it was because Max had done a service for one of Audhilde's household. That hadn't been the whole truth, as Max had discovered during her visit, when Audhilde had lent her three books on magic. The vampire had said that she thought Max was growing into her magic, and had wanted to help. And now it seemed that even that hadn't been the whole truth. There had been something else going on. Something that had nothing to do with Max herself but which was instead connected with vampire politics and power.

Another chill ran over Max's skin as she realised that, in the vampire world, Audhilde had placed some kind of claim on Max by inviting her into her household, and extending an open invitation for Max to join the household again at any time. Max had not felt threatened in any way during or after her visit, and Audhilde had never seriously tried to take any of Max's blood. Unlike Lord Kolbyr.

And yet, Max had the sense that by accepting Audhilde's hospitality, she had put herself, all unknowing, in the middle of some vampire power-struggle, and that was not a safe place for any human to be.

Kolbyr turned to her now, returned to his normal, calm and cool manner. "You did me a great service, Max Ortis. I will not soon forget it." He inclined his head.

With her mind turning on afternoon tea with Audhilde, and vampire politics, it took Max a moment to remember that she had freed Lord Kolbyr from the collar that Shivangi and Hemang had managed to place on him, and which he had not been able to take off on his own.

"It was the right thing to do," Max said, with perfect truth. Having the vampire believe he owed her something was better than him believing she owed him, but she would far rather not have any weight of obligation between them at all. "I had assumed that the demon Queran survived the collapse of the building. It's been over a week since we left him. Time enough for him to find his way back. So, you believe that the magic performed on Ivor Costen was his work?" she asked. It could be dangerous to ask vampires direct questions, particularly the old ones, but she had an instinct that Kolbyr wanted to share his knowledge. The demon had been involved in capturing Kolbyr, after all.

Talking about the demon reminded Max of the other people involved in the ritual. A pair of senior members of the Huntsman clan, who had been killed by the vampire. The Raghavan twins, only one of whom had survived the attempted ritual. And finally, most surprising of all, the city's chief of detectives. Seeing Evan Yarwood in that place, with that company, had been a shock. Even more of a shock when Max had realised that the seemingly human Evan could hold his own in a fight against not just a vampire but also a skilled warrior of the Order. Both Kolbyr and Bryce had both won their encounters with Evan, but it had not been easy.

Max looked back down at Ivor Costen's body and wondered if it was possible that Evan had somehow found his way back from the Wild and worked the ritual. It seemed unlikely, but so many things had been unlikely about the chief of detectives that she couldn't rule it out. She tried to hold in a sigh. Having told the full tale of what had happened to Faddei and Vanko, she had also then had to repeat the events, in excruciating detail, several times before the most senior law enforcement officials in the city and a few of the council members. They had openly disbelieved her, and she had no evidence to back up the story she told.

Bryce, or Lord Kolbyr, or the captives that the conspirators had gathered together as offerings for their ritual, could have confirmed the tale she told, but Kitris was refusing to let anyone have access to his warriors, and no one wanted to bring Lord Kolbyr in for questioning. Max wasn't sure if anyone had even approached the vampire to ask for his version of events. And no one had seemed interested in tracking down and questioning the homeless people who had been dragged unwillingly from their only shelter to be kept as potential sacrifices. So it had been left to her to repeat the tale, over and over until her voice was hoarse.

She had also been warned, more than once, not to discuss the events of the Wild with anyone, and to stick to the law enforcement's official tale that Evan was taking some overdue holiday. She wasn't sure how long the senior officers expected that flimsy story to hold up, but doubtless they were hoping that he would turn up soon and laugh off everything she had said.

The only three survivors of the conspiracy that she knew of were Queran, Evan and Hemang Raghavan. And somehow she didn't think that the surviving head of the Raghavan Family would have ventured into Huntsman territory to perform a dark magic ritual on Ivor Costen. Which left Queran or Evan. And of those, she had never seen Evan use any magic. So Queran seemed the most likely suspect.

"I can't think of any other being with the knowledge and skill to perform the ritual," Kolbyr said, breaking into her spiralling thoughts.

It was a more straightforward answer than Max had been expecting.

"A demon loose in the city," Audhilde muttered, her eyes on the ancient body between them. "That's not good news."

"Perhaps more than one," Kolbyr said, a trace of laughter in his voice.

"Are you trying to give me nightmares?" Audhilde asked, staring at the other vampire. "Or are you looking forward to the chaos if they decide to show themselves?"

"Chaos is interesting," Kolbyr said, a smile pulling his mouth. "No, I do not know how to find the demon Queran," he told Max.

The shift in tone and subject made her blink, but that had been the next most obvious question to ask. She nodded, accepting the answer. If the demon had performed the ritual on Ivor Costen, then he had crossed the line into open murder and it was not an issue for her to deal with, but something that the Order's Guardians should be interested in. The Marshals dealt with supernatural creatures threatening the city and its residents, but dark magic and its practitioners were in the jurisdiction of the Order of the Lady of Light.

"If you find any more bodies like this, do let me know, my dear," Kolbyr said to Audhilde.

"I will," Audhilde said. It had the ring of a binding promise to Max's ears, but one she sensed that Audhilde had no difficulty with. And it made sense. If someone was performing dark magic rituals and draining the life force from people, Kolbyr would be a valuable resource in trying to find the magician and stop him.

"It has been a delight to see you again, Marshal Max Ortis. And it's always a pleasure to be in your presence, my dear," Kolbyr said. If he had been wearing a hat, Max was sure he would have tipped it to them. As it was, he inclined his head and made his way out of the room, his departure as abrupt as his arrival, the powerful sense of his presence leaving the room feeling empty and far less dangerous.

Chapter Three

Only when Lord Kolbyr had passed through the double doors that led out of the mortuary suite did Max realise she'd been holding her breath. She took a deep breath in, careless of the chemicals and chill air, and eased her shoulders down from around her ears before turning to Audhilde.

"A demon?" Audhilde asked her, eyes very direct. "Are you in danger?"

"I'm a Marshal," Max said by way of answer. "And, yes, a demon. Queran. He seems to have taken an interest in me. I can't work out why," she said, trying for a light tone.

There was nothing light about Audhilde's expression as she stared back at Max. "You need to be really careful, Max. Demons are nasty pieces of work. Do you want to come and stay with me?"

"That's very kind of you," Max said, after a shocked pause, "but I'm happy where I am. He's had plenty of time to track me down, and hasn't done so."

The vampire didn't seem convinced, still wearing an abnormally serious expression. "The offer is open. Just let me know." She hesitated, then went on. "You seem to have settled into your magic a bit more."

The comment took Max by surprise, although it shouldn't have done. Max had suffered a series of displacement episodes after her release from hospital. She had been determined not to talk to anyone about them, but Audhilde had witnessed one and somehow connected it to a change in Max's magic. And the vampire had been right. Since Max had returned from the Wild, since she had been forced to use her magic to defend herself, there had been no more episodes.

"I think so," Max agreed. "I've read through the books you lent me. I'd like to read them again, if it's alright that I keep them a bit longer?"

"Of course. As long as you need. Was there anything in particular that stood out?" Audhilde asked. It wasn't an idle question. The vampire was looking at her with intense curiosity. Such a look from Kolbyr would have worried Max. But she liked Audhilde and even though she didn't fully understand why the vampire was trying to help her, she didn't believe Audhilde had any ill intent.

"Not really," Max said, frowning as she mentally reviewed the books she had read. "I just found it fascinating to learn about different ways magic can be used."

"I'm glad," Audhilde said. "And happy to lend you more reference material if that helps."

"I will take you up on that at some point, thank you," Max said, and meant it. She glanced down at the body. "What are you going to do about him?"

The other woman was covering Ivor Costen's body, a frown between her brows. "I'll make the call to the Order. Let them know about the ritual. And the demon. And won't mention you were here, honey," Audhilde said, in her normal, warm manner. "Hopefully, an actual death will get Kitris' attention."

"He's been ignoring you?" Max asked, startled. She had, of course, known that Kitris had refused to let the law enforcement heads and the council question any one of the Order warriors, but she had assumed that was just Kitris' power play and hadn't thought more of it.

"He's been ignoring everyone," Audhilde answered, lips pressed together for a moment. "At least, everyone outside the Order's walls. All I've been able to get from his gatekeepers is that he's very busy. I've no idea with what," Audhilde added, a snap in her normally warm voice. Max couldn't blame her. The very foundation and purpose of the Order was to contain dark magic, and the dark lord's influence and followers. It was not a good thing when the Order turned in on itself, leaving the population to fend for themselves.

"He seemed very concerned about the Darsin and dark magic on the docks," Max said slowly, remembering her recent encounter with the head of the Order.

"That's not the only thing going on," Audhilde said, then sighed, shaking her head. "A full demon is bad news."

"Kitris should already know about that," Max said. "We encountered Queran in the Wild, so the warriors that were with us will have reported back." She was quite proud of herself for not mentioning Bryce by name, even though his was the face that sprang to mind.

"Then I don't know what he's doing hiding away," Audhilde said, a frown gathered on her face. "There's too much going on for him to decide to shut himself off."

Max remembered one of the Order warriors commenting on Kitris' foul mood. It seemed that things hadn't improved. Still, she kept quiet, waiting, sensing that the vampire had more to say.

"Someone tried to get into my Vault," Audhilde said, the words flat and stark.

"What?" Max asked, shocked, feeling as if the world had shifted beneath her feet. The words wouldn't mean much to most people in the city, but anyone with magic knew about the legendary Vault. It had an almost mythical status as a repository for powerful magicians. Legend had it that every magical secret in the world was held there, although Max doubted that. Most powerful magicians had an individual Vault. It was an utterly secure place for them to store things. Max had been provided with one as an Order apprentice, although she rarely used it as it required a significant amount of her energy to gain access and close it behind her. But she knew that whatever she did manage to put into her Vault would be left undisturbed. There were a few sacred rules around Vaults, one of which was that they were personal to each magician. No one else should ever attempt to get into them.

"And I'm not the only one. There are rumours flying across the city, and I can only imagine that the Guardians have been affected, too," Audhilde said. She looked irritated.

"Did the thief get in?" Max asked.

"No," Audhilde said, a small, hard smile on her lips. "I'm old enough to have safeguards in place. But it was unsettling, to say the least."

"I can imagine," Max said, still feeling shaken. "How long ago was this?"

"The attempt on my Vault was last night. But from what I'm hearing, the magic around the Vault has been odd for the past week."

"Odd?" Max asked.

"That's the word that kept being used. As if there was something else at work. But it's only in the past day that other magicians have reported someone trying to get into their Vault."

"An escalation?" Max asked, frowning.

"Indeed."

"Do you know if anyone has had items taken?" Max asked.

"Not from what I've heard. But, then, it's not something people would admit to," Audhilde said, shaking her head. "The whole point of the Vault facility is secure and private storage."

"This is worrying," Max said, not sure what else to say.

"I've had my Vault for a long time. This has never happened before. I don't know what's going on, but it needs to stop," Audhilde said. "Perhaps I'll tell Kitris that, if he ever actually decides to speak to someone outside the Order."

Max agreed. Head spinning with speculation, she said goodbye to the medical examiner and headed out of the building, determined to look for answers.

Chapter Four

Night was gathering as Max left the building. She made her way down the steps of the mortuary building with more care than usual, as if the world might tilt under her feet. Her phone rang as she reached the bottom step. The number was unfamiliar. She answered with her customary, "Hello."

There was a short silence, then a male voice. "Is this Miscellandreax?"

It was Max's turn to pause. No one used that name for her. Not now. Not since she had been dismissed from the Order eight years before. "This is Marshal Max Ortis," she said, voice tight. "What do you want?"

Another short pause.

"Your presence is requested in the Lady's First House," the man said. "You will arrive no later than one hour from now. Her Most Gracious Lady will see you at her convenience."

Max froze where she stood. The Lady's First House meant the city's chief temple, perhaps the grandest building among the other grand buildings in the very heart of the city, and the Gracious Lady could only mean the High Priestess herself, who ruled over the entire network of temples and other buildings dedicated to the Lady of the Light. Not to mention the hundreds, if not thousands, of people who worked in the temples and their associated buildings. Which meant that Max was being summoned to an audience with the High Priestess.

"No," she said, her jaw unfreezing enough to get that one word out.

"Pardon me. I thought I heard something," the man said. Even through the telephone connection, she could hear the disbelief in his voice. "Do you need directions to the First House?" he asked in a bland, polite tone.

"No, I will not be attending," Max said, forcing each word out as clearly as she could manage.

"That is surely a joke," the man said, returning to disbelief. "Our Gracious Lady does possess a sense of humour, but she will not find this at all amusing."

"No joke," Max said. She dragged in a breath, knowing she sounded rattled, and not able to do anything about it. It had been an unsettling day so far. "The priestess will need to find something else to occupy her time. I have nothing more to say to her. Do not contact me again," she said, and hung up the call.

The phone rang again almost at once, with the same number, and Max had a momentary impulse to throw the phone away. If she threw it off the steps, it should break on the paving slabs that surrounded the basement of the building. That would satisfy her temper. Only the knowledge that she needed the phone for work stopped her. Instead, she fumbled with the settings, blocked the number and then tucked her phone away, heading for her pick-up. She said an absent-minded hello to Cas and Pol before settling in the driver's seat, caught up in memories.

Outwardly, Max was a tall woman dressed in a battered leather jacket and well-worn dark trousers with a bright, seven-pointed star telling everyone nearby that she was a Marshal. Inwardly, Max was a child again, summoned from her lessons at the orphanage to meet a tall, dark-haired, dark-eyed woman with pale skin and a forbidding expression. The High Priestess had simply been another Priestess at that point, carrying herself with a self-assurance and confidence that Max had envied.

"Do you know who I am?" the Priestess had asked.

"You are one of the Lady's servants," the younger Max had answered, earning a tiny smile from the lady.

"That is true. And the Lady has commanded me to take an interest in your welfare, Miscellandreax," the woman had said.

It had been months before Max had worked out that what that really meant was even more pressure on her to perform well in her studies. At that first meeting, she had just been awed that anyone in the priesthood would think her worthy of attention, let alone the Lady herself. She had not quite believed it. Not that she thought the Priestess had lied. Not then, anyway. The lying had come later.

Even as a child, Max had understood that the Lady's servants in the city were not some kind of other-worldly beings. They were people, and they came in the normal, full range of people. Most of the priests and priestesses passionately believed in their calling and the Lady's teachings, but many of those employed in less elevated positions, such as the teachers at the orphanages, regarded their work as simply a job. There were a few among them who enjoyed the power that wearing the Lady's robes or the Lady's symbol gave them, although they tended to not last very long, gently encouraged into other employment. And then there were a few people like Priestess Emmeline who had managed to combine an outward appearance of piety and devotion to the Lady with cold, ruthless ambition. Max had only met the Gracious Lady's predecessor once. The former High Priest had been a small, slender man stooped with age but with bright, fiercely intelligent eyes. Max had seen in him a kindred spirit to the priestess who had taken such a close interest in her, and had not been all that surprised when Emmeline had been named his successor.

Max had never understood why Emmeline had taken such a close interest in her. There had been a practice for a while of priests or priestesses taking some of the orphans under their wing, particularly those who seemed likely to remain in the Lady's service when they were too old to be housed in the orphanages. But Max was not one of those. There had been nothing remarkable about her as a pupil.

For some reason, the question that the demon Queran had flung at her crossed her mind, as it had done many times in the past week or so. *What are you?* She shook her head, as if she could rid herself of the question and the nagging uncertainty. It didn't work. One of the dark lord's demons casting doubt on what she was should have been an easy matter to shake off. Yet the question still lingered. It didn't help that she had no real information about her origins. All she knew was that she had been abandoned to the orphanage's care as a newborn, neither of her parents apparently wanting to raise her. She had always assumed she was purely human, with nothing remarkable about her. But with Queran's question ringing in her mind along with the reminder of the High Priestess's interest in her, she wondered again just who her parents were and where she had come from. And she had missed a chance to meet with the High Priestess and demand answers, she realised. Not that Emmeline was likely to have answered her questions. But Max could still have asked them.

A sharp bark from one of the dogs snapped her back to the here and now, breath catching in her throat. She was still sitting in her pick-up, the keys not even in the ignition yet. So she had not been in danger of hitting another vehicle or, worse, a person. But something had alerted her dogs.

She glanced in the side mirror and saw another vehicle waiting for her space, its indicator light flashing, the driver's door half-open. The driver - a human male - was carefully sliding back into the vehicle, eyes fixed on the back of Max's pick-up. She glanced through the window at the back of the cabin and saw both Cas and Pol on their feet, attention on the driver.

The driver had clearly intended to march up to her window and demand that she vacate the space. Max found herself smiling as she put the key in the ignition. He'd got a lot more than he bargained for with two shadow-hounds appearing.

"Good job, boys," she called to her dogs. "Lie down now," she added, putting the vehicle into gear.

Shaken by the call and the dredging up of old, unwanted memories, she realised she was too restless to stay in the city or stay still. She needed to move.

She pulled out into traffic, heading home to do something that she truly hated. She was going to go for a run.

Chapter Five

Cas and Pol had been delighted when Max had changed into running gear when she had got home. They thought her attempts at running were hilarious, alternating between chasing each other in circles around her or running ahead and lying on the road, watching her with their ears raised, mouths open in grins while she pushed her body forwards.

She forced herself to run as far as she could, taking a loop through disused roads near her house. The route took her past a few empty houses, abandoned when the Wild had expanded about a decade before. When the houses had been built, they would have been far away from the border with the Wild, the untamed land full of magic and danger that stretched as far as anyone could see into the distance. However, when the Wild had expanded, rapidly and unexpectedly, the people who had lived happily in the houses had decided they didn't want to live in sight of the Wild. If Max turned her head, she could see the dark shapes of tall trees against the night sky that marked the border with the Wild. The trees hadn't been there a decade before, but the magic of the Wild could do strange and powerful things to the growth rate of plants.

The empty streets and houses and proximity to the Wild meant that Max didn't need to worry about meeting any people on her run, so there was no one to see her slow pace or hear her laboured breathing apart from her dogs. And if she did come across any creatures who might have managed to slip through the barrier between the city and the Wild, her two shadow-hounds and the gun she carried should keep her safe.

She ran until she could barely breathe, her mind clear of questions and doubts for the first time in what felt like weeks, sheer exhaustion taking over. She arrived back at the gates to her house and garden covered in sweat despite the cool air, gasping for breath and swearing to herself that she was never going to do anything as stupid as try to run again. Not ever. Not again. There were people in the heart of the city who ran for pleasure, and she honestly thought they were insane as she finally drew to a stop, pausing to lean against the gatepost to catch her breath.

As she drew in much-needed gulps of air, she spared a moment to curse the Strump which had mangled her leg a few weeks before. The giant winged creature had razor-sharp talons on the edges of its wings and had caught her leg. It could have been so much worse, she knew. She could easily have lost her leg entirely. But knowing that hadn't helped the healing which, despite magic, had been slow and frustrating, not to mention painful.

Now that she was healed, she had to build her fitness back up. Marshals didn't generally have to chase down creatures, but she did need a certain level of fitness to be able to do the job. Right now, she was lacking. And that made her vulnerable, and a risk to her fellow Marshals if she was ever working with them. People had died around her before, and she never wanted that to happen again.

The thought of being vulnerable reminded her about the shocking information Audhilde had given her earlier. That someone had tried to access the vampire's personal Vault. Max rarely tried to access hers, as it cost a lot of magical energy and she didn't have any particular secrets to hide. But with the news from Audhilde, she let herself and her dogs through the gates, then braced herself against a gatepost and called on her magic, seeking out the connection to her Vault.

To her surprise, it was there, ready and waiting for her with far less effort than it usually took. The complexity of the Vault's own magic and the depth of spells she could sense almost took her breath away, as always. She had never been quite sure what the Vault actually was, but in her mind imagined it as a great, magical construct of impossibly complicated spells and formulas that would make even a master magician's head spin.

Satisfied that all was well and her Vault was secure, she came back to the here and now and the tremor of over-worked muscles and sweat drying on her skin.

After stretching to try to ease her muscles as much as possible, a much-needed shower and change of clothes, she was stir frying some chicken and vegetables, her stomach telling her in no uncertain terms that she needed to eat, when her phone rang. Marshals were on call at any hour, and the number that came up was the head Marshal, Faddei Lobanov. She answered on the third ring.

"Are you watching the news?" Faddei asked, with no greeting. That was unusual enough to lift her brows.

"Not right now. I'm cooking. Hold on," Max said, turning away from the kitchen and finding the remote for her television. Even this far out from the heart of the city, she still got a decent signal. There was only one news programme scheduled then so she turned to the channel and put the remote aside. The picture cleared quickly, showing her the earnest, handsome face of the news anchor. In the small picture beside his shoulder there was a picture of a protester, their face half covered by a scarf, holding up a sign that said *Take Back the Wild*. "There are more protests?" Max asked, surprised. She had seen a couple of those signs in the recent protests in response to the fuel rationing imposed by the city council. The mood in the city had been turning ugly when the council had ordered a convoy out into the Wild to gather more crude oil from the nearest oil field. Max, along with most of the Marshals, had been on that convoy. It had been a dangerous journey, but the convoy had been successful and the city's fuel supply had been restored. For now.

"Same protests," Faddei said, his voice grim. "And some new group has been targeting the city's law enforcement."

Max's brows lifted. The city's residents generally respected the police force, and expected officers to answer when they called. Law enforcement officers ran the risk of being caught up in fights, and injured in accidents or spontaneous violence, but it was rare for them to be specifically targeted.

"Has anyone been hurt?" she asked, even as the picture on her screen changed to show a hospital bed occupied by a man. Half his face was covered in vivid bruising, and one of his arms was immobilised in a heavy cast. "Oh," she said. "A police officer?"

"He and his partner responded to a call of suspicious activity. They were attacked by a masked group. The partner managed to drag him out into the street and shot one of the group," Faddei said, his voice still grim. "But it was a set-up. The second one in two days. The first pair of officers managed to get away with only minor bruising. Today's pair weren't as lucky. The partner has a broken wrist."

"Oh," Max said again, a chill creeping over her. Someone had deliberately lured police officers into an ambush. Twice. "Will the officer be ok?" she asked.

"Eventually, yes. The partner got him to hospital in time for the healing magician on duty to stop the swelling in his brain." Faddei sounded exhausted, Max realised. She wondered how many calls he'd made so far that night. Then his words sank in. Swelling in the brain. Max was no medical expert, but that did not sound good, and the officer might well owe his life to the quick reaction of his partner and the presence of a magician on the hospital staff.

"What do you need me to do?" Max asked. Dealing with human crimes was not part of the Marshals' jurisdiction, but they did work with the police from time to time. "Do you need Cas and Pol?" she asked. It was a guess. Her dogs were trained to track, and could likely follow the attackers' scent trail.

"Aurora and Ben were called in," Faddei said, naming the most experienced shadow-hound trainers and handlers in the city. Max had last seen them for dinner a few nights before, the evening full of easy conversation and good food. And now the pair were out in the city with their shadow-hounds, trying to track people who had hunted police officers. She made a mental note to send them a text and ask if they needed an extra pair of hounds, dragging her attention back to Faddei as he went on. "I wanted to warn you to be careful. So far, it's just one incident with one false call. But those signs have been appearing around the city. And the groups that attacked the officers were organised. Both were planned."

Max stood for a moment, freezing cold in the middle of her own house. Cas and Pol got off the sofa and came to stand beside her, pressing their large bodies against her, their warmth anchoring her to the here and now.

"Alright," Max said. "Consider me warned. I'll keep my eyes open."

"I'm considering doubling up Marshals," Faddei said. For most of the service, that meant sending the Marshals out in groups of four rather than the normal pairs. And in Max's case, it would mean her working with at least one and possibly two other Marshals. Something which she had resisted ever since she had joined the service. She worked alone. It was one of the concessions she had wrung out of Faddei when she had joined the service. Even seeing the injured officer on her television screen, she still wanted to work alone.

She gave a half-laugh. "Now I know why you're calling me. Look, I have Cas and Pol. They will spot any dangers well before I do," she assured him, reaching down with her free hand to pat her dogs. "And very few people are stupid enough to tackle a shadow-hound, let alone a pair of them."

"I thought you'd say that," Faddei said. She could hear what sounded like frustration in his voice. "Alright. For the moment, I'll let you work solo. But we'll need to keep it under review."

"Two attacks on police officers," Max said slowly, apprehension building, "but you're already doubling up the Marshals and warning us. What else is going on?" she asked. If someone had a problem with the police specifically, it shouldn't necessarily spill out onto the Marshals' service. They did different jobs, and most people in the city never dealt with the Marshals.

"There's a briefing tomorrow morning," Faddei said, not answering her directly, which made her even more nervous. "You'll get a text with details in a little while."

"I'll be there," Max promised.

"Be careful," Faddei said, and hung up before Max could repeat the wish back to him.

She sent a quick text to Aurora and Ben, letting them know that she, Cas and Pol would be willing to help if the more experienced handlers needed extra noses, then picked up her remote again, turning the volume up on the news report and then stood in her living room listening to the end of the segment. The news media had made a connection between the *Take Back the Wild* protesters and the attack on the police officers, although Max couldn't work out how they had done that. The next news segment went on to talk about a protest outside the last full council meeting, and in the crowds around the building, Max spotted another one of the *Take Back the Wild* signs. The reporter didn't make any comment on it, instead focusing on the supposed tension between two opposing factions on the council and the argument over road repairs in one of the city districts. That was business as usual for the council, as far as Max was concerned. The councillors were always arguing about something or other. The last show of unity had been the decision to send the convoy into the Wild to restock the city's fuel supply, and even then there had been arguments about how many people could be spared for the journey. Luckily, common sense had won, and the convoy had had enough people to keep it safe.

Max turned away from the screen, frowning, noticing that Ben had replied. *We've got all the noses we need right now, but will keep your offer in mind. Stay safe.* Max sent back: *You too.* She put her phone down and only then realised that there was a strong smell of burning from the kitchen. She fought past Cas and Pol to turn the burner off before the pan caught fire and sighed, staring down at the blackened and unrecognisable remnants of chicken and vegetables. None of it was salvageable. Not even Cas and Pol would want it. She opened the fridge and sighed again. She had been out to dinner twice in the last week, once with the Ortis family and once with Aurora and Ben, and both times had been sent home with a box of leftovers. So she hadn't done any food shopping for a while. It looked like her meal was going to be toast and eggs. Again. Assuming the bread wasn't mouldy.

Max remembered to make a stop at a grocery store on the way into work the next morning, sparing a moment of thanks for the little pieces of magic that Marshals were given as part of their jobs. The little magics included the cleaning spells that she used far more often than she had ever imagined she would need them, and a cooling spell that sat inside the food box in her truck, which would keep everything fresh until she got home. The box was also equipped with a heavy lock to stop Cas or Pol from getting inside, although she did give them both bits of chicken before she got back in the pick-up to complete the journey to the Marshals' offices.

The Marshals' headquarters were in a run-down industrial estate on the side of the city closest to the Wild, and made up of a series of square, unadorned concrete buildings made for function rather than beauty. The cracked concrete apron around the buildings was crowded with vehicles, many of which were as battered and dented as Max's own pick-up. It looked as if every Marshal on active duty was on site. Max double-checked the time as she got out of the pick-up, but she was still a few minutes early. It looked as if everyone else had simply decided to be earlier. Her dogs leapt out of the back of the truck and glanced at her, as if asking for permission.

"Go on. I'm sure Leonda will be glad to see you," Max said, and watched as her hounds sprinted away, heading for the largest building in the group, which held the armoury and the science teams. Her dogs' love for Leonda was mutual. The Marshals' armourer would be delighted to see them.

Left alone, Max gathered the bag of fresh doughnuts from the passenger seat and made her way into the office building.

As they spent a lot of time out in the field, none of the Marshals had their own desk. The common room had a series of desks that anyone could use, and a wall set up with individual shelves for each Marshal. The rest of the space was given over to comfortable seating and a miniature kitchen, which was the most-used part of the room, providing an endless supply of coffee.

The seating area was crowded with Marshals, all dressed in similar, tough clothing. A few preferred both leather jackets and trousers, but most wore tough trousers and either leather jackets or coats made of the same fabric as their trousers. All of them wore similar, heavy-soled, calf-length boots.

There was a bubble of conversation as Max came in that continued as she headed for the coffee station. Someone else had brought doughnuts as well, so she added hers to the platter, got her own coffee, and turned back to the room.

The nearest Marshals were Pavla and Yevhen, the only married pair of Marshals, who always worked together. They were both tall, slender and dark-haired, and among the most experienced Marshals on the service. Pavla lifted a hand, inviting Max to join them.

"Did you really ride a Robinsage monkey all the way up a building?" Pavla asked, brows lifting, as Max came closer.

Max felt heat rising under her collar. "It seemed like a good idea at the time," she answered.

"Do they smell as bad as Raymund's lectures suggest?" Yevhen asked with a grin as Pavla laughed.

"Worse. Much worse," Max said, with an exaggerated shudder. She had used yet another cleaning spell on her clothes the night before, just to be sure.

Yevhen joined in Pavla's laughter, then glanced aside as a wave of quiet fell over the room.

Max followed his line of sight and saw that Faddei had come in. The head Marshal looked as if he hadn't slept, dark smudges under his eyes. He was wearing similar clothing to everyone else, even though he was no longer on active service. He stood out not just for his bald head and tattoos, but also for the quiet air of authority he carried with him. Like most Marshals, he didn't look like anyone's idea of a law enforcement officer. Faddei always looked to Max as if he should be outside a nightclub minding the door or in a boxing ring, but his powerful build hid a sharp, keen mind and an almost endless curiosity. He glanced around the room, meeting everyone's eyes and exchanging a few nods.

"Thank you for coming, particularly those of you who are on your days off," Faddei said.

"Days off? What are those?" a voice from the crowd said, prompting a ripple of laughter.

Faddei managed a grin in response. It was an old gripe. A Marshal's job wasn't for everyone, and there never seemed to be enough of them. Everyone in the room had been called in from their time off more than once. They all complained about it, but every one of them had turned up for work and would do so again. And everyone in the room knew it. Someone who wanted a normal job with regular hours would not last a week as a Marshal. Faddei's grin faded, replaced by the exhaustion Max had heard in his voice the night before.

"We have a new problem to deal with in the city," Faddei started, voice serious. The room fell silent and still, watching him. Everyone in the Marshals' service liked and trusted their leader. If he said there was a problem, they all believed him. Max found herself almost holding her breath, waiting for him to continue. "I spoke to quite a few of you yesterday, but I'm going to go over it again for everyone."

No one moved, no one complained, as Faddei told the assembled Marshals about the two ambushes on police officers. The officer in hospital was expected to fully recover. Faddei didn't need to spell out that it could have been a far different outcome. Max could see the grim realisation on the faces of her fellow Marshals. Healing magicians were rare, and only had so much power they could use. It had been sheer luck that the magician had been in the hospital when the officer had been brought in.

The city's law enforcement agency had formed a task force to investigate, devoting resources to tracking down the attackers. All their officers were now going out with body armour and body cameras as extra precautions and in groups of four rather than in pairs. That meant that the police response time across the city would be reduced, but the law enforcement chiefs were not taking any chances with their personnel. It was one of the few decisions that they had made which Max agreed with. There weren't enough police officers as it was, and the city couldn't afford to lose more. Max could only hope that the task force would be able to track down the attackers quickly.

Faddei looked around the room and Max frowned as she noticed his tiredness again. The Marshals - and their leader - dealt with difficult and dangerous situations every day, and she had never seen Faddei look so worn down before. There was something else bothering him. And from the way Faddei had paused, he was about to tell them whatever it was. Max braced herself for bad news.

"None of the Marshals have been targeted so far," he said. The room was already quiet, but a deeper hush fell as everyone focused on Faddei. "But we can't assume that will continue."

"What's up?" Vanko asked, when Faddei fell silent. "What else is going on?" Max wasn't surprised by the question. Vanko was one of the longest-serving Marshals, and as close to a deputy as Faddei had. He perhaps knew Faddei better than any of them.

From the murmurs around the room, it seemed that everyone had the same questions.

"The police and Marshals have received threats," Faddei said. "Before the attacks took place. We do get threats from time to time, but these included photographs of some officers on duty and notes of their home addresses."

Max felt a chill run across her skin. That was serious. The city was large enough that police officers out of uniform were rarely recognised. As far as she knew, there had never been any targeted threats made against ordinary rank-and-file officers or their families before. Very occasionally one of the more senior officers, one of those who was the public face of the law enforcement service, would get some heckling, in the same way as the council members. The city had its share of problems, but threats to law enforcement officers had not been one of them. Until now.

"Any Marshals?" Vanko asked.

"None so far. But the threats were sent to both services," Faddei pointed out. He ran his hand over his bare scalp, a sure sign of weariness and frustration. "Most of you have very good home setups, but please take extra care. Don't hesitate to call for back-up or the police if you're concerned for your safety or your family, and let me know, too."

The room was hushed, quite a few Marshals exchanging glances, everyone deathly serious. Marshals accepted the risks for themselves, otherwise they couldn't do the job. But the idea that their families might be involved was something quite different. Max knew that about half the Marshals had partners from outside the service, and many of them had children. She could not imagine how chilling Faddei's warning must have been for them. Her own home security was better, in many ways, than that of her colleagues. Even someone wanting to hurt a Marshal would think twice about venturing so close to the Wild, and no one in their right mind would try to tackle two shadow-hounds on their own territory.

"Are these threats from the same group as the attackers?" Max asked, her voice loud in the quiet room.

"We think so," Faddei said.

"What do they want? Can we see the threats?" Max asked, frowning. Even knowing that the police could be unpopular, it made no sense to her. The police and Marshals were there to try and keep the residents of the city safe, both from other residents and from supernatural creatures. She couldn't understand why anyone would want to target specific police officers or Marshals.

"I'll get Therese to send copies to all of you," Faddei said. The Marshal's dispatcher, Therese, would be manning the phones while Faddei was here. It had been many months since Max had actually seen the woman. She was one of the coldest human beings Max had ever met, carrying out her job and running the Marshals' service with strict efficiency.

Then Faddei hesitated again, drawing the attention of everyone in the room once more. "The attackers were dressed in similar outfits. Head to toe in black. There had been reports of other people dressed like that seen around the city. This seems to be a coordinated and organised group. We don't know what their agenda is, or who is behind this, but it's very clear that they had a problem with law enforcement."

Another ripple of unease went around the room. Max had already mostly made the connection, but hearing it said aloud hollowed out her stomach. A vigilante group was the last thing the city needed.

"The news report last night seemed to suggest there was some connection to the *Take Back the Wild* signs we've seen," Max commented, her lips stiff. There had always been a few hot heads who thought the city should force the Wild back and retake the land that the city and its residents had lost over the years. They were usually seen as lunatics. The city struggled to maintain the magical barrier against the Wild as it was. Max couldn't imagine that, even with every magician in the city coming together, they would have enough power to take back even one acre from the Wild.

"That's being looked into by the task force," Faddei said, frowning. "We don't have anything to suggest there's a connection yet, but it's possible that someone is feeding the journalists information we don't have."

Max nodded. Faddei was telling them everything he knew. And it would not be the first time that someone had preferred speaking to the news media over law enforcement.

"Alright, everyone. You should all have your new assignments and rosters," Faddei said. From the nods around the room, it seemed that Therese had been busy contacting everyone else. Max glanced at her phone and didn't see any new messages. Perhaps Faddei had decided to leave her working alone with her dogs. "Any more questions?" he asked.

There were a few, practical questions about shift rotations which Faddei dealt with, then the other Marshals began drifting away, off out to their assignments, or back to their days off, until it was just Vanko, Faddei and Max left in the room. She glanced at the kitchen and saw that, despite the grim news, the Marshals had taken most of the doughnuts with them. She put her coffee cup into the dishwasher and approached Faddei.

"Something you needed, Max?" he asked.

Close up, he looked as if he hadn't slept for a week. She hesitated.

"I'm sorry to add to the bad news, but I needed to update you on a body that Audhilde asked me to look at yesterday," she said, frowning. "When was the last time you slept?"

Faddei gave a bark of laughter and shook his head. "It's been a bad few days."

"He's going home to rest and I'll keep his seat warm until tomorrow," Vanko said, his tone firm and not allowing for any argument. Max was quite sure that had not been agreed between them. Faddei sent the younger Marshal a sideways look that just drew a grin from Vanko. "If you don't go home and get some sleep, I'll shoot you up with one of Raymund's new tranquilliser rounds. I don't think we've tested it on a human subject yet."

Faddei glowered at Vanko, but didn't argue, turning instead to Max. "Dead body?" he prompted.

Max told the pair about Ivor Costen, who he was, how he was found, and what Lord Kolbyr had said about the ritual used to kill him.

Faddei looked even more worn out at the end. "Lady's light, I thought we might have seen the last of that demon. At least for a little while."

"Any word on the others?" Vanko asked. "Hemang Raghavan and Evan Yarwood, I mean. If we think Queran is back in the city, what about them?"

"I don't know," Max said honestly. "They were a really unlikely group. It's entirely possible that Queran abandoned the others and made his own way back here."

"We can't take the chance," Faddei said. "Has the Order been informed?"

"Audhilde was going to call them. She also said that Kitris has been keeping to himself," Max said.

"That's putting it mildly. He's ignoring everyone and anyone who tries to reach him," Faddei said, a hard edge to his voice. "Wouldn't even respond when the council asked to speak to Bryce to confirm the information you gave them."

"That's worrying," Vanko said, a frown on his normally cheerful face. "We might need the Order's help if this new group turns ugly."

"I think we have to work on the assumption we're not going to get any assistance from them," Faddei said, rubbing his hand across his head again. "Max, I've left you working with just your dogs for now, but please be careful."

"Always am," Max said. Taking that for a dismissal, she nodded to each of them and headed out into daylight, somehow not surprised when her phone beeped with a new message as she left the building. A text from Therese, with an address and the words: *possible creature sighting*. Given everything else the woman was juggling, with the new assignments, Max couldn't feel annoyed that the order had come by text rather than phone call. She sent a brief message back - *on my way* - and headed towards the science building to collect her dogs, hoping that the creature sighting was something less foul-smelling than another Robinsage monkey.

Chapter Six

The address Max had been given turned out to be one of the abandoned apartment buildings on the outskirts of the city, about twenty minutes' drive from the Marshals' headquarters. Max assumed that the building's former residents hadn't been comfortable with being able to see the Wild from their kitchen windows, and had fled to smaller, more expensive accommodation further into the city. It was precisely the sort of building that Marshals often ended up searching, as supernatural creatures liked to use them as quiet places to rest or nest in.

As Max drew to a stop outside the building, she saw the end of another vehicle tucked in the alleyway between the building she'd been sent to and the neighbouring one, which also looked abandoned. Frowning, she got out of the pick-up and waved Cas and Pol out of the back. They bounded a few steps to either side, looking around and sniffing the air, while Max gathered her shotgun and shoved spare ammunition into the loops of her thigh holster. That done, she took a few paces along the street so she could better see the vehicle. If the building was abandoned, there shouldn't be any cars. As she got a better view of it, apprehension slid across her skin. It wasn't just a car, but a police patrol vehicle. That particular combination of deep blue and white was only used by the police, and there was a bar of lights across the roof.

She stowed her shotgun next to the ammunition and drew her gun, making sure it was set to single fire, and then pulled out her phone, dialling the preset number for the Marshals' service.

"What?" Therese snapped in Max's ear.

"It's Max. I'm at the address you texted me. There's a police vehicle on scene. Do you have any more information?" Max asked.

"No. We got an anonymous call about a creature in the building. No mention of police. How many officers?" Therese asked. She sounded as grumpy as usual.

"I can't see any officers, just the patrol vehicle." Max read out the vehicle's licence plate. With the walls of the building in the way, she couldn't see the large numbers that would be spread along the sides of the vehicle and on the roof.

"Do you need back-up?" Therese asked.

"Not at the moment. I can't see or hear anyone else," Max said.

"I'll contact police dispatch and call you back," Therese said, and hung up.

As soon as the call ended, the hairs on the back of Max's neck lifted and her skin crawled with the sensation of being watched. She put her phone away and headed towards the alleyway and the abandoned car. Not only did she want to see whether there was any information in the vehicle, but the building walls overlooking the alleyway didn't have any windows, giving her a bit of cover from whoever or whatever was watching her.

Cas and Pol came with her, sticking close to either side, their ears lifted. They were alert but not worried, still in their normal shapes, which Max took to be a good sign. Her dogs had far keener senses than she did, and they hadn't identified a threat yet.

The patrol vehicle was empty of other people. The doors were closed, but the driver's door opened when Max tried it. The keys were still in the ignition and more unease crept over her. The Marshals always left their keys in their vehicles, and their vehicles unlocked, in case they needed to make a quick getaway from a creature. She hadn't thought the police would do the same. The police chased down human wrong-doers, many of whom would be happy to use the police officers' own vehicle as a getaway. She found the latch for the vehicle's boot and opened that, too, just in case. All she found was an empty rack that she thought had probably held a couple of powerful shotguns, and the vehicle's spare tyre.

Max waved her dogs to the driver's seat. "We need to search for the driver," she told them. "Get the scent and find the trail."

Her dogs took long, deep sniffs around the driver's seat, committing the scent to memory, and then began trotting away, Max following, her gun held with both hands, muzzle down.

She was somehow unsurprised when the dogs led her around the back of the building she'd been sent to and towards the open back door. As she set foot on the shallow step that led up to the door, her phone rang. Calling for her dogs to pause, Max answered.

"Police dispatch has no record of officers at that address. The vehicle was signed out to Sergeant Ellie Randall and her patrol partner, Cadet Robert Madison. The Sergeant is not answering her phone," Therese told Max, voice clipped. "They are sending more units to the address. Have you found the Sergeant or Cadet?"

"No sign of anyone yet. I'm just about to go into the building we were sent to, entering through the back door. My dogs have a scent of someone who was driving the car."

"I'm sending Marshals as well. Vanko requests that you don't go inside until more back-up arrives," Therese said.

"Noted," Max said, and hung up. She hesitated on the threshold of the building. Waiting for back-up made complete sense, but some instinct was telling her to move forward, go inside the building, and that she didn't have time to wait.

A low, dark growl from one of her dogs drew her attention. They were just inside the open back door, and both had shifted into their attack forms. Her dogs had sensed a threat. Max raised her gun.

A series of loud bangs came from somewhere inside the building. Gunshots. More than one weapon was firing. Max caught the lighter report of a hand gun, and the deeper sounds of a shotgun. She remembered the empty rack in the patrol vehicle. It was possible that Ellie and her cadet were somewhere inside, defending themselves. Or they might not be here at all.

A cry of pain sounded amid the shots.

Max was moving forward before the cry faded, through the door and into a wide corridor that led to the first turn of a heavy staircase that ran up through the centre of the building. She took a few slow steps to let her eyes adjust to the poorer light and to get a sense of the layout of the building. It looked like four apartments on each level, and there were at least four storeys above her. A fairly standard layout for buildings of this sort. All the doors she could see on this level were open, giving her glimpses of dimly lit interiors.

Cas and Pol were ahead of her, moving towards the stairs.

Despite the gunfire overhead, Max called them back. They needed to clear the floor first. Make sure there were no creatures or other unpleasant surprises waiting here that might follow them up into the building.

Clearing the apartments on the ground floor took mere moments with her dogs' superior senses. They ran ahead of her into each open door, made their way rapidly through each apartment and came back to her, letting her know there was no one else there. If they had found someone, whether a human or a creature, they would have barked to alert her.

Satisfied that there were no threats on the ground floor, Max headed up the stairs, Cas and Pol ahead of her again, still in their attack forms. The gunfire was still continuing. Whoever was firing was using single shots, perhaps wanting to preserve their ammunition.

The first floor above ground was in worse shape than the ground floor, with quite a few of the internal walls missing, meaning it took Cas and Pol even less time to clear the floor and head upstairs.

Max put her back to the wall of the staircase, looking up and ahead as she cautiously crept up the stairs. The stairs were closed in by the walls of the building's apartments, giving her a limited view. The gunfire was closer, and between shots she could hear a low moan of pain. At least one of the shots had hit someone.

She reached the top of the stairs, Cas and Pol crouching just behind the wall, and put her head cautiously around the corner.

Most of the internal walls to one side had gone, giving her a clear view of a ruined interior, and the indistinct shape of someone crouching behind a large pile of rubble, shotgun in hand. The shooter was protected by the rubble, her dark skin covered by dust. Despite the dust, Max recognised Ellie Randall. The Sergeant hadn't seen Max, too focused on something to the other side of the building. Max ducked her head back and then looked to the other side. One of the external walls of the apartments was still more or less intact, although the door was missing, and she could see the shadow of someone or more than one person moving behind the wall. The wall also had several large holes in it that looked like they came from shotgun shells. Ellie must be using heavy-duty ammunition.

Whoever was shooting at Ellie moved along the wall, and Max caught a glimpse of a figure dressed in black wielding a shotgun that looked very like the one Ellie was holding.

There was no cover between Max and the wall the attackers were hiding behind. But Max did have two very fast shadow-hounds beside her. They were focused on the wall and the people behind it, eyes glowing, fangs bared. Eager to get involved.

"Go get them," Max said, voice tight, unable to stop the stab of worry that ran through her. She didn't want to see her dogs injured, but they were trained for this.

Her hounds moved almost faster than she could see, surging out of the stairwell, across the landing and behind the wall before the attackers had a chance to realise there was anything there. Max followed as fast as she could.

Shocked cries and a cut-off scream of pain told her that Cas or Pol, or both, had found their targets.

Max arrived in the open doorway with her gun raised to see her dogs each grappling with a black-clad man. The attackers had dropped their weapons, which was good, and didn't seem to know what to do in response to a shadow-hound taking hold of them, which was also good.

Movement ahead of her drew her attention in time to see a third figure detach from the shadows, a gun raised. He was dressed head to toe in black, his face covered.

Max fired. She aimed for the centre mass of the gun man, and hit him dead-on. He stumbled back with a cry, but didn't go down. He must be wearing body armour. She flicked her gun to automatic fire, for greater impact, even as he aimed his gun at her.

She moved sideways, seeking the limited shelter of the wall, firing even as bullets ripped into the wall beside her, sending spurts of plaster and dust into the air. She couldn't breathe for a moment, heart thumping. She wasn't used to being shot at.

Cas and Pol left the two men they had dragged to the floor and leapt on Max's attacker, taking him down to the cracked and dusty floor, growls coming from both of their throats. The man made a sound somewhere between fear and pain and dropped his gun as Pol took hold of his wrist. The great hound gave the man's wrist a shake, all the same, and Max heard the distinct, sharp snap of a bone breaking. The man howled in pain.

Keeping her gun ready, Max took a step forward, towards the two prone men that her dogs had left. They were also covered head-to-toe in black, including masks over their faces. They weren't moving, but she didn't think her dogs had killed them. There were no wounds and no blood on the ground around them.

As she moved towards the men, they stirred, reaching for weapons lying on the ground nearby. She fired, aiming for their torsos, assuming that they were also wearing body armour. At this close range, the impact of her bullets should give them some impressive bruises, possibly even break a rib or two. But not kill them.

The men grunted.

"Stay where you are," Max ordered. "Are there any more of you?" she asked. It was almost impossible to keep her attention on all three of the men on the ground at once, even with Cas and Pol standing guard.

None of the men said anything. The one with the now-broken arm made a low sound of pain.

"Sergeant, are you alright?" Max yelled. She didn't want to use Ellie's name in front of the attackers.

A low, pained grunt sounded by way of response. Someone had been injured in the first exchange of gunfire, Max remembered, and just hoped that whatever injuries Ellie and her cadet had suffered were minor.

"More police and Marshals are on their way," Max told the men on the ground. "Stay exactly where you are," she ordered, taking a step back towards the partition wall.

"Or what?" one of the men asked, the sneer in his voice evident despite the mask.

"Or my hounds will kill you," Max told him, voice flat. "On guard," she told her dogs. They each gave her a low, sharp bark in response and moved so that they could watch the three men.

Max risked a glance over her shoulder as she reached the opening in the wall. She could see Ellie standing beside the pile of rubble that she had taken shelter behind. The Sergeant had one of her hands pressed to her side and even from the distance, Max could see the gleam of liquid between her fingers. Ellie had been shot.

"Stay there," Max called. "Help's on the way."

"How many have you got?" Ellie asked, slumping against the rubble. She had a shotgun in a loose grip in her other hand, but didn't look as if she had the strength to lift it.

"Three here," Max answered.

"There were more," Ellie said, voice grim.

"Have you got cuffs?" Max asked.

"Always," the Sergeant said.

"Alright," Max said. She glanced back at the three men and her hounds keeping watch, and risked turning her back, jogging across the open floor to Ellie's side.

Close up, Ellie's breathing was harsh, sweat beading her face. She tilted her chin down to her hip, and Max saw a pair of heavy-duty handcuffs on a loop.

"Where's your cadet?" Max asked, taking the cuffs off Ellie.

"Told him to hide," Ellie said, grimacing as she shifted her weight. "First week out of training. He's not ready for this."

"What made you come here?" Max asked. The police dispatcher had told Therese that there had been no call.

"Someone flagged us down," Ellie said, her breathing harsh, words barely above a whisper. "Told us they had seen someone lurking." She grimaced. "Trap."

Max put her hand on Ellie's arm for a moment, a silent gesture of support. She couldn't think of anything to say. She was sure that Ellie and all her colleagues would have had a similar briefing to the one Faddei had given the Marshals. That should have stopped Ellie from bringing her cadet into a building without another pair of officers to back them up. And Ellie knew it. It wasn't like her to go against protocol.

As Max lifted her hand away, she felt an odd residue clinging to her skin. She turned her hand over but couldn't see anything, and then realised that it wasn't on her skin, but something brushing against her senses. Some leftover magic. "The person who stopped you. Can you describe them?" she asked Ellie.

"Ah. No," Ellie said, frowning. "I can't remember anything about them. Not even if they were a man or woman. Strange. Rob was trying to say something to me," she said, and shook her head.

"Your cadet?" Max prompted. "What was he saying?"

"I can't remember. Everything is fuzzy. All I remember is the urgency to get in here," Ellie said, frustration clear.

"There's magic on you," Max said.

"There shouldn't be," Ellie said, glancing down at her arm where Max's hand had rested. "Someone made me come in here?"

"I think so. I need to tie these guys up. Help's on the way," Max said again. "Just hold on a bit longer, will you?"

"As long as I need to," Ellie confirmed. "Watch your back. This lot are slippery."

"How many more, do you think?" Max asked.

"At least two," Ellie said. She tried to lift the shotgun and grimaced, her whole body trembling with the effort. She dropped the large, heavy weapon and drew her handgun instead.

"Get back behind cover," Max told her, the back of her neck itching as if someone was watching her. "I'll tie these three up and go looking for the others."

She came back to the three men with no one trying to shoot at her, which was something, and then handcuffed the men together, looping the handcuffs under one of the exposed floorboards. Unless they had superhuman strength, they weren't going anywhere. She kicked their weapons out of the way and called her dogs. There were more people to find.

As Cas and Pol surged ahead of her to the hidden corner of the floor, her phone rang. She pulled it out, trying not to curse, and answered.

"What?"

"It's Vanko. Where are you?"

"Second floor. Three attackers handcuffed together. One police sergeant in need of urgent medical care. I'm looking for two more attackers and the police cadet," Max told him. "Oh, and there might be a magician nearby," she added, remembering the residue on Ellie's uniform and Ellie's hazy memory.

"Marshals and armed police are coming in now," Vanko said, sounding tense. "Are you hurt?"

"No," Max said, and hung up. Cas and Pol hadn't come back from their exploration of the corner, which meant they had found something.

She edged her way along the remaining wall to the gap where a door had been and took a quick look around the opening. The space was shadowed, her dogs nowhere in sight, but there was a too-still body in uniform lying on the ground, eyes open and staring up at the ceiling. From the crispness of his uniform, Max guessed she had found the cadet. Someone had shot him between the eyes, his face frozen in a startled expression.

She set her jaw and crept around the wall, heading across the open space with prickles of unease running across her skin. From the layout of the building, this was a dead-end corner. There were no stairs or other escape she could remember, and yet her dogs were still in the remaining room.

She came to the doorway and peered around it. There were no windows in the room ahead, the only light coming from the room she was in. In the gloom she could see her dogs, both of them still in their attack forms, standing side by side and focusing all their attention on what looked like a closed wardrobe on the other side of the small room.

There was nothing else in the room, and no other exits. Max moved across the room and took hold of one of the door handles, glancing at her dogs to make sure they were ready. Their eyes gleamed in the poor light. Unlike her, they seemed eager to find out what was inside.

She pulled the door open and took several rapid steps back, raising her gun.

A human-shaped creature made of hair and fury sprang out of the wardrobe, screaming at a pitch that drilled through the bones of Max's skull. It swiped at her with one long arm, sending her thudding into the wall, and rushed past her dogs, who growled, turning and following it. Max yelled after her dogs to halt. She didn't want them chasing the creature into a trap.

Alarmed shouts and cries from elsewhere on the floor told her that the promised back-up had arrived. Max gathered herself away from the wall and checked the wardrobe just in case. Empty. As she had expected. Which meant that the other attackers were somewhere else in the building.

She followed Cas and Pol out across the room, skirting around the body of the police cadet, and into the other space where she found a pair of paramedics taking care of Ellie, and a group of armed police officers along with Vanko and Zoya and her hounds, all staring up the stairs. Even though she had just talked to him on the phone, Max still blinked in surprise at seeing Vanko there. He was supposed to be standing in for Faddei at headquarters.

"We were closest," Vanko said, and heat ran up Max's face as she realised he must have read her expression. She looked away to check on the prisoners she had left and blinked again.

"What happened to the men?" Max asked, staring at the space where she had left the men handcuffed together. There was nothing there. Not even their weapons.

"We just found Ellie. No one else," Zoya answered. "She said there was a cadet?"

"Was, yes," Max said, and tilted her chin. "He's back there."

"Dead?" Vanko asked.

"Someone shot him between the eyes," Max said.

"Sergeant Noah Willard," one of the male officers introduced himself. Like the others, he was wearing heavy body armour, including a matte black helmet, only his face uncovered. "Is there anyone else in the building?" he asked.

"I haven't checked the upper levels yet," Max said. "I came across three armed men, and Ellie said there were at least two more."

"Did she say why she was in here with just the cadet?" the Sergeant asked, frowning. He grimaced. "I know Ellie. There's no way she would have risked a trainee like that."

"She said someone flagged them down and told her to come in here. There was magic on her uniform." Max watched the Sergeant's face tighten as he absorbed that.

"Someone used a compulsion spell on her?" Zoya asked.

"I think so. She couldn't tell me anything about the person who sent them in here, just that it was urgent she come inside," Max said.

The Sergeant muttered something unflattering about manipulative magicians which Max silently agreed with.

"They must still be up there," Vanko said.

"Right," Noah Willard said. "Compulsion spells only work one to one, yes?" he asked, eyes travelling across Vanko, Zoya and Max.

"So far as I know, yes," Vanko answered.

"So, if we stay together, we should avoid that," the Sergeant concluded, and headed towards the stairs.

"Hold up," Max said, at the same time as Vanko.

"Wait," Vanko said, as Max fell silent. "We don't know what's up there. Let Max and her hounds go first. We'll follow."

"That's not protocol," the officer said, clearly unhappy.

"My dogs will sniff out anyone before we can see them. Even a magician," Max pointed out. She glanced across to where Ellie was being put onto a stretcher with exquisite care. From the brief look, Max thought that Ellie was unconscious and hoped that she was free of pain, at least for the moment.

Noah Willard followed her gaze and his face tightened. "Fine. We'll be right behind you. With our weapons."

"Good," Max said. She checked the load in her magazine and switched it out for a full one, then looked at Vanko. "Did you see what the creature was that ran past?"

"Looked like a Seacast monkey," Vanko said, although he was frowning, "only with longer hair."

"It looked angry," Zoya commented.

"It was shut in a wardrobe on the other side of the floor," Max said.

"That explains the anger," Zoya agreed. "You didn't see any more wardrobes?"

"Wardrobes full of Seacast monkeys. There's a thought to give us all nightmares," Vanko muttered.

"That's the only furniture I've seen so far," Max said, lips twitching.

She caught sideways glances between the police officers gathered around them and bit her lip to stop a smile. Marshals were often referred to as the crazies of law enforcement, as only crazy people would voluntarily go into a building with a supernatural creature on the loose. But the police had their own dark humour, and the nickname was not meant as a cruelty.

"Lead the way," Vanko prompted. He and Zoya were wielding their shotguns. The police officers also had shotguns ready, but theirs were heavier, filled with normal ammunition.

"The attackers I came across were wearing body armour," Max told the others before she put her foot on the stairs upwards.

She heard grunts of acknowledgement from the people gathered around her. She waved Cas and Pol ahead of her. With the prospect of armed attackers on the floors above, her heart was thumping, palms damp on the grip of her gun. If she had a choice, she wouldn't go up, but the black-clad attackers had shot and injured Ellie, and one of them had outright executed a cadet barely out of police training. They couldn't be allowed to get away. So she followed her dogs up the stairs, trying to keep her breathing steady, making sure she kept glancing upwards just in case any of the attackers decided to start shooting from the higher floors down the stairwell.

They made it to the next floor without incident. Unlike the floor below, this one had most of its internal walls intact. As soon as they got to the top of the stairs, her dogs paused, low growls emerging from their throats.

"They've got a scent," Max told the others, speaking as quietly as she could. "Find them," she told her dogs.

The hounds turned without hesitation, stalking their way along the communal space in the middle of the building, heading for the apartment at what Max thought was the back of the building. The door was open, a sliver of light spilling out into the hallway. The light cut off for a moment and Max froze. There was something or someone in there.

Before she could react, gunfire sounded. From behind her. She whirled, gun raised, to find a pair of black-clad attackers coming down the stairs from the upper floors, firing into the group of police officers and Marshals. Max moved out of the way, keeping her gun raised and ready but not firing. The police had far heavier weapons. And she was behind all the law enforcement officers. She didn't want to risk shooting them. The attackers had no such hesitation. They must have realised that the police would follow them up through the building and had set a trap for them, Max thought.

Vanko and Zoya ducked to one side, against the wall, out of sight of the stairwell, even as the police officers returned fire, the sounds of their heavier weapons deafening in the enclosed space. Both of the attackers went down, shot through the head. Max forced herself to breathe. The police had been taking no chances. Or so she assumed.

"Who authorised head shots?" Noah Willard demanded, fury clear in his voice. "We wanted them alive."

Shaking heads and denials rippled through the half dozen police officers gathered in the hallway. None of them had killed the attackers.

"There's someone else up there, then," the officer said.

Max shivered as she realised what that meant. One of the other attackers had killed their own people.

Noah Willard glanced back at Max, his face pale and grim under his helmet. "We need to clear this floor first, though," he said. He left two of his men guarding the stairwell, the others following him as he joined Max. "There was something in there?" he prompted when she stood still, staring at him and the two bodies on the stairs leading up to the next floor.

"Er. Yes. Something," she agreed, turning back to the open door.

Cas and Pol surged ahead of her, going into the apartment. A shriek lifted the hairs on Max's body as she followed her dogs in.

The human-shaped creature that had been stuck in a wardrobe downstairs was huddled into a corner, its teeth bared as it chattered at Cas and Pol. Her hounds were too clever to approach it, standing a few paces away, ready to give chase if it tried to run.

"That's not a Seacast monkey," Vanko commented, coming to stand at Max's shoulder.

"No," Max agreed, nose wrinkling. "It looks like a cross between a Seacast and a Robinsage. Is that even possible?"

"Who knows," Vanko said, with a weary sigh. "Zoya, take it down, will you? I'll call Raymund."

Zoya lifted her shotgun and put a tranquilliser round into the creature's arm. It shrieked again, baring long, yellowing teeth at her, but showed no signs that the tranquilliser had affected it. "Alright. The heavy stuff it is, then," Zoya said, and switched out her shotgun magazine.

Max watched, surprised when the creature just stayed where it was as Zoya lifted her shotgun and fired again. The second round, with the more powerful drug, did the trick, and the creature slumped down against the wall, its eyes closing.

"We need to clear this floor," Vanko reminded Max. She was still staring at the creature, trying to work out what it was, and why it had just sat still while a Marshal fired at it.

Before they could move to the rest of the floor, two single shots sounded from somewhere over their heads. Max exchanged glances with Vanko, then they followed the police officers as they regrouped and made their way up the stairs, past the dead bodies and blood. Max spared a moment to be thankful that the dead men were wearing masks. She didn't have to see the damage done by the bullets.

There were two more bodies lying in the hallway of the next floor, both of them also shot in the head. One of them had a makeshift bandage around one of his arms. Possibly the man who had attacked Max and had his arm broken.

The rest of the floor was empty, as was the roof. The Sergeant still insisted that they search the whole building again, from top to bottom. The men hadn't shot themselves, he pointed out. He didn't sound hopeful that they would find anything, and Max silently agreed. Someone ruthless and determined enough to set up the ambush for Ellie and her cadet, and then ultimately kill their own people, was hardly likely to wait around for the police to find them. Still, they had to look.

Chapter Seven

By the time the search was done, night was falling outside. They hadn't found anything else in the whole building. No other bodies, no wardrobes, no other creatures. Max could practically see the tension in the air around the police officers. They had been targeted again, and one of their number had been killed.

With the search complete, the law enforcement team and the Marshals left the building, gathering outside and letting in the Marshals' science team and the medical examiner's people. Max was somehow not surprised to see that Raymund Robart himself had turned up to collect whatever the creature was, all of his team being very careful with their handling of it as they brought it downstairs and out into the customised van. He shook his head when Vanko asked him to identify the creature, apparently as puzzled as Max and the others were. He agreed it was probably a hybrid, but wouldn't speculate further.

With the unidentified monkey safely removed, Audhilde and her people were free to look at the cadet and the other bodies while the crime scene techs were setting up for a long night of combing through every inch of the building to find whatever evidence they could.

Faddei had arrived, too. He had managed to get a change of clothes and some rest, Max noted. He was in close conversation with a stout, older man in a police uniform that Max recognised all too easily. Deputy Chief Harvey James. She had gotten to know him far more than she would have liked in the last couple of weeks, since her return from the Wild. He had been one of the senior officers who had questioned her for what felt like days, interrogating her over and over about what had happened in the Wild.

The deputy chief and Faddei lined up with the other police officers and Marshals outside the building, all watching as the stretcher carrying the cadet's body was carried out. The cadet's body was contained in one of the black plastic wraps that the medical examiner's office used, so at least none of them had to look at the too-young, too-still face. Max swallowed a hard, painful lump in her throat. She had arrived too late to help the cadet. Police officers knew that their work was dangerous, and many of them were injured each year. But very few officers were ever killed in the line of duty. In fact, Max could only remember hearing about two other deaths in her lifetime. She could see the shock, and the anger, on the faces of the police officers gathered around her, the silence heavy as they all watched as the stretcher was loaded into the van to be driven back to the mortuary.

The other bodies in the building would also be wrapped in plastic, but they would be taken out with far less ceremony and, from the discussions that Max had overhead, carried to the mortuary in a different vehicle.

Audhilde paused next to Max and Vanko, watching the van doors being closed with a frown.

"Five bodies in one night, and one of them a police officer. This is not acceptable," Audhilde said, with almost unnatural calm. For a moment, Max thought that the ancient vampire was talking to her, then realised that the deputy chief and Faddei had drawn closer.

"I agree," James said, with seemingly genuine grief. "We'll set guards on the building while your people are here," he told Audhilde.

"And Sergeant Randall?" Audhilde asked.

"She's in surgery. A bullet struck her just under her body armour," the deputy chief said, looking even more worn out. His white hair, normally neatly arranged across his skull, was standing up in random tufts and there were deep lines of weariness and grief on his face, his eyes shadowed by the glare of vehicle headlights. There were no streetlights here. Seeing the feeling on the deputy chief's face, Max felt a moment of sympathy for him. However unpleasant he had been to her, it seemed he did truly care about his people. "We won't know more for a few hours."

Max's eyes prickled with heat, taking that in. Ellie might have been talking when Max had last seen her, but it seemed her injury was far more serious than that might suggest. Ellie was one of the toughest women Max knew, and the idea that she and her trainee had been caught up in an ambush felt almost unreal.

"I will send my findings as soon as possible," Audhilde said, "but from a first glance, it looks like the young man died from a single shot to the head. The others in the building were killed the same way." The vampire looked around the scene, expression tight. "I hope you find whoever was responsible, and soon."

With that, Audhilde left, getting in the van with the cadet's body and driving away. As she left, the armed officers who had been in the building headed out as well, back into the patrol vehicles they'd used to get here, the crowd of people outside the building thinning out. Doubtless they had reports to write, but Max doubted many of them would be getting sleep until they knew how Ellie's surgery had gone. The senior officers of the police force might not like the outspoken Sergeant, but she was highly respected and well liked among her peers.

With a bit of space and quiet around them, Max realised how weary she felt. Even though she had only worked one scene, it had taken the entire day and she was ready for a break. But the presence of the deputy chief and Faddei meant she'd need to wait a bit longer before she got a chance to rest.

"Faddei tells me you were first on scene," James said, turning to Max. "And you didn't wait for back-up."

Max felt heat surge up her neck. "I heard shots, and a cry of pain," she explained.

"Tell me what happened," the deputy demanded. The grief and exhaustion had been suppressed, replaced by a quiet determination that Max remembered vividly from the hours of questioning. He had been openly sceptical of her accounts of what had happened in the Wild, in particular Evan Yarwood's involvement. For a moment, she was tempted to refuse to answer his questions, not sure that there was anything she could say that he would believe or that would help matters. But Faddei was there, too, and he needed to know what had happened. He would believe her, she knew.

So she went through the events, from arriving at the address until coming out of the building, the search completed. To her surprise, the deputy chief didn't interrupt or ask questions until she was finished. Then he lifted a brow at Vanko and Zoya, asking them what they had seen and learned.

Max forced down a surge of anger. He wanted to corroborate her story, that much was clear. But Vanko and Zoya, along with the police officers, had arrived after the fire fight which had injured Ellie and after the cadet had been killed. And her fellow Marshals couldn't identify any of the attackers. Max couldn't identify the attackers, either, as she'd made clear in her story. They had been wearing masks the entire time.

When Vanko and Zoya had confirmed as much of Max's account as they could, the deputy chief looked at Max, his jaw set, a familiar expression of displeasure on his face. "You'll come to the central station in the morning to make a formal statement," he told her. Then he glanced at Faddei. "And you need to make sure your people have body cameras in future so we can verify their stories."

Max clamped her jaw shut, holding in her anger. She should have got used to his disbelief, but it still rankled. Faddei was not so restrained.

"No," Faddei said. "We don't answer to you. My people, as you call them, have done nothing but tell you the truth and do their jobs. If you want formal statements from us, make appointments through the central office."

Deputy Chief James glared at Faddei, his jaw working. His eyes slid sideways, no doubt realising that the conversation was taking place in front of an audience that included those of his own people who had been left to guard the building. "You're refusing to cooperate?" he demanded.

"We've done nothing but cooperate," Faddei said, in a mild voice that Max thought should make the deputy chief wary. That kind of mildness hid a white hot fury that Max could see reflected in Faddei's eyes. He'd displayed almost unending patience with the deputy chief's relentless questions over the past couple of weeks, Faddei's patience helping Max to hold on to her own temper. But even Faddei's even temper had its limits, and it looked like he'd reached them. "I'm sorry for your loss," the head Marshal continued, the rage banking down a little, "but we're not the enemy here." Faddei looked around, assessing the remaining police officers and the crime scene vans. "It sounds like Ellie was directed into the building by a magician. There might be some trace evidence of that magician on the street," he pointed out.

Max watched as the deputy chief's face changed colour. He hadn't forgotten that particular detail, Max thought. It was more like he hadn't thought about doing anything in response to it. She couldn't help wondering how long it was since he had run an active investigation, or been in charge of a crime scene. She could only hope that the other members of the task force were more attuned to the details of an investigation. The deputy chief jerked his chin, once, signalling that he had heard Faddei, before he turned and stalked away, heading for the nearest officer. Max could only hope that he was summoning one of the magicians who worked for law enforcement.

"And we've got other work to get on with," Faddei said, calling her attention back. He waved Max, Vanko and Zoya to follow him as he headed away from the building. Cas and Pol, who had been lounging at Max's feet, padded along by her side and she gave them each a pat as they walked. They had done good work that day and were doubtless as tired as she was.

Faddei paused by his vehicle, frowning back in the direction of the deputy chief. He looked at Max. "I'd like you to write up your impressions of the masked men," he told her. "Anything you can remember, however small."

"Alright," Max agreed. It was a reasonable request, and one she knew Faddei made with good intent. "I'll head back to the office now," she said.

"Good. Thank you. Vanko, Zoya, go to the mortuary and see if Audhilde can give us more information. I'm going to speak to Raymund about that creature we found."

Even though visiting the morgue was generally regarded as even less appealing than writing reports, neither of the other Marshals objected, simply heading for Zoya's truck. Max left them to it, going back to her own vehicle.

It took a couple of hours for Max to write up her impressions of the attackers, going over and over everything she had seen in her mind until she was beginning to doubt her own memory. And after all that effort, the most useful information she could come up with was that the masked attackers had been well-trained and well-armed. There had been no insignia on their clothing that she had seen, and they hadn't addressed each other by name or rank.

The one bright spot in the long, frustrating process was hearing from Faddei that Ellie was out of surgery and expected to make a full recovery. Max took the warm hope of that piece of news and clung to it as she looked over her notes for the millionth time.

As she finished her notes, Vanko and Zoya arrived back from the mortuary and Faddei met them in the Marshals' common room. He waved Max over, taking a copy of her notes with thanks.

It felt far too late, or far too early, for coffee, so Max got a glass of water and settled in a comfortable chair with the others. Vanko pulled a low table into the space between the chairs and set a series of high resolution photographs on its surface. Faces of dead men, all of them with gaping wounds where they had been shot. One of them had been shot from behind, his face unrecognisable. Max's stomach turned, but she forced herself to look. These were the attackers who had killed a police cadet, tried to kill Ellie, and attacked her, her dogs, and the other police officers who had come to stop them.

She didn't recognise any of them. They were all young-looking, possibly in their twenties, clean shaven, their skin tones varying from pale to mid-brown.

"Audhilde has sent copies to the deputy chief and the investigation team," Vanko said, settling back in his chair with a long, weary sigh. "But so far there's nothing. They're not in any database as far as we can tell. There were no personal possessions on any of the bodies."

"No ID?" Max asked, startled. It was one of the city's rules that everyone had to carry an identification card. Protests rose up from time to time about the infringement on freedom, but what most people didn't realise was that the identification cards were coded to let law enforcement know if the individual was something other than human. The city council thought it was important to keep track of the city's non-human population. The Five Families hadn't objected, much to Max's surprise. Of course, there were some people who refused to carry their ID cards, but most people did, as they didn't want to risk the heavy fines that would be imposed otherwise. She wasn't sure why she was so surprised that a group of men who had shot at law enforcement officers didn't have their ID cards on them.

"One of them had a Huntsman tattoo," Zoya added, pointing to the photograph of the man with the destroyed face. "Not that it's going to help us much."

The Huntsman clan was a disparate group of partly human people known for their violent, criminal activities and their disdain for the city's police. That included refusing to cooperate in providing access to members of the clan for police interviews. Very few of the Huntsman clan members were on police records.

"Was the tattoo fresh or faded?" Faddei asked, drawing Max's attention.

"It looked a couple of years old, from what Audhilde could tell," Vanko answered, in a thoughtful tone. "What are you thinking?"

"I was just wondering if he was still a member of the clan or if he might have gone elsewhere," Faddei said, and shook his head slightly. "I know, most people never get out of the clan, but we've had one or two over the years. They don't get their tattoos renewed, so the ink can look very faded."

That was news to Max. She had never heard of anyone getting out of the Huntsman clan before. "So, if the tattoo was a couple of years old, does that mean it's likely he was still a member?" she asked.

"Possibly. It's not going to help much with the Huntsmans, of course," Faddei said. He sighed, leaning back in his own chair, scowling at the photographs Vanko had laid out. "None of this is making any sense."

Max agreed. A magician had directed Ellie and her cadet into a building where they had been attacked by at least five people. Then the fifth attacker had killed the others, shooting them all, before escaping. It made no sense. Not just the ambush on a pair of police officers, but also one team member killing the others. A waste of resources, if nothing else.

"What did Raymund have to say about the creature?" Zoya asked, cutting through Max's spiralling thoughts.

"That also doesn't make sense. It does look like a cross between a Robinsage and a Seacast monkey, but he's running tests to see if he can confirm that. We've found some cross breeds before, but never that particular combination. They aren't very compatible," Faddei added.

Max nodded her agreement, reviewing what she knew of the two different breeds of monkey. Seacast monkeys tended to band in larger groups and were aggressive in acquiring new territory, and seemed to hate everyone and everything that wasn't a Seacast monkey. Robinsage tended to be far more solitary, and kept to themselves. No doubt the smell helped with that, too, she thought, nose wrinkling in memory.

The Marshals' service library held records of old experiments, which Raymund encouraged all Marshals to review from time to time. In years past, some of the wealthier city residents had amused themselves by crossing different species with each other, trying to create new species. Some of them seemed to have been done out of boredom, and some with specific intents. Max had read some of the records with horror and disgust. The experimenters had not cared one bit for the creatures that they were studying. One thing had been very clear from the notes, and from Raymund's comments on the subject, was that it was beyond cruel to force different types of creatures together. They all had different instincts, the mixed breed offspring often inheriting some of the worst traits of both their parent species, living short and unhappy lives. Neither Seacast nor Robinsage monkeys fitted into the city, with its mass of people and artificial buildings, but both types of monkey could live full lives back in their natural habitat of the Wild. A cross breed would have nowhere to go, Max thought. Neither one of its parent species would accept it.

"The creature is settling well," Faddei added. "Raymund has put it into one of the larger holding pens and it was sleeping last I heard." He shook his head again. "We'll need to consider what to do with it once Raymund has completed his tests."

Max nodded, and saw similar grim expressions on Vanko and Zoya's faces. The Marshals' service generally tried not to kill the creatures they were sent after. Some of the smaller species, like the yellow, vicious crow spiders, were kept on site, housed in Raymund's workshops. For larger, more intelligent species like the monkeys they ran across, the Marshals' teams generally returned them to the Wild. But something that was a cross breed would almost certainly not survive in the Wild, which meant Faddei and Raymund would have to consider whether the creature could be allowed to live, and where. Being kept in one of the holding pens for the rest of its life was an awful thought for a creature whose instincts would be to climb trees and move across large areas of territory.

"The task force is meeting again in the morning," Faddei said, and glanced at the clock on the wall. "In a few hours, then. From what I've heard, they don't have any more information about the magician that Ellie spoke to. I'll take them your notes, Max, and the photos, thank you," he said, and gathered the grim, glossy prints from the table. "Go get some rest. I have a feeling it's going to be another busy day."

Left alone in the room as the others headed out, Max stared at the blank surface of the table, exhaustion pressing on her. Masked attackers. Magicians using compulsion spells. Some idiot mixing up different types of monkeys. Not to mention the shocking news from Audhilde that someone was trying to get into magicians' Vaults. She didn't know what to think or where to start.

A huge yawn took her by surprise and reminded her that she needed rest. With daylight not that far away, Max opted for a blanket and a nap on one of the sofas in the common room. It wasn't the first time she or one of the other Marshals had slept there.

She slept just long enough to get some energy back, then pushed herself to her feet. She might have a head full of surprises and downright shocks, but there was one place in the city she could always go for a warm welcome and information. She gathered Cas and Pol and headed for the Hunter's Tooth.

Chapter Eight

Max pulled into the parking lot that served the Hunter's Tooth in the early morning light, surprised to see another pair of vehicles there already, parked closer to the building. The Tooth did occasionally have patrons who stayed all night, but it wasn't common. The pair of vehicles were large, rugged looking vans with no logos she could see. Her attention slid past the vehicles, caught by movement around the side of the building, where Malik kept his large, wheeled bin. There were people there. That was unusual enough to make her frown as she got out of her vehicle. As soon as she set foot on the ground, unease crept across her skin. Something was wrong. The ground felt different. There was always a sense of life and calm around the Tooth, Malik's influence extending even to the parking lot. That calm was missing.

Looking across at the bar itself, she saw that the door was hanging off its hinges. She drew her gun, waving Cas and Pol out of the pick-up, and turned her attention to the group of people standing around the bin. No, not just standing. They were kicking something on the ground. It looked like a pile of old cloth, although Max couldn't understand why anyone would want to kick old cloth. Perhaps some unfortunate creature had taken refuge under the bins and the people were tormenting it. It wouldn't be the first time.

"Hey! Stop!" Max yelled, and drew her badge. "Marshals' service," she called, heading across the cracked concrete. As she moved closer, she checked in her stride, shock coursing through her. Each member of the group was wearing head-to-toe black, and she caught the gleam of a weapon just before one of the group raised their arm towards her, the weak morning sunlight glinting off a gun barrel. She scrambled backwards, seeking shelter, ducking around the front end of her pick-up, hearing the crack of a weapon and the ping of bullets hitting her vehicle. She fired back even as Cas and Pol sprinted across the open space, heading for the group, her dogs shifting into their attack forms between one stride and the next.

Her dogs hit two of the people squarely in their chests, sending them crashing to the ground, loud snarls rising in the air as others in the group lifted weapons and pointed them at Cas and Pol. Max fired again, aiming her shots over her dogs, panic closing her throat at the thought her dogs might be shot. The shadow-hounds whipped around, tackling two more of the group, dragging them down to the ground as well, more snarls rising in the air.

Max left the safety of her pick-up and ran across the cracked concrete, gun in hand. No one was firing at her. Or her dogs.

There were half a dozen black-clad people on the ground when she got there, all of them armed.

"Clear out," one of the people said.

To Max's surprise, the half-dozen people moved immediately, getting to their feet and sprinting for the vans she had seen. She raised her gun, tracking their movements, but was reluctant to shoot, even though they had fired at her.

As she turned, she realised that the lump on the ground wasn't cloth. It was a person, Max saw, more shock coursing through her as she recognised Malik's curling hair, worn jeans and t-shirt. He was lying on his side, one arm flung forward, stretching towards the building, and every bit of skin that Max could see was covered in bruises or blood or both. Her chest hurt just looking at him, at the injuries she could see.

The sound of engines starting reminded her that Malik's attackers were getting away, but she didn't care about them. Malik looked more than half dead.

After a quick glance to make sure that the vans and the armed men were really gone, Max holstered her gun, kneeling beside Malik, heart thumping in her throat as she wondered if he was even alive. She held her hand in front of his mouth, not surprised to see her fingers trembling. This was Malik. He was warm and generous and the world was a far better place with him in it. A soft rush of warm air against her skin reassured her that he was still breathing.

"Malik," she whispered, "what happened?"

He stirred, his eyes opening a fraction, which was as much as he could manage with his face swollen from bruising. His lips formed a word, barely any sound coming out. "Max," he said.

"Yes. What can I do? You're injured. Hospital?" she asked, but stayed where she was, not reaching for her phone. Malik was not human, and she wasn't sure a hospital or conventional medicine would help him, or even if he would survive the trip. He was a male siren, and from the little she knew about them, they were closely connected to their home territories.

"Inside," he croaked, his swollen lower lip splitting as he spoke, fresh blood appearing.

"Inside," Max repeated. She followed the line of his outstretched arm. He'd been trying to get to the side entrance set into the wall. It led to an open area next to the building. She had only been in there a few times, and remembered a lush, green paradise of a garden. Malik's garden. And she remembered Ruutti meeting Malik for the first time, saying that Malik couldn't leave. Max had never seen him anywhere apart from the Hunter's Tooth and the buildings around it, which he also owned. His territory. "Inside," Max repeated, determination in her voice. "I'm sorry, I think this is going to hurt," she said, getting up. "I'm not strong enough to carry you."

She rolled him onto his back as carefully as she could, trying to ignore the moan he made. He doubtless had more bruises under his clothes. She put her hands under his arms, braced herself, and pulled, dragging him towards the side entrance.

Or, rather, she tried to. He didn't move. Not even a little bit. It was like trying to pull her pick-up, with its brakes on. She'd pulled a Seacast monkey out of a building before, and with far less effort. Malik's *other* nature must be weighing him down. She dug her heels in and tried again. He moved the smallest, tiniest fraction and then stopped. She gasped with effort, whole body straining, and managed to move him a little further. Then she had to stop and brace herself, her hands on her knees, breathing hard.

Cas and Pol crowded beside her.

"Can you try grabbing his ankles and pulling?" she asked her dogs. They brought down prey much larger than themselves on a regular basis. One non-human male should be relatively easy for them.

Her dogs moved at once, seizing hold of Malik's legs, and tried dragging him towards the side entrance. He moved a little bit further than he had when Max had tried, but not nearly far enough. Her dogs growled, panting, and redoubled their efforts. They moved another foot or two, and Malik moaned again. Her dogs were being as careful as they could be with their mouths, but between the grip on his legs and his other injuries, Max realised that moving him was causing him more pain.

"Stop, stop," Max said to her dogs. "We need another way." She tried to remember if she had any rope in her truck. She seemed to remember that there was an old tree inside Malik's garden. She might be able to loop a rope around the tree and use her pick-up to drag him inside. If there wasn't a tree there, she might need to tie Malik to her pick-up and drive through the wall if she was going to get him inside. If she had a rope, of course.

Rapid footsteps nearby and her dogs' low growls alerted her to someone else approaching.

She drew her gun on reflex, wondering if it was Malik's attackers come back to finish the job. There was only one person running towards her, the sun behind him at first. As he moved, she could make out his features and her brows lifted, recognising Bryce. She hadn't seen him since they had got back from the Wild. They had planned to have drinks together, but he had been forced to cancel as Kitris had sent him off on some mission or other.

"What's happened?" he asked, not bothering with a greeting.

"There were half a dozen men here. He's badly injured. He wants to go inside, but I can't move him. He weighs more than my pick-up," Max said, hating that she sounded weak. "Can you help?" she asked.

"Of course. Can you hold this?" Bryce asked, handing off his automatic weapon to Max. "And ask your dogs to back off?"

"Sure," Max said, taking the weapon. It was heavier than she had expected and she cradled it in her arms, not wanting to put her fingers anywhere near the trigger. She called her dogs away and they watched as Bryce took hold of Malik under his arms, as Max had done, and then dragged him across the cracked concrete to the side entrance. It was clear that Bryce was using a lot of effort, putting his whole body into the task of moving Malik, and keeping his movements slow and controlled as he dragged the injured man across the ground.

Max's jaw dropped as Malik moved. She had known Bryce was strong - he had picked her and her heavy backpack up and simply jumped them across a gap in the ground not so long ago - but seeing him manage what she and her dogs hadn't been able to do was still startling. It must be his non-human side, she realised. He might look like a tall, broad-shouldered human male, with short, dark hair and a face that had been punched more than once, but there was a subtle difference to the way he moved that would tell someone looking closely that he was not fully human.

"Wow. You're much stronger than you look. Must be the demon part of you," Max said, heat rising to her face at her unguarded words. "I'm sorry," she said immediately. It was generally rude to comment on someone's non-human nature. Not everyone wanted to acknowledge that they had something *other* in their make-up.

To her surprise, Bryce slanted her a sideways look and a smile. "It comes in useful sometimes," he admitted.

As he didn't seem offended, she gave in to her curiosity as he continued to pull Malik, slowly and carefully, the short distance to the building. "Do you know what order of demon?" she asked. She hadn't made as detailed a study of the different types as she should have done. And *demon* was a broad term, covering not just the true demons from the underworld, but also just about any human-shaped, non-human being.

"Mum and dad don't have horns or scaled skin, if that's what you mean," he said, still smiling.

Max choked on a laugh, more heat rising in her face. She was sure he was teasing her, but just in case, she said, "That's not what I meant at all."

"We all seem to have sharper senses and extra strength, so the family tradition goes that we're probably descended from rock-breakers," Bryce added, making her laugh again. That was not an official class of demon, of course, but there were definitely a few types that would fit the blunt description.

He was trying to distract her, she realised. And she had been curious enough. Pressing for more information would be rude. She cast about in her mind for a graceful way to change the subject, then realised that the side door to the building was still shut and moved ahead of Bryce, shoving the door open with her shoulder just before he reached it. There was a lip at the bottom of the door, and Bryce grunted with effort as he lifted Malik across that, but he got him inside. Max called her dogs in, then closed the door behind them.

The lush green paradise that Max remembered from her previous visits was still there, along with the tree rising over their heads. What had once been a utilitarian warehouse had been turned into an exotic garden, with fantastical plants rising above their heads with vivid pink and orange flowers, head-high plants with broad, dark green leaves swayed in the slightest of breezes, and a trickle of water sounded from the artificial stream and pond that Malik had created. Brightly coloured fish darted here and there in the water, catching Cas and Pol's attention.

There was an ancient rug and collection of large floor cushions set near the pond along with a tray with a large pitcher and several glasses. Max pointed, silently asking if Bryce could move Malik across there. He did so without comment, straightening when he had Malik on the rug and looking around, mouth open in clear surprise.

"I had no idea this was here," Bryce said. For the first time she could remember, he sounded out of breath. Even for him, moving Malik had taken an effort.

"Very few people do," Max said. She put his automatic weapon on one of the cushions and grabbed the pitcher and one of the glasses from the tray. The liquid in the pitcher looked like plain water. She tilted the drink into Malik's mouth, wincing in sympathy as the movement made the split in his lip open again. He took in some of the liquid and swallowed, though, a trail of moisture running from his eyes as he did so. Max hesitated, but then gave him more water. She didn't know how long he had been outside, or what else she could do for him.

Malik finished the glass and let out a long, heartfelt sigh, his whole body relaxing.

"Better," he said. There were still trails of tears leaking from his swollen eyes, but he was breathing more steadily.

"The men outside. Who were they? Who did this to you?" Max asked.

"Don't know them," Malik answered, his voice still weak. "Four? Five? Thought one had a Huntsman tattoo."

"There were six of them," Max said, hearing the tremor in her voice. It had taken six men to overpower Malik and drag him out of his property. "Just one with a Huntsman tattoo?" Max asked, remembering the group now lying in Audhilde's mortuary. One of them had a Huntsman tattoo as well. She shouldn't be surprised that the Huntsman clan was involved in violence, even if it was shocking that anyone had committed violence against Malik, and on his own territory.

"That I saw," Malik confirmed. His fingers twitched, reaching for the glass, and Max filled it up again, holding it to his mouth.

"Six people," Bryce repeated. He was crouched on Malik's other side, expression intent as he watched the injured man. "One with a Huntsman tattoo. Anything else?"

"Magic. One used magic," Malik said. "Don't know who. Powerful spell," he added, lip curling in disgust. His split lip bled again at the gesture. "Brought it in."

Max's throat tightened. The attackers, whoever they were, had known they would need numbers and magic to overpower Malik. They had prepared magic somewhere else, and brought it here. And they had nearly succeeded in killing him.

"Did they say why they were here?" Max asked.

"Interfering siren," Malik said, an odd inflection to his voice. Not his words, Max realised. Someone had said those words to him. One of the attackers, most likely. "Poking my nose where it doesn't belong," Malik added, voice slurring a little. He winced. Max wondered just how much damage the attackers had done.

"You need to rest. Heal," Max said, resisting the urge to put a hand on his shoulder. From the way he was lying, it looked like every part of his body hurt and she didn't want to cause him any more pain.

"Not yet. Tell me. Something about Vault," Malik said, frowning. "No. To tell you. Max. Something about Vault."

"Audhilde said that magicians have been reporting people trying to access their Vaults," Max said. "Someone tried to access hers."

Malik's eyes brightened for a moment. He gave a soft laugh that cut off in the middle and turned into a groan. "Hilda. No one messes with her."

"So I gathered. The six men were all in black," she told Bryce. "I, er, encountered a similar group yesterday." She turned back to Malik. "I was coming here to ask you what you knew," Max told him. He had drunk the second glass and she poured another, offering it to him. He shook his head, and she set it down, folding her hands together to stop herself from reaching out to him. It had been a long time since they had been together, but it hurt to see him in so much pain. "I don't know what they hoped to achieve here," she added, staring down at Malik's bruised and battered face.

"Me dead," Malik answered, lips twitching. "Almost succeeded." He turned his head slightly and looked at Max with his swollen, bloodshot eyes. "We don't do well out of territory. I was nearly gone."

"I'm sorry I didn't get here sooner," Max said, unclenching her hands and reaching out to touch his arm. The briefest, lightest of touches, trying not to hurt him.

Before Max could ask him anything else, she became aware of a scratching sensation along her upper arm, as if someone was trying to get her attention. She turned, but there was nothing there. Even as she stared at the empty space beside her, the sensation came again. No. Not on her arm. It was something connected to her, but not physically present. She could feel the snap of an invisible tether tightening and put her hand up, gathering her magic. Not just her magic. Something else. Something familiar, but rarely used. The Vault. *Her* Vault.

"What is it?" Bryce asked.

"I'm not sure. I think someone is trying to access my Vault," Max said, getting to her feet, palm out in the direction the scratching sensation was coming from. She pushed back, willing her Vault to stay closed, and the sensation faded. She breathed a sigh of relief. "I haven't checked the bar," she told Bryce, a chill running over her. She'd been so focused on Malik and getting him to comparative safety, she hadn't considered that there might be more people lying in wait in the bar. Or more people injured.

"I'll do that now," he said, picking up his weapon.

"I'm sorry," Max said. "I didn't even ask why you were here." Order warriors didn't get much free time, so he was most likely here on business, and his help with Malik would be delaying him.

"I came to see Malik. He's one of the best sources of information in the city," Bryce said, "but it will wait until he's healed. I'll check the bar," he said, and headed back out through the side door.

Leaving Max alone with Malik. She crouched down beside him again. "You're looking better," she told him.

"Given enough time, I will heal," he answered, and managed a faint smile for her. "Thanks to you."

"Thank Bryce. I could barely move you. I was considering roping you to my truck," she told him, almost giddy with relief. He was alive. He was on his own territory. He would be alright. He had to be.

Malik tried to laugh, the sound cut off again in another moan of pain.

"Can I call someone? Is there anyone who can help?" Max asked.

"I'll heal in time," Malik said, shaking his head. "If you can shut up the bar for me, that would be good. It might be a few days."

"Alright," Max said, rising to her feet. "Let me check with Bryce about the bar. I'll be back soon," she said. She waved for her dogs to stay with Malik and headed out after the warrior.

As she left the courtyard, she pulled out her phone, hesitating. There was one person she could call, although she didn't think Malik would thank her. But she didn't know anyone else of Malik's kind. And he had nearly died.

"My dear Max, were you missing me?" Ruutti Passila answered her phone with a low purr.

"A group of men came to the Hunter's Tooth and attacked Malik," Max said, not responding to the detective's teasing. "He's in a bad way."

"Did they take him out of his territory?" Ruutti asked, her voice sharp and focused.

"Yes. Onto the parking lot. He's back in his territory now. He *says* he'll be fine," Max said, hearing the hesitation in her own voice. She paused, not sure how to frame the question she really wanted to ask. Ruutti usually gave the impression that she didn't care about anyone apart from herself.

"I'm on my way," Ruutti said, cutting through Max's hesitation, and hung up.

As she put her phone away, Bryce came out into the daylight and pulled the door behind him, shoving what looked like a pool cue across the door to wedge it shut.

"Bar's empty," he told her. "How's Malik?"

"Says he's doing better. I've called Ruutti. She's on her way," Max said, glancing back at the partly open door to the garden.

"Ruutti Passila?" Bryce asked, sounding surprised.

"They're the same kind," Max said. Ruutti's quick response had surprised her, too, but the detective had seemed utterly astonished to find a male of her kind when she had met Malik a few weeks before, when Ruutti had roped Max into helping her with a case. If male sirens were rare, perhaps Ruutti had an interest in keeping this one alive. Max could only hope so. She started back towards the garden, wanting to let Malik know he was about to have some company.

The scratching sensation rose again, this time across her whole arm and shoulder, spreading across her back and down her torso. She found herself pulled, turned away from her path, a whirling mess of magic appearing in the air in front of her. Magic with a familiar resonance. The Vault again.

And something else. A brilliant, blinding white light that rang all through her to her very bones with an unheard note of peace and calm and the suggestion of something vast and undying.

Distracted by the white light, Max lost her concentration on the Vault, only coming back into her body as her feet started sliding across the concrete. This time, she couldn't stop the Vault opening and whatever force was connecting her to the Vault was pulling her forwards. As she flung up her hand to command the Vault to close again, an arm reached through the magic, a hard hand grabbing hold of her wrist, dragging her off her feet, forward into the maelstrom of magic.

The last thing she saw before the magic took her was Bryce's startled expression, her ears echoing with the barks of her dogs. Then she was pulled into a vortex of spinning colours and everything else faded from view.

Chapter Nine

Magic pulled her, spun her around and around and around until she was dizzy and nauseous and had no idea where up or down was or where her fingers or toes were. Round and round and round again. Magic washed over her in a wave of pressure that squeezed her bones, her mouth open in a scream that had no sound. A brilliant flash of light blinded her. Not the white light that had echoed through her. Something different. Camera flash?

Max hit the ground shoulder and hip first, the impact jarring every bone in her body. Not spinning any longer. Her stomach settled and she sucked in a relieved breath. There was a *down* and an *up*. She scrambled to her feet, her boots settled on something solid and firm. She couldn't see a thing, her eyes not working after the flash of light. The magic had faded, leaving a roaring in her ears. The air was wrong against her skin. She had no idea where she was, panic rising in her throat. She remembered the hard hand grabbing hold of her, pulling her through the magic into wherever this was. She reached for her gun, fingers closing around the hilt. At least that was still there. She stilled before she drew the weapon, trying to work out if there was anyone else, or anything else, nearby. Her attacker, for example.

"I can't believe that worked," the voice was too close.

Max gasped and took an instinctive step back, in the direction her senses told her was away from the voice. Her back hit something solid. She put a hand out to either side quickly, making sure there was nothing else nearby. Her fingers met hard, cool stone. A wall.

"How did you let yourself get caught? Are you really that bad a magician?" the voice asked. The speaker was male, but she didn't recognise him.

She drew her gun, holding it with both hands in front of her, blinking rapidly to try to clear her sight. She dared not move any further.

Her eyes started to clear, letting her see broad shapes. She was inside, in what looked like a rectangular room with no windows. There was a dark shadow standing not far away from her that she thought must be the speaker, and a crumpled mass of shadow on the floor near him.

"Oh, are you going to shoot me?" the voice asked, full of mocking laughter. "Can't even see me, can you?" he asked, still laughing.

He lunged towards her and she fired. One bullet. She was confident it hadn't hit him. He kept moving. She reversed her grip on the gun instead and ducked sideways, away from his charge, using the butt of her gun as a club and swinging it in the general direction where his head should be.

Her weapon connected with a satisfying thud and her attacker slumped, sliding to the ground at her feet. She backed up, holding the gun ready to fire again, her throat tight, mouth dry.

There was a roaring in her ears which gradually died as her sight cleared, letting her see more details. The man at her feet looked unconscious, but she knelt and put one hand on his neck to be sure. There was a pulse there, steady and clear.

Wiping her hand on her trousers, she straightened and cast a look over her attacker. He was wearing black combat clothing that looked to be at least a size too big for him, from the heavy-soled boots to the heavy-wearing trousers with multiple pockets and bulky jacket. The outfit reminded her strongly of the groups who had attacked Ellie and Malik. The only real difference was that this man wasn't wearing a mask. Curiously, he didn't have any weapons of his own. As she replayed the brief conversation in her head, she wondered if he might be a magician rather than a fighter. No one she knew, at any rate. He was quite ordinary-looking, with short, straight dark hair and pale skin.

She remembered the other crumpled form and turned, gun ready. As she turned, her head spun. The after-effect of whatever magic had brought her here, perhaps. She kept her feet planted on the ground until her head cleared. Her sight was back to normal, thankfully. The air tasted stale, disused. There was magic in the background, though. The familiar magic of her Vault, which was a combination of the Vault's inherent magic and her own signature.

She looked around the room more carefully, finding herself in what looked like an extremely ordinary storage room big enough to hold at least two of her pick-ups. The room had dull grey walls, floor and ceiling, and two racks of shelves against one wall. The room was lit by a strip of what looked like plastic set into the ceiling. The strip cast a diffuse, muted light through the room. The shelves were almost empty. There was a familiar-looking case which housed the rocket launcher she had bought almost on a whim many years before. And boxes of emergency rations, carefully preserved, as well as bottled water. It wasn't just a storage room, she realised, skin prickling. She was inside her own Vault. The things she could see were familiar to her, all of them marked with her signature so she could find them and pull them out as needed. When she had been sending things into the Vault, she had had some unclear notion that she should keep some basic things for survival. There were other boxes on the shelves which she knew should contain blankets and a change of clothes, along with at least one more handgun and ammunition. Not all that much, but then it had always been an effort for her to access the Vault and to deposit or remove items.

So, she was in her Vault. She had not known that was even possible.

And she had knocked out the person who might have told her what had happened, and how she had been brought here.

Or perhaps not the only person. The crumpled mass of shadow on the floor that she had seen earlier was another body. She stilled for a moment, remembering finding Malik close to death. She could only hope that Ruutti would be able to look after him and he would be back to full health soon. Right now, she couldn't do anything to help Malik.

Keeping her gun ready, she took a cautious step forward and nudged the other body with her foot, taking a quick step back in case it reacted. Nothing. Not even a moan. She tried a harder nudge and the body slid from its side onto its back, face up to the ceiling. A young man she didn't recognise, his eyes closed, a gaping wound at his hairline that was bleeding sluggishly. There was a thick trail of blood down the side of his face that had run into the cowled neckline of the robe he wore.

Max frowned, taking stock of his clothing. The vastly different attire, and the fact that he had already been unconscious when she arrived, suggested that he wasn't associated with her attacker. The robes made her pause. Normally, only Priests and Priestesses wore robes, but their robes were a soft grey colour. She had also encountered followers of Arkus wearing dark robes while they were setting up a dark magic ritual.

These robes were different. They looked to be made of rough fabric, and were a deep blue colour with silver stitching on the front right shoulder, where a police officer or a warrior of the Order might wear their badge of rank or insignia.

She took a careful step forward, gun still held ready, and took a closer look at the silver stitching. It caught the light in a flare that nearly blinded her, telling her there was magic woven into the fabric. The negative image of the symbol appeared behind her eyes as she blinked and she frowned, sure she must have been mistaken. But, no, she hadn't been. The symbol matched the one that she had used for the Vault when she had created the spells that allowed her to access it. Which meant that the unconscious man, whoever he was, most likely worked for the Vault.

So she had one man, dressed in black, who seemed to have been involved in bringing her here. And another man, already unconscious, who probably worked for the Vault.

All of which left her with questions buzzing around her mind. How had she got here? Who was her attacker? Why had he brought her here? And what was he doing here in the first place? This was the Vault. It was supposed to be a near-sacred space, where magicians could store whatever they liked with no questions asked, and be secure in the knowledge that their particular Vaults would never, ever, be accessed by anyone else. And yet she had arrived here to find not one but two people inside her personal Vault.

Panic threatened to choke her. It shouldn't be possible. None of this should be possible. And yet, she was here and everything around her was real and solid.

No one knew much about the Vault. Those who were lucky enough to have spaces in it generally did not discuss it. The very little knowledge that Max had, suggested that the Vault was most likely guarded in some way. She had always assumed the Vault was a construct of magic, and not a real place. But standing in the storage room, she could see that she had been wrong. With that new knowledge, it made a certain sort of sense that the physical Vault would need staff. Workers who were charged with the security and protection of powerful magicians' secrets, and who therefore probably possessed the means to defend themselves and the Vault against intruders.

Panic rose. She didn't need the mockery of her attacker to tell her that she was ill-equipped to deal with sophisticated magic. And she had no real idea where she was, or how to get out. She looked around, wondering if there was a way she could get out and back to the Hunter's Tooth. The only door she could see was the one ahead of her, past the unconscious man in the blue robes. She could try sending herself out of the Vault the way that she had added and removed items from it, but as soon as she tried to access her magic, a stabbing pain struck behind her eyes. She wasn't going to be using magic any time soon. In the meantime, she had managed to defeat the man who had dragged her here. She should probably try to see if there was another means out of the building before he woke up.

She put her hand on the robed man's neck, just above the cowl, checking for his pulse. It was slow and steady under her fingers. He seemed to be breathing fine, too, just unconscious. There wasn't anything more she could do for him. From the swelling around his head wound and the amount of blood, she guessed that he had been injured and unconscious for a while. A memory of a long-ago basic first-aid course at the Marshals' offices suggested it was a bad idea to leave the unconscious man lying on his back. She carefully turned him back onto his side. He didn't react, but his breathing stayed steady and his pulse was still strong when she checked it again. She had done as much as she could for him right now.

She looked back at the door. There was an ordinary-looking handle, with no apparent lock. But of course, this was the Vault, which was supposed to be the most secure facility that magicians could create. There were probably other security measures apart from a simple lock and key.

Max took a step forward and put her ear to the door. Nothing. She couldn't tell whether that was because the door was too thick and solid for her to hear through, or if there was nothing moving on the other side of it. She stared at the plain grey paint for a moment, then pulled her phone out, wondering if she could get a signal to pinpoint her location. The screen showed an error message. *Out of network.* No signal. She sighed, but she hadn't really expected anything else. Whoever had built the Vault had doubtless put in place additional security measures to stop electronic surveillance. Which left her with the door in front of her.

She glanced up at the muted light overhead, hoping that it wouldn't cast a shadow and make her a target when she opened the door, then put her hand on the door handle, her breathing harsh and loud in her ears.

The handle turned, smooth and silent, and the door eased open, a sliver of brighter light creeping around the edge. Taking another breath, Max stepped outside.

Chapter Ten

She was at the end of a wide corridor, a solid wall to her right-hand side, the corridor stretching ahead of her with another five doors - two more on her side, three on the other. The corridor was empty. For now. The gaps between the doors suggested rooms of a similar size to the one she had just left. The doors had heavy stone surrounds, with the doors set back inside the frames. More than enough space for her to keep hiding, if she wanted. Soft light was provided by domes in the ceiling overhead, showing the muted brown and sand colours of the ceiling, walls and floor. The building material seemed to be stone, but a type that Max wasn't familiar with.

Looking around, Max saw that there were markings on the walls next to each of the doors. Lines and dots and other designs that made no sense to her. She stepped out of the doorway and turned to look at the surround of the door to her Vault, and saw a set of markings formed into a square pattern next to the door. Perhaps a coding system, to identify the particular room? There didn't seem to be any other markings around the doorway that she could see, just on the walls. Taking her phone out, she snapped a picture of the markings next to the door, glad that the camera function wasn't tied in to the phone's network. It occurred to her she should probably take a picture of the two men in her Vault, too, just in case she came across someone who might be able to identify them or tell her what was going on.

Before she could go back inside, one of the other doors along the corridor swung open. She ducked back into the recess of her doorway, tucking herself into the shadow and putting her phone away so that the lit screen wouldn't give her position away. The door surround was deep enough to conceal her, if she didn't move and if someone didn't look directly at her. She thought about going back into her Vault, but she didn't want to be trapped with only one exit, and two unconscious men.

Trying to stay as still and quiet as possible, she watched as a man in black combat clothing similar to her attacker came out of the open door. He had sallow, pock-marked skin and close-cropped dark hair and a surly expression that suggested a ready temper. Someone to avoid if at all possible. He crouched briefly and marked an X on the ground with chalk. Glancing around the corridor, Max saw that all the other doors, including hers, had the same marking in front of them.

As he straightened, another man in the same clothing came out of the room. The second man was taller than the first, with close-cropped reddish-brown hair and the sort of pale skin that didn't tan. Both men were carrying automatic weapons across their chests, with pistols at their hips. The second man had a trail of magic around him that suggested a powerful magician.

"Nothing useful there, either," the second man said. The first man grunted. "You'd think that magicians would hide something useful in their Vaults," the second man complained.

Max held herself still, heart thumping from both fear of discovery and shock. Even though she had discovered an intruder in her own Vault, it was still almost unthinkable that magicians would break into other Vaults. She drew a deep, silent breath, trying to calm her mind, trying to slow her spiralling thoughts. They were searching each Vault. She wondered if they were looking for something in particular, or just things to steal.

"Any trouble?" the second man asked. "What about the other guy?"

The first man shook his head with another grunt. Max's brows lifted, wondering if he spoke at all. And also who the *other guy* was. The second man had shown no concern when asking for him, just looking for information. Max wondered if he was asking about the man lying unconscious in the Vault behind her.

The pair turned their backs to her, moving to the end of the corridor and turning a corner until they were out of sight. Max hesitated. They had left the room door open behind them, perhaps not caring about what was in it. In the shadows of the other heavy door frames, she thought that a couple of the other doors might be open as well. They all had the same large X on the ground in front of them. The pair had searched all of them. And didn't seem to have found what they were looking for as they weren't carrying anything extra with them.

Max edged carefully out of the shadows of her doorway and into the corridor, glancing at the solid wall to one side that marked the end of the corridor. No one was going to come at her from that direction, at least. She moved as carefully and quietly as she could along the corridor, hiding behind each door surround as she went, then creeping forward to the end of the corridor, risking a glance around it.

As she took a look around, the air moved slightly against her skin and she realised that the whole place was saturated with magic. It was ancient and subtle, woven into all the surfaces around her, bearing the familiar resonance of the Vault. The magic was older than anything she had ever sensed before. Centuries old. More than old enough to have seeped into the stone. There didn't seem to be any active spells that Max could sense, just the gentle presence of old spells. Her brows lifted. Whoever had built the Vault had clearly not expected to need defensive spells.

She remembered the blinding light and sense of something vast around her just before she had been pulled into the Vault. The light had borne a faintly familiar resonance, but she still couldn't place it. And it was nowhere to be found now. It was just her and the Vault.

With the magic settled and calm around her, Max looked ahead. The short, dead-end corridor that she was on opened part way along a much longer corridor which ran in both directions, openings at each end suggesting that it connected to more passages.

Apart from the length, the layout was nearly identical, with heavy door surrounds at regular intervals. The men were standing in front of the nearest door. The second man pulled what looked like a computer tablet out of his chest pocket and tapped the screen.

"Vault 17 dash 24 dash 4. Owned by Constance Farmer."

"I thought she was dead?" the first man said, startling Max with his deep voice. So he could talk.

"She is. So there shouldn't be any safeguards," the second man said, putting the tablet away and placing his hand on the square of symbols on the door surround. "Hopefully," he added.

Max could feel him gathering his magic, and wondered if she should intervene. They were thieves, and this was the Vault. But there were two of them, both armed, and the second man at least had powerful magic.

While she was hesitating, rapid footsteps sounded from the other end of the corridor. The two men turned at once, lifting their weapons.

A pair of people wearing dark blue robes ran around the end of the corridor, both of them apparently unarmed. A man and a woman, they were both short and dark-haired, the silver stitching on their robes glowing in the muted light. The pair came to a halt and raised their hands, but not to surrender. Instead, they flung glittering bolts of magic energy at the intruders.

The magic was as powerful as anything Max had come across before. The armed men were thrown off their feet, flying through the air, landing on the ground close to where Max was hiding. She pressed herself back against the wall, but as the men scrambled to their feet, one of them spotted her.

"Who are you?" he asked, weapon pointing at her. It was the first man, the surly one, who seemed far taller and more intimidating close up than he had from further along the corridor.

"Never mind her," the other man said, turning back to face the robed people.

"She's not one of us," the first argued, weapon still pointed at Max.

"Surrender," a woman's voice said.

For a startled moment, Max wondered if the woman was speaking to her. But it must be the robed woman, the one with powerful magic. She was out of Max's line of sight, but not the armed men's. The second man raised his hand, magic gathering.

Before he could act, another wave of magic slammed into him, sending him off his feet. He was quicker to rise this time, and raised his gun, sending rapid automatic fire along the corridor.

The first man turned to join him, firing on the robed pair.

Max had her own gun in her hands before she knew what she intended, firing twice, once at each man, then ducking back into her corridor as their attention turned on her. Before she had time to think about the wisdom of hiding in a dead-end with no escape, more running footsteps ahead of her signalled the arrival of another pair of black-clad men, with more automatic weapons.

Max ducked behind the nearest door surround, using the heavy stone as a cover, and held her gun ready to fire, cursing silently. What had she got involved in?

She spotted one of the intruders' heads poking around a corner ahead of her and fired, aiming slightly lower than the head. She didn't like killing. He ducked back, spitting out a curse, and a moment later the muzzle of a gun appeared. Max retreated into the door recess as automatic gunfire sounded, feeling the vibration of bullets hitting the stone she was hiding behind. Thankfully, the stone was thick enough and heavy enough to shield her, but there were four attackers and it was only a matter of time before they decided to simply charge her, guns firing.

Her eyes stung. It was such a stupid way to die. Stuck in the Vault, separated from her dogs, in the middle of a fight she knew nothing about.

More gunfire sounded, more bullets hitting the stone behind her. Then a surge of magic rose and the world went quiet for a long moment. When the magic faded, she risked a quick peek around the corner just in time to see the four men gathering at the end of the corridor. The first man, the one of few words, grinned when he saw her, raising his weapon.

Movement behind her made her turn, pressing back into the doorway on instinct. Another armed man came out of one of the Vaults. Her Vault, she recognised, blinking in amazement. It looked like Bryce. He had his weapon raised and fired ahead, at the four men at the end of the corridor. Four shots. Followed by four dull thuds as the bodies hit the ground.

Max stared at him, mouth open, as Bryce made a quick check of the corridor they were on, peering into each Vault to make sure there were no more attackers lurking. He passed her with a curt nod, heading for the four bodies.

Body shaking with leftover adrenaline and fear, Max left her hiding spot and followed Bryce to the junction and the pile of bodies. He had killed each of the four men with a single shot to the head, not bothering with trying to wound them, or hitting them somewhere less fatal. He crouched by each of the bodies in turn, patting them down and removing the computer tablet, what looked like a piece of folded black cloth, and enough spare ammunition to start a small war. He tucked the ammunition into the backpack he wore and rose to his feet.

"Are you alright?" he asked Max.

"Ah. Yes. I think so. I mean …" Max's voice trailed off as she looked around at the open doors to the Vaults, the markings on the floor, and the dead bodies. "Oh. The robed people," she said, surging forward.

Bryce put an arm out, blocking her path. "There might be more of the Syndicate," he said.

"The what?" Max asked.

Bryce tilted his chin down to the four dead men. "They've taken over the Raghavan holdings at the docks," he told her, and grimaced. "Kitris is not pleased."

"I've never heard of them," Max said. "But they look like a group that's been targeting police officers, and the ones that were attacking Malik," she told him.

Bryce's expression tightened. "That's not good news."

"Hang on. So, the Order has been aware of this group? Why hasn't Kitris told the city's law enforcement? Or the Marshals? A police cadet was shot yesterday," Max said, her voice too high. It wasn't Bryce's doing, she reminded herself. But he was the only member of the Order in front of her right now.

"I'm sorry," Bryce said, still with that grim expression. "You know Kitris doesn't like to share intelligence."

"Understatement," Max said, shaking her head. The head of the Order would far rather not deal with any of the other enforcement agencies around the city, seeming to, at best, consider them a necessary evil. "So this Syndicate has been causing problems for the Order as well as the police?"

"Understatement," Bryce said, lips twitching. The humour faded as quickly as it had risen. "We should discuss this later. Robed people?" he asked.

"Yes. I think they work for the Vault," Max said. "They were using magic against the armed men, and I think the armed men might have killed them. Round the corner," she said, and pointed, then lifted her brows at Bryce's frown. "What?"

"The Vault? Is that where we are?"

"Yes. That room you came into is my Vault," Max said, colour rising on her face as she realised he had probably seen the sparse contents of the shelves. "Erm. The two unconscious men aren't part of my collection," she added.

"Did you knock them both out?" he asked her.

"Just the one in black. He was trying to attack me. I think he's the magician who pulled me in here. And you, too, it seems."

"I was trying to pull you back out," Bryce told her, then turned away. "Let's see about these robed people."

Max stared at his back as he moved away, not sure what to make of that. He had tried to pull her out of the magic? That made warmth bloom in her chest and she followed him into the corridor.

The two magicians in blue robes were dead. They had each been hit by several rounds of automatic fire, blood pooling on the ground around them.

"They just attacked the Syndicate with magic?" Bryce asked, staring down at them.

"Yes. They didn't seem to have any other weapons."

"Brave," Bryce said, and shook his head. "And foolish."

Max nodded, a lump forming in her throat as she looked down at the two people who had been alive and channelling powerful magic not that long ago.

Before she could say anything, Bryce tilted his head. "There are more people coming. Hard boots," he said, and pointed to the softer shoes that the robed people were wearing.

"Probably the Syndicate then," Max said, throat closing again.

"There are a lot more of them this time," Bryce said. "We should try and find somewhere a bit more defensible," he suggested.

"Or someone in charge," Max suggested. "Where are they coming from?" she asked. She couldn't hear anything, but she trusted his sharper senses.

"That way," he pointed. "We'll go this way," he said, turning to follow his own suggestion and setting out at a steady jog.

Max finally remembered to holster her gun and followed him, stretching her legs to keep up.

Around the next corner they found more bodies on the floor. Two black-clad women, their faces frozen in shock, and another pair of robed men, bodies riddled with bullets. Bryce paused by the black-clad women, going over their bodies and removing another computer tablet and more ammunition. He hesitated, glancing up at Max.

"Do you want one of their weapons?" he asked.

Max looked at the automatic weapons on the ground by the bodies and shook her head. The response was instinctive rather than rational. Bryce lifted a brow, silently asking for an explanation. "I don't know those weapons," Max said. "I've never used that type before. If we can find more ammunition for my handgun, I'll stick to that."

"Good choice," Bryce said. Max's face must have shown her surprise as he tilted his chin to her. "It's always better to stick with a weapon you know, and that you know will work."

"That makes sense," she said.

"Here, this should fit your gun," he said, and handed her a pair of magazines that she didn't think had come from the black-clad women, but rather from his backpack. Max tucked the magazines away at the small of her back with the other ammunition and her back-up gun, and followed him as he set off again.

As they moved, Max could hear the approaching footsteps, too, and panic gave her extra speed to keep up with Bryce.

The end of the next corridor opened not into another hallway but into a stairwell, the steps wide and shallow and made of the same stone as the walls. The muted, domed lights that were in the corridors were set into the walls of the stairwell, providing enough light to navigate the steps. Bryce paused, brows lifting, silently asking her opinion on a direction. Her mind spun. Down or up. Up or down. She chose up. She had an instinct that they were underground, and if they went up they might find an escape. Or answers. Or both. Possibly.

Chapter Eleven

MAX'S LUNGS WERE BURNING, her legs turning to rubber, but she kept pushing herself forward, trying to keep up with Bryce. What made it worse was that he didn't even seem to be trying. He wasn't even breathing hard, and she was sweating under her jacket. She made a silent promise to herself that if she made it out of this alive, she would double down on working on her fitness. The attempts to go running and the extra walks she'd been taking with Cas and Pol clearly hadn't been enough.

Over the sound of her own harsh breathing and the steady thump of her and Bryce's footsteps, she suddenly realised that she couldn't hear their pursuers. The heavy tread of boots had been following them for what seemed like an eternity, but it was gone now. She could only hope that they had lost their pursuers in the maze of corridors and stairwells. She didn't think that meant the pursuers - the Syndicate, Bryce had called them - had given up. She needed to keep going, to see if she could put more distance between them.

She wiped her brow with the back of her hand and shoved her damp hair back from her face, wishing she could take off her jacket. But the beaten up leather would be heavy and awkward to carry, and might provide her with a small bit of protection if the Syndicate caught up to her and Bryce and started shooting again.

She followed him around another corner to find a corridor that looked similar to all the other ones they had run through. She didn't know about Bryce, but she was thoroughly and completely lost. Not only were there no clear signs to separate each corridor from the last, but the environment around them kept changing. They had almost run into walls where she didn't think there should be any, and more than once they had turned back from a dead end to retrace their steps only to find the opening they had just come through had somehow disappeared and a different opening was available. From Bryce's frown, she knew that wasn't her imagination. The layout of the building had somehow changed around them even as they were moving through it. It wasn't just the corridors. The stairs were chaotic. Some led up what seemed a long way, others went down five steps and then led to another level. As they ran, Max could feel magic ebbing and flowing around them. It had the familiar trace of the Vault, and wasn't threatening them. But it wasn't helping them, either.

Max had a vision of being trapped forever in the endlessly changing corridors. She wished her dogs were here. Even if Cas and Pol couldn't find a way out with their more acute senses, she would at least have their company. Her throat closed on a sob, eyes stinging.

The end of the corridor led to another stairwell. Looking up, Max thought she saw the faintest suggestion of brighter light overhead. The corridors and stairwells all had the same muted, diffuse light that she'd first seen in her Vault. She glanced back at Bryce. He was looking down. Checking for more enemies, she suspected. They had turned this way and that so often, she wouldn't be surprised to find their pursuers around the next corner. It wasn't a happy thought.

"It looks like there's more light above us," she told him, keeping her voice low and trying not to be too obvious in her gasps for air.

"Good. We might be able to get some answers," he said. He frowned at her. "Are you alright?" he asked.

Heat rose across her already warm and sweaty face. Her hair was sticking to her scalp, and her breathing was harsh and loud in her ears, along with the thudding of her pulse. She could only imagine what she looked like. By contrast, he wasn't even breathing hard, as calm and focused as if they weren't in a strange, ever-changing place with people chasing them. "I'm not used to all this running," she confessed.

"Marshals don't need to chase creatures?" he asked, seemingly surprised.

"The creatures we hunt are generally either too fast for us to follow on foot, or trapped. There's really not that much running involved," she said, giving in and leaning forward, resting her hands on her knees for a moment while she sucked in more air. When her heart rate had steadied a little, she straightened and nodded. "Let's go."

Another flight of stairs up - just one this time, which Max and her legs were very grateful for - and the space around them opened up into something different. The heavy door surrounds and now-familiar corridors were gone. Instead, there was a square space with a marginally higher ceiling and an open door leading off it. The stairs continued up at the other side of the space. To Max's surprise, Bryce headed across to the open door, gun ready, and took a look inside.

"This will do," he said. "We can stop here for a moment."

"Really?" Max asked. She was almost swaying on her feet. Without waiting for an answer, she headed across the space and through the door, stopping as she crossed the threshold. It looked like a communal room of some kind. There were mismatched dining chairs and tables at one side, the side they had come in on, and a few more comfortable chairs and low tables to the other side, along with what looked like a snack machine and a coffee station. The faint aroma of coffee and baking trailed across the room, pulling Max forwards.

"Staff break room?" Max speculated.

"It's got one door with good visibility to the space outside. We've only got two points of access in the stairs up and down, and good lines of sight," Bryce told her.

"Alright," Max said. Now that he had pointed it out, she could see what he meant. "Does that mean we can get a drink and sit down for a few moments?" Not that Bryce looked like he needed a rest, she added silently. But she certainly did.

"Yes," he agreed. He pointed to a chair close to the door but out of sight. "Somewhere near there would be ideal."

"Ok," she said, and headed across the room to the coffee pot, telling her legs to stop complaining. "Do you want coffee?" she asked. There was a filter machine, with a full pot sitting on the warming plate and a stack of heavy-duty recyclable cups next to it.

"Thank you. No milk or sugar," Bryce added from just beside the door.

Max poured two coffees. Plenty of milk for her, none for Bryce. She spotted half-drunk cups along the counter and paused, chest hurting as she remembered the dead they had seen. She wondered how many of the cup's previous holders were now dead downstairs. There was a plate of what looked like home baking as well. Telling herself that she needed the fuel, and feeling more than a little guilty about the minor theft, Max balanced the coffee cups on the plate and carried everything back across the room.

Bryce had moved one of the mismatched dining chairs closer to the door and had settled into it back-to-front, resting the muzzle of his weapon on the chair back. He had the computer tablet he had taken from one of the dead men and was scowling at the screen.

"Anything useful?" Max asked.

"It's an inventory of some kind. There's nothing else on the drive," he answered, handing the tablet over to her. He lifted a brow as he saw the baking. "I didn't realise Grandma Parras did deliveries," he commented, taking the coffee and one of the pieces of cake. He dug into his pocket and pulled out the other computer tablet he had taken off the second set of dead bodies, frowning at the screen.

Max settled into the more comfortable chair he had pointed out earlier and tried to ignore the sting in her eyes. Mention of Grandma Parras had reminded her of the strange situation she was in. She had no real idea of how she had got here, and not a single idea of how to get back. And she missed her dogs. She shook her head, blinking to clear her eyes, and reminded herself that she wasn't actually alone. Bryce was here. If he hadn't come through the magic after her, she had no doubt she would be lying dead on the stone floor not far from her Vault.

Seeking a distraction from her gloomy thoughts, she looked at the tablet Bryce had handed her and her brows rose. The document on the screen was a basic table with a list of numbers that made no sense to her eyes in the left-hand column, a name in the middle and an X or a blank space in the last column. It didn't make sense to her until she saw a newly familiar name.

"Wait. I heard them say this one. Constance Farmer. Numbers 17, 24 and 4. Oh, those numbers must be the Vault number," Max said, tracing the line with her finger. There was no X next to it, but all the entries on the list above that line had an X. "This must be a list of the Vaults and who owns them," she said, and looked up at Bryce. "This information is supposed to be secret. Not even other magicians know the identity of people holding a Vault," she said, more shock running through her. "The ones with an X are the ones they've already searched, I guess," she said, holding the tablet out to Bryce.

He was frowning at the second tablet. "This is the same. Just the list. It looks like a different set of names, though," he said, and switched tablets with her.

None of the names on the second list were familiar, and Max shook her head. "This is a different list. Different numbers. Different Vaults?" she speculated.

Bryce was staring at the screen he held, brows lifting, and glanced at the one Max held. "The numbering makes no sense, but, between them, that's a long list."

"So they've been at this for a while," Max said, giving him back the second tablet. He tucked both of them away. "You picked up something else," she remembered. "What was it?"

"I'm not sure," he said, pulling the cloth out of the pocket where he had stowed the computer tablets. "It just looks like fabric to me."

Max took it, and felt the spill of magic across her skin along with the softness of velvet. The texture reminded her of her dogs' ears and she had to breathe through a stabbing pain in her chest. She shook out the fabric with one hand, trying to ignore the way her fingers trembled, and stared at it. "It's a null pouch. A nullification pouch. The spells in it feel new. They haven't settled into the fabric yet," she said, frowning. It took a lot of skill with magic to craft the detailed spells needed for a nullification pouch. There couldn't be more than a handful of magicians in the city with the necessary skills to make a new one. "And it's larger than any I've seen before."

"Can we assume that whatever the Syndicate is looking for, they are going to put it into a nullification pouch when they find it? So the object is magical?" Bryce asked.

"I'd say that's reasonable, although some magicians like to carry null pouches just in case. The Marshals usually have a few on hand," Max said, setting her coffee and cake to one side and folding the pouch up again before handing it back to Bryce. "But if they are going to use the pouch to hold whatever it is they are looking for, it's a big object. Most magical trinkets are actually quite small," she added, and picked up her cup.

Max cradled the coffee between her hands. The material of the takeaway cup insulated her from the heat of the drink, but she still hoped that some warmth would seep out and into her. The efficient lists, with their marked-off Vaults, were somehow more chilling than the presence of armed men with automatic weapons in the building. Whoever the Syndicate was, they had impressive resources to be able not only to get a list of the Vault numbers and owners, but also to have searched so many, and overcome the resistance they had encountered so far. She remembered the dead bodies on the floors below and shivered. The robed people might be powerful in magic, but they had not been prepared to withstand the intruders.

"Can you tell me more about the Syndicate?" she asked Bryce and took a sip from her cup. The coffee was adequate, her eyes stinging again as she compared it unfavourably to Malik's almost-lethal brew. Her mind skipped back to the Hunter's Tooth and Malik lying in the midst of his own personal oasis. She hoped that he was recovering, and that her dogs were alright. Luckily, Bryce answered her question before she could dwell on what she had left behind for too long.

"I don't know much about them. They appeared seemingly out of nowhere about a week ago. Well organised. Well armed. Well trained. Disciplined. They cleared out the homeless warehouse on the docks practically overnight and took over the Raghavan territory. When they were challenged, they told the team that they were the Syndicate and they had claimed the territory as their own."

"A week? That's all? And they've claimed the docks already? How did they do that?" Max asked, astonished.

"We're not sure. And, yes, we are confident about the timeline. We've been sending regular patrols out along the docks ever since we learned about the Darsin," Bryce said. He shook his head slightly. "If I hadn't seen it happen, I wouldn't believe it, either. Some of the powerful dark magicians have their own security teams, but nothing like this."

A chill ran over Max's skin at that thought. From what little she had seen, the Syndicate was extremely well-resourced. She couldn't imagine how they had been formed so quickly. A week ago. That would have been shortly after they had got back from the Wild. The Marshals had been kept busy since then, as usual, but still she was disturbed that she hadn't heard anything at all about the new armed group, or the disturbance of the homeless population. Those were both major events in the city and word should have spread. Then she remembered the other critical thing Bryce had said. "They cleared out the warehouse? What happened to the people there?" Max asked, remembering the crowded, chaotic space full of people who had nowhere else to go.

Bryce made a low, dark sound. "They moved into one of the abandoned factories across the road from the docks."

"I can't imagine that the council is happy about that," Max said, a sour taste blooming in her mouth.

"They aren't. I think they are finally trying to work out proper accommodation for the people," Bryce said.

"About time," Max muttered, staring into her coffee. The city had more than enough abandoned and empty buildings which had utilities still attached to them to house every single one of the people who had taken shelter in the warehouse. But the council had not wanted to deal with the issue, not wanting to spend the city's limited resources on people who, in their view, didn't contribute to the city's economy. It made Max angry just to think about it.

"I agree," Bryce said, surprising her. He took a drink of his coffee and grimaced. "I prefer Malik's, but this will do."

"I was just thinking the same thing," Max said, on a half-laugh.

"So, the Syndicate," Bryce said. He hadn't taken his eyes off the doorway, Max realised, keeping watch on the outside even while he rested and talked. "They have some powerful magicians. And they seem fond of dark magic. That's all we've really been able to learn so far. No one has been able to get onto the docks since they took over."

Max absorbed that information with another drink of coffee. She knew just how well trained the Order warriors were. If they hadn't been able to get past the Syndicate's perimeter, that suggested the new group had a similar level of training and discipline. Which was impossible, she told herself. The Order had been training its warriors for centuries. A new group could not simply spring up in the space of a week and take over.

Unless it hadn't sprung up out of nowhere, Max realised, another chill working its way over her skin. Unless this had been planned. It would have required a lot of resources, a lot of organisation, and an incredibly cunning leadership.

"There have been attacks on police officers," she told Bryce. "People dressed in a similar way to the Syndicate here, except that they have all been wearing masks. At least one of them was a magician and lured an experienced officer into an ambush. The officer was shot and their training cadet was killed." She had to pause then, remembering Ellie and the dead cadet. Although Ellie should make a full recovery, that would be little consolation for the Sergeant. Ellie would blame herself for the cadet's death.

"You think it's the same group?" Bryce asked, frowning.

"Same outfits, anyway. And the people who were trying to kill Malik were wearing the same outfits, too," Max said, a tremor running through her.

"They knew who and what Malik is," Bryce said thoughtfully. "That suggests a knowledge of the city, and a lot of planning. They knew how to weaken him."

"True," Max said. The attacks on the police were taking on a more sinister aspect in her mind, with the suspicion that they might be connected to the Syndicate. "There were at least five people in the group that attacked the police officer and cadet. One of them shot four of the others before running away."

Bryce absorbed that information in silence, expression tight. "Killing your own people is not a good long-term strategy," he said.

"There's no sign of a leader?" Max asked. She wasn't really sure how newly formed and sinister-sounding armed groups worked, but she was fairly confident that there would be some kind of hierarchy.

"There must be a chain of command. There always is. They're too well-organised not to have one. But they all wear the same outfit, and we've not heard any of them referring to each other by any kind of rank, so we've not been able to pinpoint the structure so far."

"A week?" Max asked, pushing down an unexpected urge to smile. Bryce sounded quite disgusted that he didn't know more about the new group. No doubt he wished that he also knew all the names, biographies and abilities of every member of the group.

"That we noticed, yes," Bryce confirmed. She took a sideways look at him, now that they were still and quiet. He looked tired. She wondered just how much work he and his fellow warriors had been doing to investigate the Syndicate. The stupid little sliver of hurt in her chest that she had been trying to push aside eased a little bit. He hadn't been ignoring her. He had probably been on duty without a break.

Max made her way through two pieces of cake, which were good but not as good as Grandma Parras' baking, then got up and handed the plate and last remaining piece to Bryce. He probably needed the energy more than she did.

"Thank you," he said, sounding surprised. He glanced across at her as she took her seat again. She lifted her brows, wondering what he wanted to say. He put the empty plate on the floor near the wall, along with his empty cup. "I'm sorry I haven't been in touch," he said, straightening. He wasn't looking at her. "We got into a fire fight with the Syndicate a week ago, and they shot my phone."

"Your phone?" Max asked.

"They were trying to shoot me, but got the phone," Bryce said, mouth twisting in what might have been a smile. "I got a replacement, but all the data from the old one hasn't been recovered yet," he said.

"They don't let you backup your phones?" Max asked, the question out before she really understood what he was saying. Thanks to Faddei's love of information and knowledge, all the Marshals' phones were automatically backed-up on their network so nothing was ever lost.

"No," Bryce said, the humour gone from his face. "And I haven't been able to get the technicians to recover its memory."

"So, you lost my number," Max said, and felt warmth surge up her face, embarrassed at her hurt feelings. He had been in a shooting match and she had been worried he was ignoring her.

"Not on purpose," he said. Max was thankful he was still looking out the door as she was sure she had a silly expression on her face. She was stupidly pleased he had not been ignoring her. "I volunteered to ask Malik if he'd heard anything about the Syndicate, but I also hoped he'd give me your number again."

She definitely had a silly expression now. Before she could think of a suitable response, or any response at all, his whole posture changed, going from almost relaxed to focused and intent in a heartbeat.

"What?" Max asked, as quietly as she could.

"There's someone coming," he answered, speaking softly. He gestured for her to move back a little, then slid off his chair and moved it out of his way in silence, crouching down beside the door frame.

Max moved as he had asked, getting out of the chair and taking a step back along the wall, further out of sight of the doorway. She drew her gun, checked that it was set to single fire, then held it ready, muzzle pointed to the floor.

After a moment, when she realised that her breathing was too loud again, she heard footsteps. More than one set. Coming up the stairs, she thought, and not bothering to be quiet about it.

"No Vaults on this level," a voice said. "We can set up a base here."

Max frowned. The voice was faintly familiar, but she couldn't place it immediately. A magician, she thought, although her memory wasn't giving her a face or name.

"Yes, sir," a second voice said. Max definitely didn't know him, but he had the crisp way of speaking she associated with warriors.

"There's a room over there we can use," the first voice said. "Go secure it."

"Sir," a third voice answered, and there was the sound of booted footsteps moving across the floor. Towards the doorway where Bryce and Max were hiding.

Chapter Twelve

Max's mouth was dry, stomach uneasy, hands sweaty on the grip of her gun, and she was sure her heartbeat could be heard a dozen paces away. She held herself still, pressed against the wall. On the other side of the doorway, Bryce was motionless. Waiting. He had blended into the shadows next to the door, his weapon held ready to fire.

The footsteps came closer. Max hated not being able to see anything. There wasn't even a mirror or pane of glass she could catch a reflection from, just the ominous sound of boots getting closer.

Bryce opened fire. Single shots, evenly spaced. Five of them. There were shouts of alarm, dull thuds, and running footsteps from outside the room. Max had seen enough of Bryce's expertise to know that the thuds were from bodies hitting the ground. Her stomach twisted again. She didn't like killing, even people who would happily kill her.

"I thought you said the Wardens didn't have automatic weapons?" the first voice asked, hissing with fury. The voice was from further away. They must have retreated. Max frowned. She did know that voice. If only she could remember from where.

"They don't. That wasn't the Wardens," another man answered. One of the armed men, Max thought. So there were still some of them left alive, then.

"If you come out, we'll let you live," the first voice said.

Bryce didn't answer the offer. Perhaps recognising it for the lie it was. He simply held his gun and waited.

The others were quiet, too. The space between Max's shoulder blades itched as she wondered what they were up to. What were they planning now? It was clear that whoever was outside the room hadn't expected to meet resistance here, and even though she and Bryce were in a good, defensible position, they also didn't have any means of escape apart from out the open doorway.

The silence dragged on and the itching sensation grew worse. Max was tempted to shift position, to try to scratch her back and forced herself to stay still. The crawling sensation was spreading over her skin and as it crept across her shoulders under her clothes, she realised that it wasn't her own tension, but the approach of magic. Subtle and powerful dark magic. The magician who she thought she might know was sending magic into the room. It was sliding around the door frame and across the walls, spreading out as if looking for them. Max took a hasty step away from the wall, and gestured Bryce to step back as well. She wasn't sure what the magic would do if it actually came into contact with her skin, but she didn't want to find out.

On the other side of the doorway, Bryce had taken a clear step away from the wall, but was still shrouded in shadow, his focus on the outside of the room, ready to fire again at any attacker foolish enough to come close. Max drew a deep breath, trying to calm her heart rate and focus enough to get a better look at whatever spell the magician was spinning. There was a jagged trail to the spell and it was sending tendrils out, hunting as it unfolded. Some kind of trap, Max guessed.

With the little bit of space and time, she managed to gather her own magic and instinctively started to plan out one of the elaborate formulas that the Order's magicians used, and which she had been taught was the only proper way to use magic. Her mind slid away from the symbols and patterns that made up the framework of a counter-spell and she almost cursed out loud. Several years of training, and she couldn't even manage a simple counter-spell. But then she had never been good at the formal, complicated magic that Kitris and the Guardians used. And now she knew that was not the only way to use magic, no matter what Kitris said. There were other ways.

She thought about what she wanted. A counter-agent to the spell. Something to neutralise it and keep Bryce and her safe. She freed one of her hands from her gun and cupped her palm in front of her, imagining her magic gathering against her skin. Little sparks of light formed in response to her wish and she almost gasped aloud. She hadn't been sure it would work. But it was working. Far better and more smoothly than anything she had ever tried with the Order's magic.

When her palm was full of sparks, she moved her hand, turning it so that the sparks of light flowed out towards the wall and door frame. The little motes of light fizzed when they came into contact with the dark magic. Rather than dying, the sparks grew and multiplied, coursing along the trails and jagged edges of the dark magic, lighting the spell up. The trap was far more extensive than Max had realised. It had completely smothered the door frame and was rising up to the ceiling. As she watched, the light she had created reached the edges of the attack spell, hanging in the air for a moment before they flared and turned, scorching back along the lines of the spell, burning away the dark magic.

The light didn't stop at the door frame, blazing out of the room and out into the open space, following the trail of magic that Max could barely sense.

Max heard a cry of alarm and then a low sound of fury that sent more chills across Max's skin. An instinctive response that she couldn't help. It sounded like her lights had reached the magician, and he was not happy about it. He also sounded like he might not be human. She should be afraid of him. She knew that. And yet she was holding on to anger of her own. The intruders, including this magician, had broken into the Vault, where they had no right to be. They had killed the Wardens who had tried to protect the Vault and the magicians' privacy. And they were trying to kill Bryce and her.

Her hand felt warm and she looked down to find that there was more light gathered there. The bright, blinding light of the Lady. Ready to use. Her mouth curved up in a hard smile. She should be afraid of the more skilled magician, but she wasn't.

She heard movement and voices, too low for her to catch the words spoken.

On the other side of the doorway, Bryce straightened, catching her attention. He signalled something to her that she didn't understand. It seemed urgent.

As she was frowning, trying to work out what he was trying to tell her, several hard objects clattered across the floor outside. Before she could react, Bryce had moved across the open doorway. Rapid gunfire sounded as he crossed the open doorway. He didn't check in his forward movement, grabbing her around the waist, dragging her further away from the door and the wall.

Just in time. As they moved, a series of loud explosions sounded, destroying the wall they had been hiding behind. Unlike the Vault walls below, this wall appeared to have been made of lathe and plaster, jagged fragments of wood and chunks of plaster hurtling into the air along with vast quantities of dust.

The force of the blast sent Bryce and Max tumbling off their feet onto the ground, landing awkwardly between a large sofa and an upright armchair. Max hit the ground with a thump, her ears ringing, the air full of plaster dust and smoke from the explosives. She still had her gun in one hand, magic in the other. And she was in one piece. Bryce must have taken the main impact of their fall, she realised, turning to check on him.

Bryce was on his feet already, weapon ready, apparently uninjured. She heard the sharp crack of gunfire and scrambled to get to her feet. Bryce moved so that she was partly shielded by him. She tried to protest and ended up coughing instead.

There were shapes moving through the dust and smoke. Armed men. Four of them. Not enough, was Max's immediate thought. Four armed men were nowhere near enough to take down Bryce. Particularly not when he was ready for them.

She was right. Four quick, single shots later, and the men had crumpled to the ground.

Bryce was moving, out of the room, through the ruins of the wall.

Magic rose around him. Bryce stopped as if he had run into something solid.

Max scrambled across the ruins of the wall to join him, the dark magic trying to wrap itself around her, too. It shied away from her hand, though. She lifted her light-filled hand and pressed it against the dark magic.

Somewhere nearby, the magician screamed. An awful sound that stirred up memories she didn't want to think about. And he was definitely not completely human. No human throat could make that sound.

Bryce was moving again, firing as he went. Max ran to keep up with him. He crossed the open space, now littered with dust and debris, to the stairs going up. After a brief look he turned back, facing the way they had come. He gestured for Max to go ahead. She ran up the first few steps, her legs protesting, and then paused, realising Bryce wasn't with her. He was still facing into the open space.

The magician was standing in the middle of the chaos. He was wearing a black outfit like the men Bryce had killed, but not carrying any weapons. Max did know him. One of the Forster Family, and one of the most powerful magicians not just in that Family but in the entire city. Oliver Forster. That was it. The Forster matriarch's oldest son. Max had only ever seen him from a distance before, but the aura he carried had left an impression on her. He was staring up at Bryce and Max, his face tight with concentration. He lifted his hands slowly. Even at the distance, Max could feel magic gathering. It was far more powerful than anything she had felt before.

She reached out and grabbed Bryce's shoulder, pulling him back towards her. Or trying to. It was like trying to move a building.

"Run!" Max shouted through the ringing in her ears and the echo of gunfire.

Chapter Thirteen

To her surprise, Bryce did as she asked, and started running up the stairs. She pushed herself to try to keep pace with him, listening for the tell-tale sounds of pursuit from behind them. It would only be a matter of time before Oliver Forster gathered his resources and what men he had left to follow them.

They ran up another two flights of stairs before they found a doorway. As they ducked through it, Max realised it looked different from the others. There was a control panel to one side, and a gap in the top of the door frame that looked like there was some kind of gate suspended there. She grabbed Bryce's arm, pointing to the control panel, her lungs still choked with dust and too out of breath to speak.

Bryce looked at the doorway and the control panel, and aimed at the control panel, firing a quick burst of shots into it. The control panel lit up an alarming shade of red and the gate slammed down. It was a solid chunk of metal which sang with magic in Max's senses.

"Nice," Max managed, voice rasping.

"That should take them a while to get through. Are you hurt?" Bryce asked, casting a professional, assessing look over her.

She shook her head, tried to speak again and coughed. "No," she managed. "You?"

"Bruises," Bryce said, unexpected humour lighting his eye. "I didn't see the sofa before we nearly landed on it. Got the arm of it in my back."

"Ouch," Max said, wincing in sympathy. "And thank you. I think you saved my life back there."

Bryce nodded, as if he had just been doing his job. "We should keep moving," he said.

Max agreed, looking around the new floor they were on. It was very similar to the one that Oliver Forster and his people had destroyed, with an open area and another set of stairs leading upstairs. There was no open door here, though. "I guess we go up," she said, and had to pause to cough again. "I don't suppose …" she began, voice trailing off as Bryce held out a flask she recognised. Order brandy. She took a sip, letting the liquid trickle down her throat and clear it, then took another sip for good measure, handing the flask back to Bryce. "Thank you," she said. She drew a deep, steadying breath. "That was Oliver Forster. The magician. Do you think he might be in charge of the Syndicate?"

Bryce took a drink of his own before storing the flask in one of his pockets, a slight frown letting Max know he wasn't ignoring her question, but giving it some careful thought.

"He could be. But I doubt it," Bryce said eventually, "although I can't tell you why, not really. I would have thought it more likely that if one of the Forster Family was setting up their own militia, they would do it away from the city, perhaps closer to the Wild where they wouldn't come across other people."

"Interesting," Max said. "I don't know anything about him other than he's a powerful magician. Oh, and he's not quite human. I wonder what he's doing here?"

"If we see him again, we can ask him," Bryce said, "but I'd like to get some more distance between us for now." He checked his weapon and switched out the magazine for a fresh one, then headed off, going up the stairs. Max followed him, hoping that they had successfully left one of the city's most powerful magicians and the armed men behind, and wondering what lay ahead of them.

Max never wanted to see another staircase again in her life. Her legs were trembling, lower back aching and lungs burning with effort, and they had only climbed another two flights. She had lost count of the total number of stairs she had climbed today, but it was far too many in her view.

Bryce still wasn't out of breath, she realised, trying not to glare at his back as he went up the stairs in front of her. He wasn't fully human, she reminded herself. His non-human nature clearly gave him extra strength and stamina, along with sharper senses. It didn't help her feel better. She still felt horribly unfit and ill-prepared.

They reached the top of that flight of stairs and she paused, hand on the wall, trying to catch her breath.

"This looks promising," Bryce said.

Max looked up, realising that they had arrived at another open space, the ceiling noticeably higher than the floors below. It looked a bit like the entrance hall for a busy building, with plenty of room for people to bustle about going to and from their important business. The surfaces had been formed from the same soft sand and brown coloured stone that they had been walking through, and around the space she could see what looked like more open doorways. More open rooms than they had seen so far. The stairs they were on continued upward, but she agreed with Bryce. This did look promising. Perhaps they would find some answers here.

She managed to straighten away from the wall, grimacing as her lower back protested and her feet stung when she took a pace forward to stand shoulder-to-shoulder with Bryce. He was coated in plaster dust and she glanced down, realising that she was similarly covered. It seemed frivolous to waste a cleaning spell on harmless dust, so she just ran a hand through her hair, dislodging a few pieces of plaster and more dust, and wiped her damp hand over her face, grimacing as it came away coated in gritty dust. She wanted a shower. Better still, a bath she could lie in for about an hour. She'd settle for a comfortable sofa to sit on, while she was thinking of things she almost certainly couldn't have.

"It looks like there's brighter light over there. Shall we? Maybe there are more chairs?" Max asked, then bit her lip. She hadn't meant to say that last part aloud.

Bryce just nodded and kept pace with her as she walked, slowly, across the hallway towards the brighter light.

They reached a doorway with no obvious door, and no magic blocking it. It opened onto a large room filled with what looked like natural daylight, except

Max couldn't see any windows. The room was full of the whirring sound that Max associated with computers, a series of large screens showing various different images of similar-looking corridors. Apart from the screens, the only furniture seemed to be what looked like a large, semi-circular table, the curved edge towards Max and Bryce.

"A pox on them," an angry voice said.

Max jumped, and reached for her gun, halting when she realised she couldn't see anyone to fire at.

"Damned interfering sons of-"

"Hello?" Max said, before the speaker could finish.

"What? Who's that?" There was a soft thud followed by: "Ouch. Lady's light, who put that damned thing there?"

A head rose from the other side of the semi-circular table. Bright orange-red hair bundled up into an untidy knot presided over a broad, square face wearing a ferocious scowl. The rest of the woman emerged a moment later. She was wearing the now-familiar dark blue robes, the silver stitching glowing.

"Who in the name of the dark lord are you?" the woman demanded.

Max hesitated before answering. The woman was not human, that much was clear, but Max had never come across anyone like her before. Her head would barely reach Max's chest, her shoulders as broad and square as her face.

"I'm Max. This is Bryce. May we have your name?" Max asked.

"Names. No. You can call me the Armourer," the woman said, still scowling. The air around her crackled with power and Max realised that the Armourer was a powerful magician in her own right. "You're not dressed like the others."

"No, we're not with them," Max said, being careful to stand still and keep her voice calm. The amount of power she could sense radiating from the Armourer meant that the woman could most likely destroy her and Bryce with little effort.

"The people in black have been trying to kill us," Bryce added. He was standing quite still and although he held his automatic weapon, the muzzle was pointing at the ground, carefully away from the Armourer.

The Armourer made a noise somewhere between a huff and a snort, and the magic around her dimmed. Max tried not to relax too much. The woman might have decided not to kill them just now, but she could change her mind. The

Armourer looked from Max to Bryce and back again. "How did you get here? Oh, hells. Step aside a moment, will you?" she asked, sounding angry.

Max quickly moved out of the doorway to stand against the wall. The self-styled Armourer drew something from under her robe and threw it at the space where Max had been standing. The piece of metal flew out of the room and hit something outside with a thump.

"Damned thieves. I think that's the last one on this level," the Armourer said, stomping across the room and out into the hallway. "Inigo! Make yourself useful, and take this one to the cells," she said.

Max followed the Armourer's movements, looking out onto the open space in time to see another blue-robed figure appear and cross the floor to where a black-clad man was lying, apparently unconscious, a heavy metal tool on the ground next to him. The Armourer picked up the tool and inspected it.

"No damage. Good." She waved away the other blue-robed figure, who was openly staring at Max and Bryce. "No. Off with you. And reinforce the cell doors. We don't want them breaking free."

Max looked across at Bryce, and murmured, "Cells?" She had never imagined the Vault would have such things. But then, she had never imagined that the Vault would be like this.

"Now, where were we?" the Armourer asked, coming back into the room before Bryce could answer. "Oh, yes. How did you get here?"

With a wary eye on the tool that the Armourer still had in her hands, Max answered. "I'm not sure. I think someone pulled me into my Vault."

"And I was trying to stop her from getting pulled through, and somehow ended up here as well," Bryce said.

"Pulled through?" The Armourer's brows had almost disappeared into her hairline. She lowered them, staring at Max. "What kind of magician are you not to have safeguards in place?"

"Honestly, no one told me it was possible to get pulled into the Vault," Max said, spreading her hands. She didn't want to have to discuss her failings in magic with another person, particularly not the angry woman still holding a potential weapon.

The Armourer snorted - disbelief, or disgust, Max couldn't tell - and turned to Bryce, assessing him. "Well, you'll know better next time."

"We dropped one of your reinforced doors to block some of the intruders," Bryce told the Armourer. "Two flights of stairs down."

"I noticed," the woman said, her voice dry. "Made a hell of a mess."

"That wasn't us," Max protested. "The other people set the bombs."

"Bombs? What? I was speaking about the warrior here shooting the control panel. What bombs? And do you know who these people are?" the Armourer asked, glaring at Max.

"Small ordinance," Bryce answered. "Four or five of them, most likely grenades. They were thrown against the wall of what I think was the break room downstairs. The wall came down."

"That explains the dust," the Armourer said, her nose wrinkling. She took a deep breath. "Alright. That's not a critical wall. Now, the people?"

"The magician we saw was a man called Oliver Forster. He's from a powerful Family, and is a very strong magician. I don't know much about the others apart from they seem well-organised," Max said and looked at Bryce. He was standing with his weapon pointed at the ground, but still alert for possible danger.

"They call themselves the Syndicate," Bryce told the Armourer. "My people first came across them about a week ago. They seemed to come out of nowhere, and they are dangerous."

The Armourer made a low, disgusted sound. "Tell me something I don't know," she muttered. "There's been someone sniffing around the outer defences for a few days. They managed to stay out of sight for a while, until they found a way in." She paused, face full of anger as she took a breath. "That shouldn't have been possible, but they're inside now, and spreading like rats. They got in yesterday and every time I think we've cleaned them out, more appear. They keep popping up everywhere."

"There did seem to be a lot of them," Max agreed. "We saw perhaps ten, but I'm sure there are more." She looked at Bryce. He nodded in general agreement.

"Your people had dealt with a few of them, and we dealt with a few more," Bryce said to the Armourer. Max sent him a sideways glance. She hadn't really had a hand in that, but it didn't seem helpful to argue.

"I haven't been able to track them all," the Armourer said, sounding frustrated. She gestured to the screens behind her. "We've never bothered with security cameras," she added, sounding disgusted.

"But you have cells," Max said, hesitant to mention them just in case the Armourer decided a cell was an excellent place to put her and Bryce.

"The designers were paranoid," the Armourer said, then made a rude noise. "Clearly, not paranoid enough."

"Erm, is it common for there to be people trying to break into the Vault?" Max asked. She had never heard of a secure storage facility in the city that didn't have cameras and other security measures in place. But this was the Vault, so perhaps the rules were different here.

"Common? No, it is not common. Three hundred and eighty seven years this facility has been in operation and not one single breach before yesterday. Not one, do you hear me? And now-" The Armourer broke off, pressing her lips together, visibly struggling with her temper.

"Your people seem very capable," Max said. It was true, but she also thought it might be a diplomatic thing to say.

"We are trained to deal with magic threats. But they have guns. They've already killed seven of the Wardens. And another four are missing," the Armourer said, her voice cracking. Somewhere between fury and grief, Max thought.

"There was an unconscious man in my Vault when I arrived. He had a head wound," Max said. "He looked like one of your people. Unfortunately, there was one of the intruders there, too. I, er, hit the intruder and left him there, too," Max said, her face warming, feeling that she should have at least tried to help the Warden or get him out of there. But she hadn't understood what was going on then, and knew that, even with Bryce's help, she would not have managed to carry the Warden through the Vault and escape the armed men.

"Oh? Really? Which Vault? What level?" the Armourer asked, putting her hand on the desk beside her. The surface of it lit up and Max realised that it was, in fact, an interface of some kind. From the computer noises, and screens, it looked like most of the desk was electronic, although she could also sense magic. In other circumstances, she would have liked a closer look. She had never heard of someone integrating magic and technology in that way.

"I don't know. Er. I took a picture of the door," Max said, pulling her phone out. She opened the photograph and held the phone out to the Armourer. The Armourer didn't glance at the phone, staring at Max instead.

"You don't know what your Vault number is?" the woman asked, looking and sounding as shocked as Max had been when she had been told that someone was trying to break into magicians' Vaults. As if the natural order of the world had been unsettled.

"No," Max said. "Should I?"

"It was on the paperwork."

"Paperwork?" Max repeated, frowning. "There wasn't any paperwork. I just had to complete the spell to open my Vault, and that was it."

"No paperwork? Of course there's paperwork. What kind of an outfit do you think I'm running here? Things aren't normally like this. You'd have been given your paperwork when you opened the Vault," the Armourer said. She sighed, shaking her head, and looked at Max's phone screen. "Level 17, corridor 23, Vault 6," she said. "Inigo!"

The abrupt shout startled Max, and was followed moments later by running footsteps. The same blue-robed man appeared in the doorway, having apparently disposed of the black-clad intruder. He was of similar build to the Armourer, but his deep red hair was cropped close to his head.

"What is it now?" he snapped at the Armourer.

"One of ours is injured and down in one of the Vaults. 17, 23, 6. Sounds like one of the intruders is there, too. Take whoever you can find and go get our man out," the Armourer ordered.

"Why can't you do it?" Inigo asked.

"Because I'm still trying to fix the interface and get our defences back up," the Armourer answered, a sharp edge to her voice that made Max want to step away. "And I've got this pair of tourists to deal with."

Inigo looked Max and Bryce up and down, not seeming to be impressed by what he saw. "Fine," he said, sounding like a surly teenager. He turned and stalked away.

"Is there anything we can do?" Max asked.

"I don't know. Is there?" the Armourer snapped and went around to the other side of the desk, disappearing from view for a moment. There was a loud thump and the desk display lit up. "Right, that's got that loose wire."

"We don't want to get in your way," Max said.

"Good. Go and stand over by the wall, then," the Armourer said, her voice muffled by the heavy desk.

Max moved so she could see around the end of the desk instead. The back of the desk was open, revealing a mass of wires and blinking lights that made no sense to her eyes. The Armourer was on her knees, head deep inside the desk, muttering to herself.

A soft touch on Max's arm drew her attention back to Bryce. He'd been standing quietly, taking in everything that had happened. He inclined his head towards the wall and Max followed him. They wouldn't be out of sight or hearing of the Armourer, but it gave them the illusion of space. And it also gave Max something solid at her back to rest on. She leant against the wall with a sigh of relief. A chair would have been better, but this was better than standing. Or more running. The brief stop for coffee and cake felt like an eternity ago rather than just a few minutes.

Bryce handed her a protein bar and her brows lifted.

"I look that bad?" she asked.

"I've a feeling we're going to be busy again soon. Take on fuel while you can," he told her. He had a protein bar, too. After the refreshments earlier, Max wasn't hungry, but she knew it was sensible to eat something else while she had a chance.

"I really hope we don't have to run anywhere else," Max grumbled, unwrapping the food. "Or climb many more stairs." Her lower back was still complaining, and leaning against the wall was pressing the extra magazines and her back-up gun into the small of her back. She sighed and bit into the protein bar. It was easier to complain about the little things rather than dwell on the bigger issues, like the fact they were in the Vault with the Syndicate, and Oliver Forster.

Bryce said nothing, quietly eating his food.

With some energy creeping back into her body, Max frowned across the room to the desk. The Armourer was still hidden in its depths and, from the occasional swearing, her attempts at repair were not going well. Then the Armourer gave a low, satisfied sound and the lights on the desk flickered, then shone more brightly than before.

"That's done it. Thank the Lady," the Armourer said, getting up from behind the desk. "Are you still here?" she asked in surprise.

"I'm not sure where here is," Max said honestly.

"Oh, are you from one of the islands? A few of the magicians on the mainland know roughly where we are, although they do keep it to themselves," the Armourer said. She frowned. "Actually, that would explain the lack of paperwork, too. The postal service has a bad habit of ignoring the islands on its routes."

"Mainland?" Max asked, glad she was braced against the wall. The word was strange on her tongue. It was not something she had ever said aloud before. She'd come across the word in books before now, and had only the vaguest idea of what it meant inside fiction. Outside a book, it made no sense. There was the city and the Wild. Nothing more.

"Islands?" Bryce asked, sounding equally shaken.

The Armourer frowned at both of them. "Well, yes. Where are you from?"

"The city," Max said. She was quite sure of that, at least.

"Which one?" the Armourer asked.

"What do you mean, which one? Do you mean which district?" Max asked, the food she had eaten turning in her stomach.

"District?" the woman frowned in turn. "Why would I care about that? No. Which city?"

"There's only one city," Max answered, voice faint. It was a truth of the world. There was the city, there was the Wild, and there was the fog at the edge of the world. Nothing more. That was all there was. She had always known that. Hadn't she? She looked at Bryce, to find him looking equally confused.

"Nonsense," the Armourer said cheerfully. "I mean, we're a bit out of the way here, but there's at least a dozen cities on the mainland, and at least one on each of the islands."

For a moment, Max's mind gave her an image of a great expanse of land, seen from above, with the silver-grey trails of roads snaking across it, peppered by cities - some larger than the city - and towns and farms and forests and mountains and lakes and deserts. She shook her head. That all seemed familiar, and yet she had never seen it before. And then the image was gone, and she remembered the truth. That there was just the city and the Wild.

The city and the Wild. That was all. But here was a living, breathing person talking about other cities. Islands. Mainland. And Max knew that no one had ever mapped the full extent of the Wild. It might go on indefinitely.

Her breath caught as she wondered if there might be another edge to the Wild. Another city, at the other side of the Wild. Another group of people who thought they were alone in the world. Perhaps that was where they were just now?

All at once, the walls and ceiling seemed to be closing in on her. She needed air. Fresh air. Daylight. To see outside, to reassure herself that she wasn't going mad. That this was real.

"Are there windows?" Max asked, her voice too high. "Can we see outside?"

"Well, we're still underground here. But if you go up two flights, you'll find windows," the Armourer said slowly, eyes travelling between Max and Bryce. "You really don't know about the other cities?"

There was a roaring in Max's ears and she had no voice to answer. She turned to Bryce and he nodded. They set off together, out of the room and up the nearest flight of stairs they could find, Max ignoring the protest in her legs. Two flights, the Armourer had said. Two flights up to see what was outside.

Chapter Fourteen

Two flights up, there was a similar hallway to the one outside the Armourer's office, only with fewer, larger doorways. There was one ahead of them that showed a glint of glass through the shadows, and Max headed for it.

She stepped into a room that was similar to the break room downstairs, now destroyed by the Syndicate's bombs. There were chairs, tables, armchairs, sofas and side tables, with a long sideboard against one wall that held coffee cups and what looked like trays of food. She ignored all of that, instead looking ahead.

One wall of the room was entirely made of glass, showing a view outside. It was dark, the stars and moon vivid in the sky overhead, more than bright enough to highlight the landscape below. Max walked forward, feet dragging on the rug underfoot as if they didn't want to take her onwards.

She stopped when she was close enough to touch the glass. And stared, not breathing.

She didn't know the landscape outside. She had never seen it before. Not in her imagining, not in paintings, not in life.

There were high, bare mountains surrounding them, formed of the same sandy-coloured rock as the Vault. Ahead of them, the barren mountains curved, steep sides jagged in the moon and star-light, to form a valley that opened up to the land beyond. In the depths of the valley were hints of life. Trees swaying in a gentle breeze, a trail of water that must have come from somewhere in the mountains, the river trailing out along the end of the valley to the world beyond.

And the world was vast. It stretched far further and wider than the city, with hints of rises and falls showing hills and valleys. Here and there was a flicker of light, indicating possible buildings. Farms, towns and, at the farthest edges of what Max could see, the muted glow of a vast city sprawling halfway across the horizon.

Max's breath caught and she sank to her knees, still staring outside. She was vaguely aware of Bryce beside her, but nothing else.

She had no idea what she was looking at. No idea where she was. She had never seen this world before. It was not possible. It wasn't. There was the city, the Wild, the fog. Nothing else. And yet, she knew she was not imagining the scene outside. It was as real as everything else around her. It was real. It was impossible.

"Max, come and sit down," Bryce said. He put a hand under her elbow, gently encouraging her to get up. She followed his suggestion and found herself in a large, comfortable armchair, facing the windows.

"Did you know?" she asked Bryce, her voice a harsh whisper. "Do you know where we are?" Her voice cracked.

"No," he said. "I thought the city and the Wild was all there was. Like you. I've never ... I never imagined ..." His voice trailed off.

"The stars are wrong," Max said. Amid all the other strangeness, she had looked into the sky for familiar constellations.

"Yes," Bryce agreed.

"You two really aren't from around here, are you?" the Armourer asked from somewhere behind them, her voice softer than it had been.

In the midst of all the other shocks, Max didn't even react to the woman's abrupt appearance.

"No," Max answered, forcing the word past the lump in her throat. She couldn't turn away from the landscape outside. It was strange and beautiful and terrifying for all that it meant. There was more to the world than the city and the Wild.

"Do you know where you are from?" the Armourer asked.

"The city," Bryce said. Out of the corner of her eye Max saw him shake his head. "I know that's not helpful, but it's the only answer I've got."

"Does the city have a name?" the woman asked.

"It's never needed one," Max said, her face stiff. "It's just the city." She tore her gaze away from the windows and looked at the Armourer. It had never occurred to her that it was strange the city didn't have a name until now. "What is this land called?" she asked.

"This is Argana. All of what you can see," the Armourer answered. "We call the world Lumina."

"Argana. Lumina," Max repeated, the words heavy and strange on her tongue and tasting odd in her mouth, and above all, unfamiliar. A collection of sounds she had never heard or imagined before. "I don't know those words," she said, her eyes stinging as she looked back at the view.

"Look, I don't know where you came from, but you got here somehow. I'll do my best to send you back once I've sorted out whatever is going on," the Armourer said, in a gentle tone that made Max's eyes sting.

"Assuming that you can send us back," Max said, her chest hurting at the thought of never seeing her dogs again. Never feeling their soft fur or watching them play. Of never seeing and touching and smelling and tasting all that was familiar to her.

"Of course we can," the Armourer said more briskly. "The Vault is connected everywhere in the world."

"And when I woke up this morning, I believed that the world was just the city and the Wild," Max said, scrubbing her hands through her hair.

There was a short pause, then the Armourer moved, coming to sit in a chair nearby, facing Max. "But we all live by the Lady's grace, and I do not believe that She is so cruel as to send you here without a means to return," the woman said, her voice soft.

"The Lady. Our Lady Bethell?" Max asked, leaning forward a fraction. The Armourer had called on the Lady before, but Max had been too caught up in all the strangeness to pay it much attention.

"Of course. Why, do you have another Lady?" the Armourer asked, astonished.

"No. She is our Lady as well," Bryce confirmed. "Although, the way you spoke, I've only really heard our Priests and Priestesses talk like that."

"Hm. Well. I wasn't always the Armourer," the woman said, looking away, voice gruff. "But we go to serve where we must."

"Lady Armourer," Bryce started.

"Call me Cira," the woman said. "Although I do like Lady Armourer. I wonder if I could get the Wardens to call me that?" A trace of mischief entered her eyes.

The gleam of fun in the Armourer's eyes drew a small smile to Max's face. Now that she was looking away from the strangeness outside, the panic subsided a little.

"The armed men. The Syndicate," she began, "they seemed to be searching for something. They were looking through each Vault, and then marking the floor outside them," Max said. "Oh, and they had a list." She glanced at Bryce and he pulled the computer tablet out of his pocket, holding it out to Cira.

The Armourer took the tablet and glowered at the list, her expression making Max glad it was directed at the screen and not at her. The Armourer muttered a few spectacular curses that made Max's brows lift and one that even drew heat to her face.

"No one is supposed to have this information," Cira said, glancing up at Bryce and Max, "but you knew that already."

"Where is the information kept?" Max asked.

"In the Vault records. And only there. Oh, the magicians' guild protests and kicks up a fuss every few years, wanting a list of the Vault holders, but it never goes anywhere. Not least because as soon as they start making a fuss, the non-magicians then want to know what's in the Vault, and none of the magicians want to share their secrets," Cira said, voice loaded with scorn.

Max's head spun at the idea of a magicians' guild. Somehow, that was just as shocking as the idea that there was more to the world than the city and the Wild. She dragged her focus back to the matter at hand. The list. "Has someone accessed your system?" she asked.

"I didn't think so, but I'm not a computer tech. We're mostly cut off from the outside world, but we do have network access." The Armourer sighed. "Can I keep this?"

"Yes. I took it off one of the intruders. He's dead," Bryce said in a matter-of-fact tone.

"Good," Cira said, a hint of savagery to her tone.

"They seem to be looking for something," Max said again. "None of the Syndicate members that I saw were carrying anything, so I don't think they've found it."

"This is the Vault," Cira said. "It holds the possessions of some of the most powerful magicians who have ever lived. And one of the absolute rules that we have is that whatever is in a magician's Vault is their business. No one else's. So, to answer your next question, no, I don't know what the Syndicate or this Oliver Forster could be looking for."

"One of your Wardens was in my Vault. Is that common?"

"No," the Armourer said, voice clipped. "My predecessors and I have only ever authorised three entries into a Vault. And only when the integrity of the structure was under potential threat. The first time a magician had decided to get rid of his possessions by burning them. One of the Wardens spotted smoke coming out from around the door. It took an age to put the fire out. The second was for a noxious smell that unfortunately turned out to be a body that the magician had decided to store without any attempt at preservation. And the last occasion was about ten years ago when there was an explosion in one of the Vaults. A grenade, we think, although why any magician would try to store such a thing without its pin, I don't know."

"So, only three times in over three hundred years." Max shook her head, impressed by how seriously the Armourer and her predecessors took their jobs. "Which makes me wonder just what the Warden was doing in my Vault."

"I've been wondering that myself, and I'm going to ask him as soon as he wakes up," Cira promised, scowling.

"So, we don't know how many Syndicate members are in the structure and we don't know what it is they are looking for," Max summarised. "Do we know how they got in?"

"Somewhere on level 15, I think. There's a maintenance tunnel that leads to the outside," Cira said. "We're on level 3 here. The office where you found me is level 5," she added. "The level where you blew up my wall is level 8. From level 8 upwards there are no Vaults, but there are twenty eight levels of Vaults underneath," she said.

"So, the maintenance tunnel is twelve levels down from here?" Max asked, frowning as she tried to make sense of the numbers. It was as confusing as trying to remember one of the Order's magical formulas.

"Not quite. The Vault doesn't follow a conventional shape," Cira said, a brief grin flashing.

"Is that a defensive measure?" Bryce asked, eyes sharp.

"It is," Cira said, tilting her head as she looked at him. "You've got some experience of this sort of design?"

"Some," Bryce said, grimacing. "There's a labyrinth under the Order that we use for training. The levels are mixed up and the walls can move. It's a challenge."

"Then you'll be right at home here," Cira said.

Max's nose wrinkled in turn, remembering her panicked run through the Vault, the ever-changing layout and cut-off corridors and stairs. "You can change the Vault at will," she realised, remembering the Armourer's powerful magic. "How do you find anything?" she asked.

"There's a knack to it, but it takes a while to learn." The Armourer sighed, shoving a hand into her hair and clutching a fistful of the red-orange strands. "I need to find what's left of my people. Inigo and the others should be back by now," she added, getting to her feet.

"We may be able to help," Bryce said.

Cira eyed Bryce from head to toe and back again, doubtless taking in the various weapons he carried, including the large automatic weapon he held across his chest, and the body armour he wore. "We've never needed any armed assistance," she said, sounding distressed. "We guard against the possibility that someone might try and break in, but it's never happened before."

"We can help," Max said, staying where she was in the comfortable chair. "Or, more accurately, Bryce can help," she added, a wry twist to her mouth. She wasn't sure what she could do against armed men, but she was willing to try.

"You look half dead on your feet," the Armourer commented.

"I'll move when I need to," Max answered, trying out a smile. It didn't feel very convincing, but the brief stop earlier, and the protein bar, had helped. She no longer felt sore all over.

"There's food and drink over there. Get some supplies, then come and find me." The Armourer headed for the door.

Max watched the square, determined shoulders of the woman as she left, then turned to the sideboard that Cira had indicated. Refreshments. Amid all the shocks and strangeness, that was homely and familiar. There might even be more coffee. That thought got Max to her feet and across the room.

Chapter Fifteen

Fuelled by some surprisingly good coffee, and with Bryce's backpack now stuffed full of extra snacks and a pair of water bottles, the first thing that Max heard when she approached the Armourer's office was colourful swearing. She exchanged glances with Bryce before they went through the door.

Most of the screens on the wall were now showing static. The vast desk was brightly lit, the Armourer hitting buttons seemingly at random, muttering curses under her breath.

"What happened?" Max asked.

"They managed to find most of the few cameras we had in the stairwells," the Armourer said, glaring at the blank screens. "I'm blind now. Can't see a damned thing."

"Do you know how many intruders were left?" Bryce asked.

"No," Cira said, voice gruff. "Every time I thought I had a count of them, more appeared."

"What about your Warden in my Vault? Any news on him?" Max asked. It still troubled her that not only one of the intruders but also one of the Vault staff had been there. She had nothing worth stealing, as far as she knew.

"Inigo got him out, which is something, at least. He's still unconscious. He's in one of the rest rooms above us," Cira said, voice and face tight. "So, no, I don't know why he was there. All the Wardens have been here for at least a decade, and none of them should have been in any of the individual Vaults without express permission. Or a damned good reason," she added, scowling.

"Has anyone been to check the maintenance tunnel to see if that's where the Syndicate is getting in?" Bryce asked.

"No," Cira said, face and voice grim. "We've not been able to get close."

"If they are still able to get in ..." Max began, not finishing the thought as she saw from their expressions that both Bryce and Cira had already worked the implications of that out for themselves. There could be an entire army on its way into the Vault.

"We should at least check out this tunnel," Bryce said. "Stop that route in, if nothing else." He glanced at Max and then Cira, frowning. "Max has her handgun. Do you have any weapons?"

"We've never needed them," the Armourer answered, then her eyes gleamed and she straightened, "but we do have some weapons, yes." She stalked to a blank space on the wall and put her palm on it, saying a word that Max didn't know. There was a sharp click and a hidden panel opened.

Max blinked at the gleam of metal revealed. Rather than the modern weaponry she had been expecting, there was an array of more traditional weapons. A great battle axe, similar to the one that appeared on Bryce's insignia, along with a giant hammer, and various other battle axes and war hammers. Cira picked up the hammer. It looked too big and too heavy for her to even hold, but she held it as if it weighed nothing. She pulled out a harness made of supple leather and strung a pair of war hammers through the loops provided, then took a step back, closing the door again.

"Let's go," she said, striding towards the door.

Wondering just how a great hammer would help against automatic weapons, Max followed the Armourer out of the room and into the Vault, Bryce bringing up the rear.

With Cira taking the lead, striding out with purpose and determination, they made their way down one flight of stairs and along a corridor that Max could have sworn was not there when she and Bryce had made their way up that same set of stairs. The ancient magic that she had sensed earlier was stronger now, reacting to the Armourer's presence, and Cira was doing something, magic gathering around her. It wasn't any kind of magic Max had ever felt before, and it was working with the power of the Vault. Max tried to follow what was happening and grew dizzy, feeling as if the floor and walls and ceiling were shifting, changing their shape as she walked. She put a hand on the wall nearest her and drew back quickly. Rather than the cool stone she had been expecting, the wall was warm to the touch, magic coursing through it.

"Are you doing something to the Vault?" she asked Cira.

The Armourer sent a glance over her shoulder to Max, eyes lit with power. "I'm creating a shortcut for us. It's how we normally get around. Do you really want to go down ten flights of stairs?"

"No. Thank you," Max said, concentrating on keeping her feet on the floor, and trying to combat the dizziness.

"You're sensitive to magic," Cira commented. "Walking through the Vault when it's changing is unsettling the first few times. Try looking at the floor ahead of you. It will help with the nausea."

"Thank you," Max said again, and focused on the floor ahead of her as if her life depended on it.

Ahead of her, the Armourer turned the next corner and promptly ducked back, bullets hitting the wall beside her.

"Thieving scum," she yelled, raising the hammer. The great head of it lit up, symbols etched into the metal surface glowing with magic. Cira glanced back at Max and Bryce, her eyes gleaming with magic and fury. She lowered her voice. "We're on level 15. The maintenance tunnel should be at the end of the next corridor."

"Behind the armed men?" Max guessed, drawing her own gun. Bryce already had his automatic weapon ready.

The Armourer didn't answer, instead holding the hammer in front of her, sparks of bright magic coursing along its surface.

"For the Lady!" she yelled, and ran forward, around the corner, into gunfire.

Bryce ran forward to the corner, crouching there so that he was as small as possible, sticking his head around the stone and beginning to fire. Single shots, one after the other.

Screams of pain and yells of fury punctuated the gunfire, along with a static crackling noise that Max thought must be from Cira's hammer. Apparently, the hammer could defend against automatic weapons, because she heard Cira give another roar of fury rather than pain. Bullets flew past Max and Bryce, thudding into the walls.

Max pressed herself against the wall behind Bryce, gun ready. With no body armour, and armed only with a handgun, there wasn't much she could do just then. Her heart was thudding loudly in her ears, body tense.

Bryce got to his feet and moved around the corner. There were no more bullets flying, Max realised, and followed him, her own gun held ready.

The corridor ahead of them was short and wide, with no doors or hiding places anywhere along its length. At least eight black-clad, armed men lay dead or dying on the ground. About half had obvious bullet wounds, and the rest had searing burns that looked like they had burrowed through to their bones. The man closest to Max looked like he had been in his early twenties, his blond hair cut short enough she could see his scalp, the black clothing seeming too big for his skinny frame. His face was unmarked, and too young to be as still as it was, blood pooling under him from bullet wounds. Max forced herself to look away and tried to harden her heart. The man was dead, and if he had been alive, he would happily have killed her.

Cira was nowhere to be seen, but the static crackle of magic was still in the air, coming from ahead of them. Bryce glanced over his shoulder, as if making sure Max was there, and then moved forward, cautiously, to the end of the corridor.

The corridor opened to another open space, this one full of what looked like a random assortment of crates and boxes and dimly lit in comparison to the rest of the Vault. Max had to blink, trying to get her eyes to adjust to the lower light. Amid the shadows of the boxes and crates was movement. People. Armed people.

Light surged, almost blinding her, and she saw Cira in the middle of the space, swinging the great hammer. Magic still coursed along its surfaces. The hammer struck one of the armed people and the man flew back, thudding into a wall and sliding to the ground. Dead or unconscious, Max couldn't tell. Bryce kept moving forward, tucking himself behind the nearest crate, Max following him. The crate smelled faintly of machine oil and as she rested her shoulder against it, a soft *clink* sounded. Metal moving on metal. She just hoped that whatever was in the crate would be solid enough to stop bullets and wouldn't explode.

As Cira continued to batter her way through the armed intruders, Max held her own gun ready but didn't fire. She didn't want to hit the Armourer by mistake. She drew a steadying breath and took a more careful look around. Opposite where she and Bryce were hiding was a dark opening that she guessed was the tunnel entrance. Even as Max watched, another half dozen armed men and women poured through, raising their weapons to fire as soon as they saw the Armourer and her glowing hammer. The magic around Cira blazed in Max's sight, highlighting the modern weaponry held by the attackers. The Armourer spotted them, spinning out of the way of a trail of bullets, whirling her hammer and catching the nearest attacker off guard, throwing the man off his feet and back into the wall.

Next to Max, Bryce fired into the rest of the newly arrived group, all his bullets avoiding the Armourer, sending the attackers scattering for cover behind more crates and stacks of boxes. Max knelt next to him, hidden by the crate, looking at the tunnel opening and its surround, trying to see if there was a control panel. She might not be able to hit a moving target without risking hitting Cira, but she should be able to fire at a stationary control panel. If she could close the door, that would help Cira and Bryce.

Magic surged in the air. Not the clean, bright magic that Cira had been using or the ancient magic of the Vault, but something dark and sinuous. And familiar. The surge blasted through the chamber, thumping into Cira, sending her off her feet, sliding across the floor. Bryce reached out and grabbed hold of her ankle as she travelled past him, dragging her behind the cover of the crate before any of the intruders could take a shot at her.

Max took hold of Cira's arm, trying to pull her further into shelter, and couldn't move her. The woman was a lot heavier than she looked. Or perhaps that was the hammer, still held in Cira's fist. The magic on the hammer had died, leaving faint traces of the symbols. Max put a hand close to the other woman's mouth, relieved when she felt a puff of breath on her skin.

On the other side of the crate, the guns had fallen silent. The air was still full of the aftermath of magic, both the bright magic that Cira had used and the dark magic that had thrown her. Max's nose itched at the dust all the bullets had thrown into the air as well as the combination of opposing magic. The bright magic had carried the zest of citrus and cool water. The dark magic was rotten and smelled like something burning. The combination was foul.

"Is this your idea of having things under control?" a man's voice said into the quiet. Not the voice that she had expected, the one that belonged to the dark magic. But a familiar voice nonetheless, even if she couldn't place it right now.

"You're early, sir," another voice answered, one more recently familiar. Oliver Forster. And he was addressing the new speaker as a superior. Max exchanged glances with Bryce. They were both tucked down behind the crate, out of sight. He was frowning, as if he was also trying to work out who the new arrival was and what was going on.

"You're behind schedule," the new voice said. Max frowned. She did know that voice. Not someone she was very familiar with, but someone she knew.

"Was that the last of them?" a second new voice asked. That was one Max did know, and one she had been expecting. It went along with the dark magic. Queran. The watcher demon who seemed to have made it his personal mission to interfere in her life. She wasn't sure why she was surprised he was here. Breaking into the Vault seemed like something a demon would do. Max's fingers tightened on her gun, but she held herself still. She had once emptied an entire magazine into the demon to no effect. She needed to save her ammunition for something that would be effective. The demon needed something more than bullets. The only thing she had found that would injure the demon so far was the Lady's light. Max put her free hand on her chest. When she had last called on the Lady's light, it had burst forth from inside her. But there was nothing there now. She was drained and hollow. She closed her eyes briefly, trying to remember the spell for calling light. Or indeed any spell.

"I'm not sure," Oliver said, his voice clipped. He didn't like Queran, it seemed. Max had some sympathy for that.

"What do you mean?" the unknown man asked, sounding displeased.

"We've dealt with eight of the Wardens, but according to one we questioned, there should be a staff of twelve," Oliver answered. "We haven't been able to find the others. Sir." That last word was most definitely an afterthought. Oliver might be deferring to the newcomer, but Max suspected he wasn't used to deferring to anyone. As one of the Forster matriarch's sons, he would be used to almost unlimited resources and power.

"And they have got automatic weapons?" the unknown voice asked.

Max's breath caught in her throat as she finally placed the voice, cued partly by Queran's presence. The newcomer was Evan Yarwood. The chief of detectives in the city. She hadn't had much to do with him until he, Queran and their co-conspirators had tried to open a portal and bring Arkus into the daylight world. Evan had proved himself surprisingly resilient, holding his own against Bryce in a fight. Something that should have been impossible for the ordinary human that Evan appeared to be.

She glanced across at Bryce again and mouthed the words *Evan Yarwood*. He nodded, frown gathering. Perhaps wondering, like her, just what Evan was doing here. And how he had managed to acquire a position of authority over Oliver Forster.

Not just that, but how Evan had managed to get out of the Wild and back into the city before establishing himself as Oliver's superior. It had been about ten days since she and Bryce had flown off in a helicopter leaving Evan, along with Queran and Hemang Raghavan, in the middle of a crumbling hillside far into the Wild. The trio had had no obvious means of transportation to get back to the city and while Max had no difficulty in believing that Queran could have made the journey, she was surprised Evan had managed it. Which also made her wonder about Hemang. Bryce had said that the Syndicate had taken over the Raghavan territory. But if Hemang was alive, and had made it back to his territory, he might have invited them in. Or been forced to.

"Not them, sir," Oliver said, sounding displeased. "We came across another pair. Not Wardens. They had weapons."

"Describe them," Queran demanded.

Max tensed, wondering just how good a look Oliver had gotten at her and Bryce.

"I didn't see them clearly. A man and woman, I think. He moved like a warrior. The woman used light magic."

Despite the circumstances, Max's mouth tilted up in a smile at the irritation in Oliver's words. She had hurt him when she had counter-acted his spell.

"Miscellandreax," Queran said, voice silky smooth, sending chills along Max's spine. "I thought I felt something familiar in the air. What an unpleasant surprise. I know you can hear me. Do come out of hiding and let's talk."

"Why are you surprised?" Max asked, not caring if it gave away her position. Queran could find her quickly enough if he needed to. There weren't that many places to hide. She stayed behind the crate along with Bryce and Cira, Bryce scowling at her, the Armourer still seeming to be unconscious. "Didn't you assign your thugs to bring me here?"

There was a short pause, which Max couldn't interpret, then what sounded like a dry laugh. "Bring you here? Why in the world would I have wanted that?"

"Marshal Ortis, I assume," Evan's voice said. He sounded displeased. "Come out, along with whoever else is in there with you."

"Why? So you can try and kill me again?" Max asked. "No, thanks."

"You really are troublesome," Evan said. There was a coolness to his voice that Max didn't like. And something else had changed. Queran now seemed to be taking his orders from Evan. The last she had seen, Queran had definitely felt he was the one in charge. She wondered what had happened to reverse that, and how Queran felt about taking orders.

Next to her, the Armourer stirred, frown gathering. She put her free hand up to her head, her other hand still holding the great hammer. "Sweet Lady," she murmured, "I feel like I've been hit by a truck."

"Close to it," Max said, speaking softly. "There's a demon here."

Cira's eyes opened and she glared at Max. "A demon? A full-blood servant of the dark lord? Here? Why?"

"Good question. I'll ask him," Max said, and tilted her head back towards where she assumed Queran, Evan and the others were standing. "Why are you here?" she asked, raising her voice to be heard.

"That's none of your concern," Evan answered, surprising her. She had expected to be ignored. His voice sounded as if he was a bit further away. Across the other side of the open space at least. She frowned, wondering what he was up to. She, Bryce and Cira couldn't stay tucked behind the crate forever, but she was also quite sure that Evan wouldn't want to stay in this space forever, either.

Next to her, Bryce made a gesture, encouraging her to keep talking. He was listening intently. She didn't think he was concentrating on the conversation, but rather on other sounds that she couldn't hear.

"Oh, really? Well, one of your thugs dragged me into my own Vault and then tried to kill me," she told him, "so I feel very concerned about what you're up to."

"You have a Vault?" Evan asked. Although Max couldn't see his face, the shock in his voice was clear. "Demon, how does she have a Vault?" He hadn't known. Which made her wonder just what had prompted the magician in her Vault to drag her here.

"I don't even have a Vault," Oliver Forster complained.

"Little Miscellandreax is just full of surprises," Queran said. He was standing near Oliver and Evan, Max thought, based on the direction of their voices. And she couldn't feel his magic, she realised, which made her worry about what he might be planning.

"We found Ivor Costen, you know," Max said, remembering the shrivelled husk of the man on Audhilde's mortuary table. "I assume that was you?"

"Ivor who?" Evan asked, sounding impatient.

"The Huntsman clan member that Queran drained of his life force," Max called in response. Somehow, she wasn't surprised that Evan didn't know the name of the dead man. "He was Nati Ortis' boyfriend and Ynes' father. You know, the mother and daughter you were going to use as a sacrifice in the Wild?"

"Oh, him," Evan said, the dismissal in his voice clear. "He was useful. Nothing more."

"Barely worth the effort," Queran confirmed. "Although it was good to practice that ritual. I haven't done it for a while."

Max had to pause for a moment, remembering the dried-out body. She hadn't thought much of Ivor Costen. He'd been a cruel bully and a coward when faced with her and her dogs. But he hadn't deserved that death. No one did. And all it meant to Evan and Queran was that he had been useful.

"So, why are you here?" Max asked, returning to her original topic.

Whatever Evan or Queran might have said was cut off by the crackle of a radio transmission. Max frowned. She hadn't seen radios on the armed intruders before. She glanced at Bryce to find him frowning, too.

"They've found it," Oliver said, voice full of excitement. And possibly some relief, too. "Level 18. Not far from here."

Next to her, Max felt Cira gathering her magic and connecting with the ancient power in the Vault, and suspected that the Armourer had just rearranged the Vault so that the intruders would find level 18 very far away.

"Make sure that no one touches it with their bare hands," Queran said, voice tight.

"We have nullification pouches. We know what we're doing," Oliver said, his tone flat, bordering on insulting. Max remembered the empty pouch that Bryce had taken off one of the dead intruders earlier. And wondered again just what it was that they were looking for that should only be handled with a nullification pouch.

"Take us there now," Evan said.

"What about them?" an unfamiliar, female voice spoke up. Perhaps one of the armed women.

"Kill them and then follow us," Evan ordered.

"My pleasure," the unknown woman said.

Footsteps sounded, fading into the distance, followed by the unwelcome sound of objects clattering onto the stone floor. Max knew that sound. She had heard it recently, a few floors above them.

"Move," Bryce growled at her and Cira.

Max moved. Faster than she would have thought possible, a headlong run for the open corridor they had left behind, Cira on her heels, Bryce at the rear, running backwards, firing to cover their escape.

As they reached the opening of the corridor, the bombs behind them exploded.

Chapter Sixteen

Max was flung forward, thudding against a stone wall that came up far too fast for her to avoid. Something crunched, and she slid down to the floor amid a cascade of stone fragments and distorted metal pieces. She curled into a ball, tucking her head into her arms as the fragments rained down on her, trying to breathe through the assault.

Her ears were ringing as the bits and pieces stopped falling on her and she uncurled, coughing against the dust in the air.

"I am getting fed up of people throwing bombs at me," she said to no one in particular, and managed to wobble to her feet, looking around.

The corridor opening ahead of them was almost completely blocked by massive chunks of stone and an array of twisted metal.

A faint glow on the ground nearby proved to be the Armourer's great hammer. Cira herself was underneath what looked like an entire side panel of one of the crates. Max lifted the heavy wood off the Armourer with some care, worried about what damage she might find. To her relief, Cira seemed to be in one piece, beginning to stir as Max set the crate panel to one side against the cracked wall.

The stone and metal in the opening shifted, and she thought she saw something moving in the clutter.

"Bryce? Is that you?" Max asked, and then had to stop and cough.

"They're not dead," an unfamiliar voice said from the other side of the pile of rubble.

"Then kill them," the female voice from before answered.

Max flung herself back against the cracked wall just before bullets flew out of the opening, narrowly missing her and Cira. She lifted her gun, thankful that she had managed to keep hold of it, and stretched her arm around the corner, returning fire blindly with several single shots. A few curses let her know that she probably hadn't hit anyone, but she had definitely annoyed them. Good. She was quite annoyed, too.

The pile of rubble shifted again. A hand and arm appeared, reaching forward into the empty space. Max grabbed hold of the hand and pulled, as best she could.

Bryce emerged from the rubble covered in stone dust, a deep gash bleeding heavily above one eye, his eyes glittering with his *other* nature and irritation. He still had his main weapon, too, and lost no time in turning and firing over the top of the rubble, careless of the fact he was standing in an open space, clearly visible to the attackers Evan and Queran had left behind.

He emptied an entire magazine into the chamber, then reloaded and paused, eyes moving as he scanned the area in front of him. Looking for movement, Max realised. Checking that every one of the attackers was down.

"Are they all dead?" Cira asked.

"No one is moving," Bryce told her. That wasn't a yes, Max knew. He shouldered his weapon and put his foot on the bottom of the pile of debris. The stone and metal shifted, sending him sliding sideways.

"We'll need to clear it first," Max noted, and coughed again. Bryce's slip had stirred up more dust.

"If my head wasn't aching like it had been split in two, I'd help," Cira said. She had managed to get to her feet and was leaning against the wall, her hammer at her feet. She looked far paler than she had been, and even through her tangled hair, Max could see a large swelling on one side of her head.

"You need medical attention," Max told her. "And I'm sure you should be sitting, not standing."

"I'm not really standing, girl," the Armourer said, glaring at her. "And I'll be fine."

"You have a lump the size of a lemon on one side of your head," Max pointed out. "I don't think that's fine in anyone's definition."

"Oh, so that's why my head hurts," Cira said, putting her fingers up to touch the lump and wincing. "Yep. A lemon is about right. Bastard demon. You seemed to know him?" Despite the obvious pain she was in, her eyes were sharp as she stared at Max in the dimly lit corridor.

"He calls himself Queran," Max said. "Apparently, he's a watcher demon, although I don't know what that means, and he seems to have taken a special interest in me."

"A watcher demon," Cira repeated, still staring at Max with that intent look. "And he's fixed on you? Why? What's so special about you?"

"I don't know," Max said honestly, her ears ringing with the question Queran had flung at her in the Wild. *What are you?* She shoved it to one side again. There was no time for her to pause and reflect right now. "I can't get a straight answer out of him."

"Watcher demons are pesky things. They tend to get ideas of their own if left alone too long," Cira said.

"It sounds like you know a lot about them." It was Max's turn to stare at the Armourer.

"Studying demons was part of my training for this job. Never thought I'd have to face one, of course. Watchers are supposed to blend in. They have a reputation for being sneaky. They aren't always the most powerful of demons, but yours seems strong to me."

"Yes," Max agreed, choosing not to object to having Queran categorised as *her* demon. She turned to Bryce to see what he made of the conversation and found that, while she and Cira had been talking, he had dismantled most of the barrier between them and the chamber. "I'm sorry. Let me help," she said to him, taking a step forward.

"It's alright. Take a moment to rest," he told her, hefting a piece of stone about the size of Max's torso and throwing it to one side. Max was quite sure she wouldn't have been able to move that block, let alone throw it.

"So. Queran. Watcher demon. And the other man? You knew him, too?" Cira had slid down the wall and was sitting, the hammer tucked in beside her. Max looked at her with some concern. She seemed to have grown paler, and her eyes weren't staying still.

"Bryce, do you have any healing patches with you?" Max asked. Although she had some, the ones the Order produced tended to be much more powerful. One of the benefits of having some of the strongest magicians in the world working within the organisation.

"A few," he said, and paused in his work, digging into one of his trouser pockets and handing a strip of paper across to Max. "It doesn't need magic to activate it. Just press it onto the wound and hold it for a moment."

"Thank you." Max took the paper and went across to Cira. The Armourer started when Max knelt in front of her, her eyes wavering as they tried to focus on Max. "It's alright. It's Max. I've got some healing for you. Stay still a moment. This is probably going to hurt," she added, pressing the slip of paper to the side of the Armourer's head where the lemon-sized lump was. The paper warmed under Max's fingers, turning into a thick creamy substance that adhered to Cira's hair and skin. Max straightened and moved back.

Cira made a low sound, full of pain, and turned her head away, tears running down her face. "Hurt? Lady's light, woman, it's like someone took a hammer to my skull."

"I'm sorry," Max said. Now that she had a moment to think, she remembered the cracking sound she'd heard as she had thudded against the wall. Nothing seemed broken or too badly bruised across her body. She patted her pockets and sighed, fishing her phone out of her jacket pocket. The screen was fractured. When she pressed the power button, it did light up, the display slanted off to one side, but nothing worked when she tried touching the screen. She muttered a curse. Even if she could find a network, she wasn't going to be using her phone any time soon. The only bit of good news was that all the information should be backed up at the Marshals' headquarters, so she should get it all back.

"We're not having much luck with phones," Bryce commented, a smile crinkling the corners of his eyes.

"No," Max agreed, warmth rising to her face. She put the broken phone away.

"You two are just too adorable," Cira muttered.

More heat coursing across her skin, Max turned back to the Armourer. The healing patch seemed to have done its job. She was sitting a lot straighter against the wall, her eyes staying focused on one thing at a time. She cast a glance between Bryce and Max, mouth tilting in a smile. "Too adorable," she said again.

Carefully not looking at Bryce, Max focused on the Armourer. "You were asking about the other man. Evan Yarwood. He was the chief of detectives in our city. We last saw him when he was part of a group trying to open a portal and bring

Arkus to the daylight world," Max told her. "He looks human, but I'm pretty sure he isn't."

"No, he's not," Bryce agreed. "There's at least some demon in him. He's much stronger and quicker than a human."

"A full demon and a part demon. You keep the most delightful company," Cira said, tilting her head so she could look up at Max. "Anything else you'd like to tell me?"

"I'm not sure what else is relevant," Max said, "but we need to stop them. If Queran and Evan are hunting for something, it's going to be something incredibly dangerous that shouldn't be let loose on the world."

Cira tilted her chin, looking up at Max. "Stop them? The demon and part demon with the armed escort? And we're just going to stop them? Just the three of us?"

"We have to," Max said, urgency taking hold of her. The shock of realising that Evan Yarwood seemed to be behind all of this was wearing off, replaced by a sick feeling of dread. He had been an active participant in a ritual to bring Arkus up to the daylight world, and he was now involved in something else, with Queran assisting him. Max had no idea what the pair might be looking for in the Vault, or what they might have actually found, but she was absolutely certain that it would be a terrible thing for the world if they succeeded in getting it out of the Vault.

"We can get through now," Bryce said, pointing at the rubble. He hadn't cleared all of it away, but he'd moved enough that they would all be able to get through the gap.

Max followed Bryce's taller, broader form through the gap, her feet sliding on the debris. As she got to the other side, her foot slipped again on a piece of polished sheet metal. She righted herself and looked down, brows lifting as she saw what she had been climbing over. She had just slid on what looked like the front door for a very expensive range cooker. Kitchen equipment. Not what she had expected.

Before she could ask Cira about it, movement caught her attention and she turned.

There were bodies littered around the space, including a pair of black-clad women who were huddled together on the ground against one of the other crates, blood pooling around them. One of the women was dead. The other was barely alive. Her fingers were twitching as she apparently tried to reach the handgun that had fallen to one side.

Bryce had his own weapon levelled at the pair before Max could raise her gun.

"Where are the others?" Bryce asked.

The conscious woman glared back up at him, and stayed silent.

"There are more bodies over there," Cira said. The Armourer was making her way, slowly but steadily, across the debris, using her hammer as a crutch. Max followed her line of sight and saw several more black-clad intruders strewn across the floor, whether from her or Bryce's bullets, she couldn't tell. Most likely Bryce, as he'd fired more bullets and with better aim. Still, Max didn't like to think she'd killed people. Not even people who had been trying to kill her.

"I think there were more of them," Max said, looking around the space. The crates and boxes had mostly been tumbled over, a lot of the contents spilling out onto the floor. "You were using this area as a delivery site?" Max asked, glancing at Cira.

"A gathering point. We have a warehouse in the nearest big city, and a delivery portal outside the Vault. At the other end of that tunnel. We transport stuff from the city to the outside, then bring it in by hand. We don't like too many people knowing where we are. There are locks on the external doors," Cira added, and shook her head. "I've no idea how they got past them. Or how they know about the delivery portal or tunnel. We work very hard to keep the Vault and its location a secret." Cira grunted with effort as she knelt by one of the bodies. "We need to review our processes. Clearly, something went wrong."

"A review seems sensible," Max agreed. "Although it still doesn't explain how Queran and Evan and the others got from the city to here."

"They wouldn't have needed to use the tunnel to start with," Cira said. She was rummaging through the pockets of the nearest body. She wasn't finding much, Max saw.

"What do you mean?" Max asked.

"Girl, the entire Vault is littered with portal spells. How else do you think magicians get their belongings in and out? I don't think anyone has ever tried to send a living person through before now, but I'd say it's possible."

Max ignored the sharp, displeased edge to the Armourer's tone. They were all having bad days. Instead, she turned that idea over in her mind. "Alright. So, someone with a Vault sent one of the intruders inside. And then they brought others through? Then why use the tunnel?"

"The delivery site outside the tunnel is basically a large portal spell. It's normally connected just to the warehouse, but a competent magician could rework it," Cira said, struggling back to her feet and glaring at the tunnel opening. "We need to seal the door off just now. I'm going to need to send Inigo and the Wardens who are left to check on it, but not while there are armed intruders about." She turned back to Max. "I'm guessing that it's only possible to bring one person through at a time in the Vault."

"But it's possible to bring more people through on your delivery site," Max finished, nodding. It made sense. Even if there were still unanswered questions. Such as, how Evan or Queran or Oliver Forster had known about the delivery site, and what they were looking for. "Wait. Oliver said they'd found what they were looking for. Level 18," she remembered.

"They're a long way from it," Cira said, with a certain grim satisfaction in her voice.

"Apart from her, everyone here is dead," Bryce said. While Max and Cira had been talking, he had made a quick inspection of the cluttered space. He came back to stand in front of the bleeding woman, his face grim. "And I don't think she's got long."

"Does she have a radio?" Max asked, remembering the crackle of a radio transmission they had heard.

"No. I checked." Bryce didn't take his eyes off the dying woman.

"So they left her and the others here?" Max moved to stand next to Bryce.

"It looks that way," Bryce agreed.

The woman glared up at them, and as she lifted her chin, Max saw the familiar markings of a Huntsman tattoo on her neck. "So, you're one of the Huntsman clan," Max said, crouching down so she was eye level with the woman. "Why are you following a demon and the former chief of detectives?" she asked.

"We will do what the weak could not. We will take back the Wild," the woman said, glaring at Max.

The hairs on Max's body lifted. She'd only ever seen those words painted in signs held by protesters. Hearing the phrase spoken aloud, and with such utter conviction, was chilling. "You're not going to be going anywhere now," Max said, a weight landing in her chest. There had been far too much death today. Far too much.

"I serve at the dark lord's wish," the woman said, her words slurred and slow. Her eyes were losing their focus, even as she glared at Max. "And I will be rewarded."

"Really? What kind of reward are you expecting?" Max asked. "I only ask because your boss here on this world left you to die to cover his retreat, and the dark lord's realm is full of demons. Not exactly rewarding." The hairs were still standing on end across her body. The woman was a follower of the dark lord, and wanted to take back the Wild. That seemed like a very dangerous combination.

"He will grant me power as I die in His service," the woman countered.

Max was going to say more, but the woman's eyes glazed over and she slumped, her last breath leaving her body.

"Why do fanatics always think they're going to get some power and riches in the next world?" Cira asked, mostly to herself. "Never seems to occur to them that everyone else is being given the same promises. The dark lord's realm can't all be made up of piles of gold."

Max stared at the dead woman's face, memories of smoke and screams and pain rising up. She hadn't seen a single piece of gold or any evidence of riches or power anywhere in the underworld. She wondered how many of Arkus' followers raged against him in the world below when they realised they had been fooled, how many of them screamed their anger even as they died, over and over again, to please him and his court of demons.

"She made her choice," the Armourer said, voice softer. She was standing beside Max, her face full of sorrow as she looked down at the dead woman. "I'll never understand the fools that follow Him. But it's their choice." It sounded to Max as if the Armourer was trying to convince herself.

"It is," Bryce said, surprising Max. She straightened and looked at him.

"You heard what she said? The Syndicate is part of the Take Back the Wild movement in the city, and following the dark lord," Max said. She couldn't believe Bryce was so calm. He was still on alert, eyes travelling around the space.

"I heard. But there's nothing we can do about that right now. We need to seal the tunnel, and quickly if we want to catch up to the others."

He was right. Evan and Queran and whatever they were after were the immediate threats. Not a protest group in a city that she wasn't sure she could get back to.

"A pox on them," Cira spat out, startling Max. The Armourer was looking past the dead women to what might once have been a control panel next to the tunnel entrance. The panel was hanging off the wall, a tangle of wires showing where it should have sat. "That's how they got into the system, and got the information," Cira said, striding over to the panel and the tangled wires.

"Your system is integrated?" Max asked.

"It shouldn't be, I know. Something else to deal with as part of the repairs. But the panel here was linked to the mainframe," Cira said, and muttered more curses under her breath.

"So the intruders could have accessed the Vault records from here?" Max asked, taking Cira's tight nod and continued cursing for confirmation. "At least that clears one question up," she said to Bryce. He nodded, but his eyes were still on the tunnel doorway. Trying to work out how to seal it up, she guessed.

She looked around the space again. The tunnel might have a locking door at the other end of it, and possibly there had once been a door on this side. Right now, this end was just an open space. They needed to find a way of sealing it off. She looked around the space again, at the broken crates and scattered equipment, wondering if there was anything there they could use, pausing as she remembered the piece she had stepped on. "You were bringing in kitchen equipment?" Max asked Cira.

"We were. Our kitchens here haven't been renovated for about a hundred years. Time for an upgrade." The other woman frowned at Max, looking confused.

"Does your upgrade include the gas cylinders for cooking?" Max asked, eyeing the various boxes and crates still scattered around the space.

"It does. Good thing they were in a different crate to the one we were behind, eh?"

"A very good thing. But more to the point, they are highly flammable," Max said, looking at Bryce. His expression lightened into a small, satisfied smile.

"Good thinking. Hopefully there's enough to seal the tunnel here, and then even the odds a bit," he said. He slung his weapon across his shoulder and started investigating the contents of the crates.

"Wait a minute. You're not thinking of blowing up more of the Vault, are you?" Cira said.

"Only the bits with the intruders in," Max said, trying not to think about the damage that a gas cylinder explosion could cause. There had been more than enough death and destruction already, but Evan wasn't finished. And she didn't want him getting his hands on whatever it was he had been looking for. She had a feeling that, if he did, the damage to the Vault would be the least of their worries.

Chapter Seventeen

It took a while for her ears to stop ringing from the explosion that Bryce had rigged. It had been effective, though, to collapse the end of the tunnel into the Vault. Max had been impressed by just how big a bang the gas cylinders could make.

The Armourer had not seemed impressed. Cira had muttered something about wanton damage, but she hadn't raised any strong objection. No sooner had the tunnel been dealt with, than Bryce was pushing them to move out. Even with Cira guiding them, and using some of her magic to clear a path through the Vault, it still took a while to wind through the corridors of the Vault to level 18. The Armourer was breathing hard. The lump on her head had gone down, but she was moving as if she hurt in other places. She had refused the offer of another healing patch from Bryce, insisting she would manage.

Bryce hadn't used all the gas cylinders to collapse the tunnel, suggesting instead that they take some with them. Max had volunteered to carry two, and quickly began to regret it as the heavy cylinders kept bumping against her, no matter how she tried to carry them. She didn't complain. Bryce was carrying another four cylinders, strapped together on top of his backpack and weapons. She wasn't quite sure how he was going to make use of them, and just hoped that they didn't get into a fire fight while he and she were carrying the explosive material.

Breathing hard, her legs protesting the effort, Max almost bumped into Cira's back when the Armourer halted at the top of a set of stairs, a corridor intersection ahead. Max couldn't work out how or why they had needed to climb up so many stairs to get to a level which was supposed to be beneath where they had started. She had tried not to think about it. Trying to map out the internal structure of the Vault was giving her a headache. Before she could ask if they were getting close, a wash of ice-cold magic slid across her skin, raising every hair on her body and making her muscles twitch, wanting to turn and run away. Far away. Very far away. She would even go up more stairs if it meant getting away from that awful sensation.

Cira threw a frowning glance over her shoulder, as if checking that Max could feel the dark magic, too. Max nodded.

Bryce had stopped with them. "What was that?" he asked, his voice pitched low. "Felt like something crawling over my grave."

"Dark magic," Max said. Bryce didn't have any magic sensitivity, but the dark magic had been strong enough that even the dead would have felt it.

"Very powerful dark magic. Whatever it is, they've got it out of the Vault. They beat us here," Cira said. "We're on level 18, and I think they must be in the main corridor, which is not far." She drew a steadying breath, squared her shoulders, and took a step forward. Bryce put a hand on her shoulder.

"A moment," he said. He shed his backpack, and untied the gas cylinders, then put his backpack on. The cylinders were roped together and he grabbed the top loop, holding his rifle with the other hand. "Ready," he said.

Max followed Cira's square, stocky form and Bryce's larger bulk around the corner and along the next corridor, shifting the pair of cylinders she carried so they were bundled under her arm. If there was any gunfire aimed at them, she was prepared to drop the cylinders and run.

At the end of the next corridor, the sound of voices drifted towards them. The crawling sensation of foul magic was still in the air. The magic seemed inert rather than active. It was still terrible. Max didn't want to get closer, yet crept forward with the others. Whatever it was, she definitely didn't want Evan and Queran to have it.

Bryce took a quick look around the end of the corridor, then continued forward, surprising Max. She followed. When she reached the corner, she saw why he had moved. The corridor ahead had the bulky stone surrounds around each door, and some of the doors had been ripped off their hinges, left to rest against the stone surrounds, providing even more cover. There was an intersection with another corridor and then more doors beyond that. At the far end of the corridor, there was a group of people, including Evan and Queran. There were only three

Syndicate members with them, and Max couldn't help wondering if that was all that was left of however many Evan had brought with him. She and Bryce - mostly Bryce - had left a significant number of dead bodies in their wake. Even though they had been trying to kill her, she felt uneasy about the amount of death. Although she didn't see Oliver, which suggested there might still be more of them. Somewhere.

Bryce was tucked behind a door on the other side of the corridor, the gas cylinders at his feet. Max moved to the door closest to her, pressing herself against the wall, losing sight of the group. She was surprised that no one had noticed either Bryce or her, but they all seemed transfixed by whatever Evan was holding in his hands.

"It seems you were not lying after all, demon." Evan's voice drifted towards her. He was speaking in a normal tone, not bothering to hide his presence.

"I rarely lie," Queran answered. From the tone of his voice, Max thought he was sneering. "I have kept my end of the bargain," he added.

"Not yet. You still have to show me how to use it," Evan said.

Max risked a peek around the door frame. The group was outside the last Vault on the long corridor. Evan was holding what looked like a massive, ancient book in his hands. He was wearing gloves, but apparently not affected by the cold, black magic that was seeping off the thing into the air. As Max watched, Queran held open a nullification pouch like the one that Bryce had found earlier. Evan put the book into it and the crawling sensation of foul magic disappeared at once.

"Ah," Evan said, rocking back on his heels. "It's so powerful. Hard to believe a simple pouch could contain it."

"It won't contain it for long," Queran warned, tying the top of the fabric together. Evan held out his hand, and Queran put the book into it with what looked like reluctance to Max.

Worried she might be seen, Max ducked back against the wall, frowning. So the object that the Syndicate had been searching so hard for was a book steeped in dark magic. It had looked old. Ancient, in fact. She had only seen books that size once or twice before. The Marshals' library had an ancient text on demons that was about that size and weight. But the Marshals' book was simply a guide. There was no magic attached to its pages.

Her earlier sense of urgency returned. If that book was emitting that much foul magic when it was closed and inert, she did not want to learn what it could unleash when it was opened and being used. She had to stop Evan and Queran from taking the book out of the Vault and using it. There were only five people. Or, rather, three people, one demon, and she still didn't know what Evan was. Bryce was more than capable of dealing with the armed people. And if Max could find a way of summoning the Lady's light, she might be able to deal with Queran, or at least set him back long enough for her to grab the nullification pouch and its contents from Evan. It wasn't a great plan, but she couldn't think of a better one right now.

"I've opened a portal for us." Oliver Forster's voice sounded. Make that six people. She'd forgotten about him. And Oliver was a powerful magician. She couldn't deal with him and Queran at the same time. Max leaned forward a fraction and saw him emerge from the intersection. "It's along here."

"Well, let's get going," Evan said briskly.

They were going to leave, Max realised, panic drying her mouth. They had to be stopped. She drew her handgun. Bryce was ahead of her, throwing a pair of the gas cylinders he had been carrying. His aim was excellent and the metal tubes landed in the mouth of the intersection Oliver had emerged from. As they landed, Bryce fired. Trying to collapse the corridor mouth the way he had brought down the tunnel earlier.

The explosion sent Max back against the wall, hitting her head hard enough to see stars. There were several ominous cracking sounds and great pieces of stone fell into the corridor opening, blocking the way. Clouds of dust rose into the air from the collapsed walls and ceiling.

"Give me the others," Bryce said, gesturing towards her. His words were distorted, but Max caught the meaning well enough. She rolled the two cylinders she had carried over the floor to him. Bryce threw his last two and then hers as well, raising his rifle. A moment later two further explosions rocked the ground under their feet. The second and third explosions set fire to the dust that filled the air. Vivid blue and yellow flames formed a wall across the corridor, blocking not just the escape for Evan and his people, but also stopping Max from seeing him.

Underneath the echoes of the explosions and the surge of flames that filled the corridor, Max could hear furious shouts from Evan and the others. Their only way out of the corridor was towards Max and Bryce.

Bullets flew out of the flames and smoke, followed by a jagged, black lightning bolt of dark magic. Queran, Max thought at once, pressing herself back against the wall to stay out of its path. But, no. It didn't feel like Queran's magic. Possibly Oliver. Or Evan. Her stomach turned at the thought. She didn't know what he was, so she couldn't be sure what he was capable of.

Bryce was firing back.

Something small and metal rolled out of the smoke and flames towards them and Max stumbled back, recognising the sound. One of the small bombs that the Syndicate carried. No, more than one, she realised as more shapes rolled towards her. Before she could get out of the way, the bombs went off.

The force of the explosions sent her back against the wall, jarring every bone in her body. She slid down to the floor, unable to move, dark magic seeping around her. On the other side of the corridor, she saw a slumped figure that had to be Bryce. He looked unconscious. She managed to turn her head the smallest fraction and saw Cira lying against a wall not far away. The Armourer didn't move. Max could only hope she was alive and simply unconscious.

The smoke and flames shifted, parting ways to let a group of people through. Evan. Queran. Oliver. And one of the intruders, face set in grim determination, the trace of a Huntsman tattoo showing at his neck.

"You really are troublesome," Evan said, coming to stand in front of her. "But I have been planning this for too long to let you stop me." He had the great book tucked under his arm, the nullification pouch still working to hide the foul magic. He crouched down and Max noticed that he didn't seem to have a scratch on him, or one single bit of debris. In contrast, her clothes were covered in dust and ash, her lungs full of the smoke filling the corridor and she could feel bits of stone in her hair. Breathing hurt, too. She might have broken a rib. Or two. "You have failed," Evan told her.

He looked human. Absolutely, utterly human. Her mind darted this way and that, thoughts scattered. There was nothing special about him. There was no aura of power around him. And yet he had just walked through fire without a scratch, and had fought Bryce before, holding his own. And he had held the book with no apparent ill effects.

"What are you?" Max asked, the words slurred. It was only after she had spoken she realised she'd asked him the same question that Queran had asked her. And she didn't have an answer for Queran. But it seemed that Evan had an answer for her.

"Not what. Who," Evan said, lips peeling back in a smile that reminded her eerily of Queran. The demon produced the same kind of false expression. "Perhaps you would like to tell her, demon?" he asked, not even bothering to look at Queran.

"Certainly," Queran said. His expression was almost forbiddingly neutral, a mask he was wearing to hide some strong feelings. "Lord Evan is a descendant of the progeny of the great lord himself."

"Progeny?" Max repeated, old-fashioned word unfamiliar on her tongue. Her nose wrinkled as she stared at Evan. "That means you're a direct descendant of Arkus?" she asked. The words were still slurred, and her mind was struggling to accept the concept. There had been rumours. There always were. Rumours that both the Lady and the dark lord had - separately - produced offspring in the daylight world. Most people dismissed such rumours as works of fantasy. But then, everyone that Max knew also believed that the city and the Wild were all that existed in the daylight world.

Evan smiled again, this time with apparently genuine pleasure. "That is so."

"Bad luck for you, eh," Max said over Evan's shoulder, addressing the demon standing oh-so-quietly and oh-so-patiently behind the apparently human former detective. "I mean, a full demon is a rare thing in this world, but even you have to bow to one of Arkus' descendants."

Queran's face shifted, unseen by Evan, more than a hint of anger and disgust showing through. Max had guessed correctly. Not happy about having to defer to Evan. Not happy at all. She wondered how long it would be before Queran found a way of turning against his new master.

Evan was still smiling as he straightened to his feet, looking down at her. "You're interfering in matters that don't concern you. Don't feel bad about failing. It was inevitable. Kill her," he said. The last was said so casually and in such a matter-of-fact tone that Max almost missed the meaning. Evan was already moving on, away from her, Queran trailing in his wake.

Max tried to move, but her body wouldn't obey her and she stayed where she was, slumped against the wall, the world tilting at an alarming angle as she tried to turn her head to follow Evan. He couldn't leave. She needed to stop him. She needed to get up. To move. But no matter how she fought internally, her body still wouldn't move.

The remaining Syndicate member raised their gun, ready to fire. Unable to do anything, Max stared up at them, watching in horrified fascination as their finger tightened on the trigger.

But another shot rang out and the Syndicate member slumped to the ground, a shocked expression on their face. As her would-be killer fell, Max saw Bryce struggling to his feet, handgun held in one hand, the other hand bracing himself against the wall. He looked as if he might fall over at any moment. He had saved her life. Again. She was losing count.

A surge of dark magic flew through the air and knocked Bryce off his feet, into the blue and yellow flames that were still blocking the corridor.

Max yelled a protest and tried to get to her feet, but her body still wasn't working. Anger filled her, along with the faintest spark of light. She drew the light out of her, screaming as it tore through her flesh, and threw it along the corridor in the direction that Evan and the others had gone.

Cries of pain and alarm and fury told her that she had succeeded in hitting someone. She could only hope she had done enough damage that they wouldn't be able to take the book out of the Vault.

A wave of agony coursed through her and she hissed, darkness rising up and dragging her down before she could see if Bryce was alive or not.

Chapter Eighteen

Max *hurt*. Ribs, back, legs, head, neck, and the back of one of her hands. She tried opening her eyes and couldn't see much. There was smoke around her, drying out her mouth and filling her lungs, clouding the air. She blinked and then coughed, trying to sit up and hissing as a stabbing pain woke up in her neck and her ribs protested. She fumbled for a painkiller patch and found one, grabbing it with trembling fingers, putting it on the bare skin of her neck. The patch flared hot, discharging all of its magic in one burst that sent a wave of agony through her body. After she had breathed through that, her eyes stinging, she could move. The pain was still there, just dulled.

She managed to get to her feet, bits and pieces of stone falling off her as she moved. The blue and yellow flames were gone, leaving grey smoke in their wake. The smoke was thinning out as she looked around, letting her see the destruction that Bryce's improvised bombs had caused. She saw Bryce half-lying, half-sitting against the opposite wall. He was unconscious, but she thought he was breathing. The relief made her shaky and she put a hand against the wall to hold herself up. Apart from her and Bryce, the corridor was empty of life. Evan, Queran and Oliver had gone. The Syndicate member who had aimed his gun at her head was lying dead in front of her, eyes still open and staring at nothing. Max shivered. Too many dead. Far too many dead.

And worse was to come, she feared, cold washing over her. Evan had got away. She had failed to stop him from taking the book. She didn't know how long she had been unconscious, but he could be anywhere by now if he'd used the portal magic that seemed to saturate the Vault.

"Still alive, I see," the Armourer said. She was looking about as bad as Max felt. She was gripping her great hammer with both hands, staring past Max at the chaos. "I'm seriously considering revoking your right to have a Vault," the other woman said, face and voice grim.

Max grimaced. She couldn't blame the Armourer. The Vault had operated and remained intact for over three hundred years, and she and Bryce had been in it for less than a full day. Or so she thought. She had no real idea of how much time had passed. And in their short visit, several bombs had gone off and a huge amount of destruction had been caused. Max could only hope that the Vault structure was still intact, apart from the damaged sections. Her eyes stung. Not only had she failed to stop Evan, she had also damaged one of the oldest and most revered institutions in magic.

"I'm joking," Cira said, reaching out and putting a hand on Max's arm. "Don't look so distraught. We can rebuild. It'll take time, but it's possible."

"I'm sorry," Max said, her throat tight. "All this chaos. All the damage. All the death. And I don't think we did any good."

"They were all followers of the dark lord, weren't they?" Cira asked in her usual brisk manner. "Well, then, I'd say a few less of them in the world is a good thing. How's your man doing?"

"I haven't checked," Max said, looking across at Bryce, then frowning at Cira. "And he's not mine. We're not … I'm not …"

"You'll figure it out, I'm sure. You both seem smart enough. If you want to try waking him up, I'm going to see if I can get hold of Inigo." The Armourer stalked off, away from the destruction.

Left alone for a moment, Max reached up to scrub her hands over her face and hair, only then realising that she was still holding her gun. She put it away, grimacing as her hand cramped. She must have been holding it too tightly. Running her fingers through her hair told her that she was just as sweaty and dirty as she felt, more stone fragments cascading off her and clattering on the ground along with another cloud of dust.

She went across to Bryce and crouched down beside him, putting a hand on his arm.

He woke at once, going from unconscious to fully alert so quickly that Max almost jumped back. But this was Bryce. And somehow she knew that he would not hurt her.

He looked straight at her. He had dark eyes, to go with his hair, but there were bright flecks in the darkness she had not seen before. She couldn't tell if the flecks were silver or grey, and it suddenly seemed important for her to know.

He put a hand on her face, his skin warm and rough and vividly alive. "Are you alright?" he asked her, voice low.

"No," she said honestly. "We didn't stop Evan. We damaged the Vault. Too many people are dead. And I hurt head to toe," she said. That last bit slipped out, and she wanted to pull back, hating to sound like she was moaning.

Bryce's eyes brightened with an unexpected smile and he leant forward. She was too surprised to move for a moment, then realised what he was doing and met him halfway.

The man could *kiss*. Max forgot all about her sweaty hair, filthy clothes, and the various bruises across her body and leant forward, snaking an arm around Bryce's neck, letting him pull her closer. She forgot absolutely everything for a few blissful moments. She had never been kissed like this before, with absolute focus and commitment and she wanted to stay right where she was, curled up against him. She moved, trying to get closer, and something metallic stabbed her in her already-bruised ribs, causing her to pull back with a gasp of pain. She didn't go far, just enough to get out of the way of the muzzle of Bryce's automatic rifle. Her arm was still around his neck, one of his hands on her waist, the other tangled in her hair. His eyes were brighter still as he looked back at her.

"We should try this again without weapons," Max said.

Bryce smiled, his eyes crinkling at the corners, white teeth gleaming, unexpected mischief on his face. He kissed her again, far too briefly, then disentangled from her. Max tried not to feel too disappointed. It wasn't the time or place for kissing. Unfortunately. She stayed where she was, kneeling on the stone floor, as he got up.

"I can hear Cira coming back," he said, and offered her a hand.

She let him pull her to her feet and paused, lacing her fingers through his, staring up at him. She wouldn't have survived her time in the Vault without him. And she wasn't ready to let him go. Not yet.

"Inigo is on his way," Cira said.

Max let go of Bryce and turned to the Armourer. The woman was standing at the head of the stairs, sharp eyes travelling between Max and Bryce.

"Is Evan still in the Vault?" Max asked.

"No. There were only three of them at the end that I saw, and they all used one of the portal spells in a Vault room to get out. This room here," Cira said, pointing to the nearest open door. "I don't know where they've gone."

"Can you send us out the same way?" Max asked.

"You look like a strong wind could blow you over, and you want to go after him?" Cira asked, staring at Max in a way that suggested she was trying to decide if Max was crazy or stupid, or possibly both.

"If he's gone back to our city, we have allies there," Bryce said. He stepped up to Max's shoulder and glanced down at her. "Kitris will need to move on this, at least."

Max shook her head slightly. In all the rushing about the Vault, and the strangeness of this world, she had all but forgotten the head of the Order and all the internal politics and power struggles she had left behind in the city. It was true that Kitris would want to know what had happened here. Every magician in the world would want to know that someone had got into the Vault. But Max was less certain that Kitris would take action.

"The Marshals will help," she told Bryce. Of that, she was quite certain. And if Faddei got involved, there was a good chance he could prompt Kitris into action. Faddei had a way with people that Max envied, and didn't fully understand.

"It would be a lot more sensible to send you back through Max's Vault to where you started from," Cira said. "We can be sure of that destination, at least."

Max wanted to object to the idea, but a pair of robed Wardens came up the stairs after Cira. One was the red-haired Inigo, looking just as displeased as he had the last time Max had seen him. The other was slightly familiar, sporting a brilliant white bandage around his head and short, dark hair.

"You were in my Vault," Max said, recognising the other Warden.

"Yes. And I must thank you for alerting Cira that I was there," the Warden said.

"You need to hear him, Cira," Inigo said. Max couldn't read his expression.

"Alright. What were you doing there?" Cira asked.

"I saw light coming from around the door," the unnamed Warden said.

"That's impossible," Cira said at once, the response fast and seeming to be instinctive. "No one should be in the Vaults." Then she grimaced, looking back at Max and Bryce, as if remembering how they had come to be in the Vault.

"I know. But there was light," the Warden insisted. He folded his hands at his chest, expression changing into one of wonder, a smile pulling his lips. "It was extraordinary. As if the Lady Herself was smiling."

"Oh, really?" the Armourer asked, voice laced with cynicism.

"You don't believe me, Cira?" the Warden asked, still smiling.

"You did get hit on the head pretty hard," the Armourer responded. "So, you saw a light. What then?"

"It drew me forward. When I reached the door, it opened for me and I walked into the light," the Warden said.

He believed what he was saying, Max said, watching the man. His whole body looked like it was lifting up, ready to float away, and his expression held more peace than Max had ever felt in her life.

"What then?" Cira asked, a little less abruptly than before.

"I could see that there was a portal open. The light was around it. I reached up, and then something hit me on the side of the head and I lost consciousness," the Warden said. He was back to being an ordinary man, albeit a powerful magician. He swayed back on his heels a little and looked around the group. "I can't explain it, but I am telling the truth."

"I believe you," Max said.

"I do, too," Cira said. She lifted a brow at Max. "It makes no sense. The Syndicate were using dark magic, not light. Unless there was someone else in your Vault?"

"No one that I saw, and I've never sent anyone there," Max said slowly. Through the exhaustion and pain, she was remembering the sensation of light and love and peace when she had been pulled into the Vault. The sensation that there was something vast and all-encompassing there, just out of her reach. A shiver ran through her. The Warden was describing the Lady's light, normally found in Her temples, carefully tended by Her priests and priestesses. "I remember feeling some kind of presence as I was pulled through," she admitted, realising that the others were staring at her.

"The Lady Herself?" Cira asked, brows lifting to her hairline. "In your Vault?"

"I don't know," Max said, wanting instinctively to move away from the idea. "I can't explain it. But there was something else there."

The Armourer stared at Max with an unreadable expression but with what looked like old wisdom in her eyes, and Max remembered her saying that she hadn't always been the Armourer.

"The Lady Herself," Cira said again, only this time it wasn't a question. "Well, She had sent you here for a reason, and I am grateful to Her."

"I'm not sure I did any good," Max protested, then glanced at Bryce. "Not me, anyway. I'm pretty sure Bryce could have sorted the Syndicate out for you, given time."

"It needed both of you," Cira said firmly, in a tone that left no room for argument. "You with your magic and him with his weapons."

"Our work isn't done," Bryce pointed out. He had stayed quiet under the discussion of the Lady and Her ways, but now focused on the unfinished business of dealing with Queran, Evan and Oliver.

"That's true. Come on, first we need to get to Max's Vault, and then see if we can send you home," Cira said.

Home. The word rang through Max, stirring up a fierce longing for familiar things and her hounds. All at once she missed them so much it hurt to breathe. With Bryce beside her, she followed Cira further into the Vault, hoping for a way home.

Chapter Nineteen

With the swirl of Cira's magic fading around her, Max hit the ground with a thump, the world spinning around her, too-bright lights stabbing her in the eyes, every part of her sore and bruised, the impact of the landing waking up old hurts, a cacophony of discordant noise ringing through her head, making her wince.

She managed to get to her knees and stopped, nausea rising. She braced her hands on her knees and took a long, slow breath, drawing in familiar scents. Exhaust fumes. The faint trace of green growing things. Stale beer. The fresh static charge of clean, powerful magic. Not the Vault. The city. Cira's attempt to send her out had worked. Relief made her weak and she was glad she was still on the ground. Home.

More noise assaulted her ears. Barking. Dogs barking. *Her* dogs barking.

She opened her eyes to see two blurry forms rushing towards her.

Cas and Pol hit her at full speed, spilling her backward across the car park's worn and cracked surface, their bodies wriggling with delight as they sniffed her head to toe and back again, pausing for the occasional lick at her face, their tails wagging so fast that they were still blurred even as Max's vision cleared.

"Good dogs." Her voice cracked. She had missed them. So much. She managed to sit up again and flung an arm around each of them, burying her face into Cas' shoulder and then Pol's, not surprised to find that she was crying. There had been moments in the past however-long-it-had-been in the Vault when she had wondered if she would ever see them again. And here she was, battered and exhausted, but back with her dogs. Cas made a happy little sound, still wriggling with delight as he lay down beside her, warm and real, resting his head on her shoulder. Pol stayed standing, his head on top of hers. She could feel the vibration of his heart thumping against her ear. They were soft and solid and warm and real. Back where she belonged. She hugged them tighter.

A low moan sounded from nearby and she turned, ducking under Pol's head to see Bryce lying on the ground not far away. He sat up, putting a hand to his head.

"That felt a lot worse the second time around," he commented, and looked across at her. "You ok?"

"Yes." Max smiled, despite the tears on her face and the dogs pressing around her. "The landing hurt a bit, but the welcome made up for it," she added, hugging her dogs again.

"There you are." A crisp, familiar voice cut across anything Bryce might have wanted to say. Max turned to find Ruutti standing a few paces away. She couldn't read the detective's expression, but she saw dark smudges under Ruutti's eyes, which she had never seen before, and the woman's short blonde hair was messy rather than artfully arranged.

"Here we are," Max agreed. She managed to get to her feet despite her dogs' best efforts. They each pressed into her legs, stopping her from walking forward. "Are you alright?" she asked Ruutti.

"Am I alright?" Ruutti repeated, and gave a short, incredulous laugh. "You and the man mountain disappear completely for nearly two days and then you ask if I'm alright?"

"Two days?" Max had lost all track of time in the underground, but still she was taken aback. "I'd no idea it was so long."

"And now you're back," Ruutti said.

By that time, Max had had a chance to look around at the familiar sight of the parking lot at the Hunter's Tooth. Her pick-up was still there, along with a sleek, shiny car she had no difficulty in identifying as Ruutti's. "How's Malik?" she asked.

"He's fine," Ruutti said, her tone and face softening to a fond expression that Max had never seen on her face before. "Thanks to you, he's recovered well. He's not opened the bar yet. Come on, he'll be glad to see you," she said, half-turning away.

Max looked past her shoulder and saw that the bar door was still closed, but the side entrance that she and Bryce had used the last time was open, a glimpse of lush green plants peeking out in sharp contrast with the bland concrete walls of the building.

"I need to call Faddei," Max said, staying where she was for the moment. "But my phone broke."

"Here," Ruutti said, holding out her own sleek and expensive-looking phone.

Max eyed the offering with some suspicion, trying to work out what angle Ruutti was playing.

"Take it. Call him. He's been calling me almost every hour, wanting to know if there's any sign of you. I've tried not answering, but he just keeps calling. I'm surprised he hadn't set up camp next to your, er, vehicle," Ruutti said.

That explained the eagerness to help, Max realised. She took the phone and dialled the Marshals' number from memory.

"What?" Therese's sharp voice had never been more welcome.

"It's Max. I need to speak to Faddei."

"Max? What's wrong with your phone?"

"I landed on it and broke it," Max said, rolling her eyes. Trust Therese to ignore the fact she'd been missing for nearly two days and instead focus on the equipment.

"I'll put you through to Faddei," the woman said. The line went quiet for a moment.

"Max? Are you alright? We've been looking all over the city for you." Faddei's voice was full of human warmth and concern.

"I'm in one piece," Max said. "Is everyone else alright?" she asked, a sharp spike of concern rising. The police and Marshals had been under threat.

"We're all alive. A few bruises, but we'll heal."

"Good. That's good," Max said, glad of the weight of her dogs holding her up as she went weak with relief again. "I have a lot to tell you. Can you meet me at the Hunter's Tooth?" she asked.

"I'm on my way," Faddei said, and hung up.

"Thank you," Max said, giving the phone back to Ruutti.

Movement in the doorway behind the detective drew her attention and she saw Malik standing there, carefully inside the boundary of his building. He looked fine, Max saw, relief coursing through her. He raised a hand and she waved back.

"Do you need to call Kitris?" she asked, turning to Bryce.

"I will do. Meet in the bar?" he suggested.

"Yes," she agreed, and took a step forward, the dogs parting company just enough to let her move towards the building.

"Your dogs refused to leave," Ruutti said, falling into step beside Max. "They've been keeping watch. And refusing to eat anything apart from chicken and steak."

"Cheeky beggars," Max said, rough affection in her voice. "Thank you for taking care of them," she told Ruutti, then looked down at her hounds. "It will be back to dog food now, hear me?" she told Cas and Pol. They looked back at her with quizzical expressions, as if they knew what she was saying and didn't quite believe it could possibly be true.

Then she reached the doorway and Malik. She stepped inside and found herself folded into a warm, familiar hug. Malik smelled of freshly baked bread and cinnamon. When she let him go and took a step back, she could see that he was thinner than he had been, his face shadowed, but there was no sign of the awful bruising on his face and his smile was bright as he looked at her.

"We've been worried," Malik said, holding out a hand to Ruutti. To Max's surprise, the detective put her hand in his and moved closer to his side. "Where have you been?"

"I'm happy to tell you, but I'd rather just go through it once. Faddei is on his way. Can we use the bar?" Max asked.

"Of course. This way," Malik said. "Are you hungry?"

Max's stomach made a loud growling noise, drawing a smile to Malik's face and heat to Max's. "I am starving," she said honestly. "Ruutti said we've been gone nearly two days."

"That sounds right," Malik agreed, and grimaced, "although I was out of it for about a day."

"I'll organise some food," Ruutti said, pulling her phone out and stepping to one side, letting Max, her dogs and Malik keep going.

"Thank you," Malik said, tone more serious than she was used to hearing from him.

"For what?" Max asked, her mind full of the events of the Vault and her return.

"You saved my life," Malik said, and put his hand on his heart. "I owe you a great debt."

"I'm glad to have been able to help," Max said. "But you don't owe me anything," she added, uncomfortable with the idea. "You've helped me plenty over the years."

"It's my pleasure to help where I can," Malik said, drawing a smile to her face. She felt the knots of tension across her back ease, along with the lump of anxiety she had been carrying for what felt like days. She breathed in air laced with familiar scents and felt herself relax even more. Between her dogs' welcome and Malik's steadfast warmth, she knew she was home. Back where everything was familiar, and the world made sense.

They had reached the other side of the garden and Malik pushed open a door, revealing a dark space. He went through first, flipping a light switch to reveal an ordinary-looking corridor which Max recognised. They were in the back of the Hunter's Tooth. There was a swing door ahead of them which led to the bar. Malik headed through and flipped more switches, letting light into the bar.

It was strange being in the Tooth when it was so empty, and seeing it from this angle. The air felt stale and lifeless, with no customers inside. Malik moved behind the bar, pressing more buttons which raised more lights around the space, giving it the soft ambience Max was used to. He left the shutters across the windows, perhaps not wanting hopeful customers trying to get inside. He wrinkled his nose as he looked around.

"Barely two days away and it feels like a different place," he said. "There isn't even any coffee ready."

"I've ordered food," Ruutti said, coming into the bar. "It'll be here soon. Do you want me to put the coffee on?" she asked Malik.

Max took a seat at the bar in one of the familiar stools, watching as Ruutti moved behind the bar and set up the coffee machine. It was odd seeing the detective doing something so ordinary, almost domestic. When Max had called the other woman to come and help Malik, it had been out of an instinct that

Ruutti might be able to help a fellow siren. Two days later, Ruutti was still here and seemingly very comfortable with Malik and his property. Max was curious, but kept her questions to herself. It was not her business. She was just glad that Malik was alive and well.

Malik moved away from the bar, going over to the main door and opening it to reveal Bryce. The door was still damaged and creaked ominously as it opened. Malik pulled a sign from a slot in the back of the door which read *Closed for Private Event*, and put it on the outside, letting Bryce inside.

"Kitris is on his way," Bryce said, coming across the bar.

He seemed as comfortable in this space as she was, Max realised. It made a certain sort of sense. Malik was well-known, liked and trusted among the non-human community. People told him things, and he shared information with people he trusted. It wasn't just Max's questions he answered.

"Are you really healed?" Max asked, as Malik came back to the bar. He was moving more slowly than she was used to, and with less than his usual grace.

"I really am," he assured her, smiling again. "Just need a day or two to get my full energy back. And no more visits from men in black," he added, with a hint of dry humour as he settled on a bar stool near Max. He didn't meet her eyes, though. Not wanting her to see him as weak, she thought. Malik had never been an overtly powerful figure, just quietly confident and assured in his own territory. That mild exterior expertly covered up the depth and extent of his power, and Max could only imagine how shocking it had been for him to be attacked and overwhelmed enough in his own territory that the attackers had been able to drag him outside, beyond his border.

"The Syndicate," Max said, voice heavy.

"You've come across them?" Ruutti asked, voice sharp.

"You could say that," Max said, exchanging glances with Bryce. "We should probably save the full story until everyone is here." She hesitated, looking back at Malik. He seemed calm, and he had never refused to answer a question from her before. Still, she didn't want to hurt him.

He met her eyes, a glint of humour in his own. "You want to know what the Syndicate were after here," Malik said. He shook his head slightly. "I don't remember much. They kept shouting at me to stop asking questions, but nothing more specific than that," Malik said, the tightness in his jaw and throat lessening. He looked back at her, frowning. "I thought it must be about the Vault at first. I'd heard about the Vault being interfered with and had been asking about that. I almost didn't believe it at first, but I kept hearing the same story." He drew a breath, "But they didn't ask about the Vault, just wanted me to shut up."

Max exchanged glances with Bryce again, remembering the extent of the Syndicate's interference in the Vault. She wondered if they had believed that no magician would want to talk about their Vault, to reveal a vulnerability, but Evan and Queran surely could not have believed that their search would go unnoticed. And anyone who knew anything about the magical community in the city would know about Malik's love of information. She had never thought that would get him into trouble before now. Along with his network of connections, he maintained an open door policy at the Hunter's Tooth. Everyone was welcome. No one had ever tried to interfere with him before now. Before the Syndicate.

Before she could ask any more questions, there was a tentative knock at the patched-together front door. Malik went to answer it. He opened the door to reveal what looked like a mountain of paper bags with two legs underneath.

"Ruutti, how much food did you order?" he asked, half-laughing. He directed the packages to one of the tables in the middle of the floor. The packages moved, the legs carrying them over and setting them down on the table to reveal a young man in one of the bright uniforms of a well-known fast-food chain, slightly out of breath.

"There's more in the van," the man said and headed out.

Max eyed the mountain of fast food bags and boxes on the table and her stomach growled again.

"I hope it's enough," Ruutti said. "Remember, it's not just you and me and the dogs, we've got the man mountain and Max as well."

"Bryce," Max said, still looking at the packages.

"What?"

"His name is Bryce. He's a warrior of the Order," Max said, and glanced across at the detective, "as I'm sure you know."

Ruutti smiled. It was an old, familiar smile full of sharp edges. It was oddly reassuring to see. The detective might have softened around Malik, but she was still very much herself. "You keep such interesting company," she murmured.

By then, the food delivery was complete. The paper bags and boxes took up three tables. Cas and Pol left Max's side for the first time and headed for the tables, sniffing curiously. The table tops were lower than their heads, but to Max's relief, they didn't try to grab anything. It seemed that, despite their rich diet for the past days, they had still remembered their manners.

Malik enlisted Bryce's help in pulling tables together to make one big enough for them all to sit around, then moving chairs into place, while Ruutti produced plates, cutlery and napkins from somewhere behind the bar.

While they were doing that, there was another knock at the door. With everyone else busy, Max went to answer it, Cas and Pol leaving the food alone to trail after her. She had a feeling that they would be sticking close to her for the next few days at least.

She opened the door to find both Faddei and Kitris outside, a few other people gathered behind them.

"Max. I'm glad to see you in one piece," Faddei said, stepping forward and giving her a brief, heartfelt hug. "We were worried when we couldn't find you," he said, resting his hand on her shoulder. "Are you alright?"

"Bruised and tired," Max said honestly, wrinkling her nose. "But I'll recover. I'm glad to be back."

"Back?" he asked, brows lifting. "I want to hear all about it. But before I forget, here," he said, handing her a sleek metal and glass object. "Therese said your phone is broken. This one is a clone, so has the same number and all the data you'd backed up."

"Oh, thank you," Max said, tucking the phone away and stepping back to let Faddei and the others into the bar. "Kitris," she said, dipping her head in acknowledgement.

"Miscellandreax," he said, his voice clipped. His gaze travelled from her boots to her hair and he didn't look pleased with what he saw. But then, he never really had, Max remembered. She had long ago decided it was stupid to be hurt by Kitris' indifference towards her.

As Faddei and Kitris filed past, Max realised that they had each brought extra people with them. Faddei had brought Vanko and Zoya, both the Marshals also pausing to give Max brief hugs. The warm greeting was unexpected enough to make Max's eyes sting and she ducked her head as Kitris' entourage filed in. There was a senior warrior whose name she couldn't remember, a pair of junior warriors, and Orshiasa. The inclusion of her former master made her stiffen, and she wondered just what Bryce had told Kitris that had made him think a Guardian was needed.

Max closed the door and followed the others back to the table. Malik was welcoming everyone with his usual warmth, passing around glasses of what looked like fruit juice as well as mugs of coffee.

Amid the bustle of getting everyone settled, Max took note that the two more junior warriors stationed themselves away from the others, with a clear view of the exits. The senior warrior stayed near Kitris and Orshiasa, but refused a seat, standing behind them, next to one of the screens that Malik had used to break up the open space of the bar. Ready to intervene, Max sensed, although she wasn't sure what he was there to intervene against. And he wasn't just a senior warrior, he was *the* senior warrior and Kitris' second-in-command. And she couldn't remember his name right now.

When the others were settled, Max realised that she and Bryce had been sat at opposite ends of the table, whether by accident or by design. Malik put a plate of food in front of her, along with a tall glass. There was cutlery and a napkin already there. She found she had Faddei on one side and Zoya on the other, Vanko on Zoya's other side. Kitris and Orshiasa were at the other end of the table with Bryce. Her brows lifted. It seemed more adversarial than she had anticipated.

"Well?" Kitris said, cutting through the murmur of conversation and clatter of plates.

He was staring at her, so Max lifted her brows. "Well, what?" she asked, and heard Vanko turn a laugh into a not very convincing cough.

"You were gone for nearly two days," Kitris said, face tight with displeasure. He was ignoring the juice and coffee that Malik had given him, staring along the length of the table at Max. She could feel power gathered around him. He was angry enough to use it, too, despite this being Malik's territory. And with Malik so recently healed, she wasn't sure if he had the strength to combat a magician of Kitris' power.

"The report I had said you were sucked into magic," Faddei said, in an easy tone that Max was sure fooled no one. "Tell us what happened."

Max met Bryce's eyes. He inclined his head, indicating she should go first. She took a sip of the juice. Fresh and tart, and very necessary.

"I was pulled into the Vault," she started.

"Don't be ridiculous," Orshiasa said immediately, bristling with as much temper as Kitris. "Are we here to listen to fanciful tales?"

"Guardian, I am here to listen to what my Marshal has to say. I agree it is a startling piece of news, but I want to hear the full account," Faddei said. "If you don't want to listen, you know where the door is."

Max had to bite her lip to stop a smile. Faddei was good at playing politics when he needed to, but he also believed in getting to the point as quickly as possible. From Orshiasa's expression, he was not used to being spoken to in such blunt terms.

"The Vault had been breached," Max went on, and glanced at Kitris and Orshiasa. "Bryce was also drawn in and recognised the intruders as members of the Syndicate."

"Is this true?" Kitris demanded, not looking at Bryce.

"Yes," Bryce confirmed. He had managed to eat some food, Max saw, although there were still dark smudges under his eyes. He had been tired before they had been drawn into the Vault, and they'd spent most of their time there running. Or so it felt like.

"Wait. What is the Syndicate?" Faddei asked, frowning down the length of the table at Kitris. "Why have we not heard of them before now?"

"They are not your concern," Kitris said in a dismissive tone that sent prickles down Max's spine. The Order was notoriously difficult about sharing information, but even Kitris had to realise that armed militia within the city limits was something that every law enforcement agency in the city needed to know about, not just the Order. She wondered just why he had been withholding the information for so long, even with one of his warriors missing for two days.

"Unfortunately, they are now everyone's concern," Max said, and turned to Faddei. "It seems to be the same group that's been attacking police officers," she said.

"What?" Faddei asked, the word exploding out of him.

"What attacks on police officers?" Kitris demanded, his face even more pinched than before.

"If you would answer your damned phone once in a while, you'd know," Faddei snapped at the head of the Order, then turned back to Max. "Sorry. Go on."

Max nodded, trying not to notice Kitris' displeased expression. "Apparently, the Syndicate appeared about a week to ten days ago. They've taken over the Raghavan territory, and sealed it off. The people living in the warehouse were displaced."

"I'd heard about the eviction," Faddei said, still frowning, "but the council seemed to think that was done by the Raghavans' soldiers."

"No," Bryce said. "Since the Syndicate appeared, we haven't seen any of the Raghavans' security."

"Is this relevant?" Kitris asked.

"How did a new group manage to take over the Raghavan territory so quickly?" Faddei asked, addressing the question to Kitris and Bryce impartially. From his frown and the edge to his tone, he was not happy that he had not been told. Max did not blame him.

"I think it's been planned for a while," Max said slowly, remembering Evan Yarwood standing over her, telling her that he had been planning this for too long to let her stop him.

"This isn't your jurisdiction. There are no creatures for you to deal with," Kitris snapped at Faddei, ignoring Max. Her brows shot up, and she was sure she wasn't the only one. In public, on display as he was just now, Kitris was normally careful to pay deference to other public authority figures in the city. In his own way, he was as skilled at politics as Faddei.

"Perhaps we should let Max and Bryce tell us what happened," Malik suggested, before Faddei could respond, his tone full of calm reason, soothing the bristling tension in the air. He might not be fully healed, but this was his territory. He and Ruutti seemed to be holding hands under the table, and Max couldn't help wondering if Ruutti was sharing her energy with Malik somehow. It would run counter to what she knew of the detective, who had always appeared to be quite focused on her own personal interests. It seemed that some things had changed in the short time Max had been absent.

"Careful, siren, I don't appreciate being manipulated," Kitris snapped, glaring at Malik now. And some things had not changed at all, Max reflected, trying not to roll her eyes. Kitris was more than happy to manipulate or outright order other people to do his bidding, but did not like the tables turned. Not at all. She ignored him and looked back at Faddei and her fellow Marshals, who were all waiting for her to continue.

"The Syndicate had appeared in the Vault not long before we got there," Max said. "They were looking for something, although it wasn't clear what. They had magicians skilled in dark magic, along with warriors. Quite a few of the armed ones had Huntsman tattoos," Max added, glancing at Faddei to make sure he took note of that. She need not have worried. He was listening intently. "The Syndicate got hold of a list of the magicians who hold individual Vaults and were searching them. The Vaults, I mean. The Vault is managed and protected by the Armourer and her Wardens. A good number of the Wardens were killed," Max added, the weight of loss heavy in her chest.

"The Armourer and her Wardens are powerful magicians, but they were facing automatic weapons," Bryce added. "They put up a very strong resistance, but they were not able to stop the intruders."

"Then the leaders of the Syndicate turned up," Max said, and was abruptly aware of Kitris, Orshiasa and the warrior whose name she couldn't remember leaning forward, intent on her next words. "Evan Yarwood is the head of the Syndicate," she said simply. "He has the demon Queran and the magician Oliver Forster working for him. Oh, and did you know that Oliver Forster is not quite human?" she asked. It wasn't the most important thing she had to tell them, but it seemed relevant.

"Lady Forster had very, er, varied taste in husbands," Faddei commented, shaking his head slightly. "So, no, I didn't know about Oliver. But it doesn't surprise me."

"Evan Yarwood? You're sure? The chief is head of some secret society?" Ruutti asked, leaning forward, looking and sounding as astonished as Max had ever seen her. "That's ridiculous."

"There's more," Bryce said, glancing between Kitris and Orshiasa. "Evan Yarwood is a descendant of the dark lord himself."

Kitris and Orshiasa froze, with almost identical expressions of shock followed by disbelief.

"How do you know this?" Ruutti asked, eyes fixed on Max's face. She had grown a little paler.

"Evan and Queran both confirmed it," Max said. Her mouth was dry and she took another sip of juice. "Queran is taking orders from Evan now."

She heard the collective intake of breath around the table as everyone absorbed that piece of information. Not everyone would fully understand the implications, but she hoped that Kitris and Orshiasa at least were paying attention to the fact that a full demon was walking in the daylight world and taking his orders from one of Arkus' descendants.

"Max, I think you'd better tell us in detail what you saw and heard when Evan arrived," Faddei said.

She did her best, with Bryce chipping in to add the occasional detail she had missed, describing Evan and Queran's arrival, the conversations she had overheard. And then she got to the part where she tried to describe the book that the Syndicate had been searching for and saw more disbelief on the faces all around her.

"They left the Vault somehow," Max said at the end of her recital. "We don't know where they've gone."

"And how did you get back here?" Orshiasa asked unexpectedly. His voice was calm and level on the surface, but Max didn't trust that calm. He was watching her intently.

"The Vault's Armourer managed to reverse the portal spell in my Vault and send me and Bryce back through it," Max told him. "She is an extremely skilled and powerful magician," she added. Even though she had been battling injuries of her own, Cira had held the portal spell long enough for first Max and then Bryce to get back. Max held herself still under Orshiasa's stern gaze, pointedly not moving her hands to her pockets. As Max had passed by her on the way to the mouth of the spell, Cira had pressed what felt like a key infused with magic into her hand. It would open a deposit box in the Vault, Cira had said. She and Max could exchange letters through that box. The Armourer had fixed Max with a gaze just as stern as the one Orshiasa was levelling at her right now and had demanded a promise from Max to let her know how things turned out. Max had been happy to make the promise, and to have a means of keeping in touch with the Armourer. They might only have known each other a short time, but Max hadn't wanted to completely leave her behind.

"A portal spell?" Orshiasa's brows lifted, as if he didn't quite believe her. "Where was the Vault that such a spell was necessary?" he asked.

Max hesitated. Her former mentor had a sharp mind, and she wasn't surprised that he was the first one to ask that question. She just wasn't sure she would be believed.

"It's in another part of the world," she told the group around the table. The words felt awkward and heavy in her mouth, as if there was a resistance in the air to her speaking them aloud. "Far from here."

Apart from Bryce, everyone was looking at her as if she had just grown a second head, or done something extremely stupid.

"Another part of the world?" Faddei repeated slowly, forming the words carefully, as if tasting a foreign substance. "You mean further into the Wild?" he asked.

"No. Somewhere else," Max said, and looked at Bryce.

"It's true. We weren't in the city or the Wild," Bryce said. He got the same disbelieving looks that Max had received.

"There is only the city and the Wild," Kitris said dismissively, the rote words flowing from his tongue. It was the universal truth.

The truth pulled at Max's mind, drawing her away from the memory of the Vault, the Armourer and the Wardens. They could not be real. They could not possibly be real. There was the city and the Wild and the fog that was the edge of the world, and that was all.

And yet, she remembered the force of the explosions, being thrown against walls, the different taste of the air in the Vault, and the incredible and unsettling sight of a strange landscape opening out ahead of her. The Vault was real. The land around it was real. There was more to the world than the city and the Wild and the fog. Even if her instincts were still telling her that it could not be true.

No one else believed her and Bryce. She could see that clearly on their faces. She couldn't blame them. If she hadn't been there herself, she wouldn't have believed it, either.

"It doesn't matter precisely where," Max said, "only that the Vault is not in the city."

The disbelieving expressions disappeared. She had given them a story. A suitable alternative to the impossibility that there was more to the world than the city and the Wild.

"Very well. So you and Bryce were sent back here by the Armourer. Where do you think the others went?" Faddei asked.

"There was more activity spotted on the docks earlier," the unnamed warrior spoke for the first time. Max wished she could remember the warrior's name. He was in charge of the warriors of the Order. He had always been a distant, forbidding figure when she had been in the Order, and she could not remember ever speaking to him before.

"Do we know if Evan or the demon have been seen?" Kitris asked, glancing over his shoulder at the warrior. The two of them were almost always seen together, Max remembered. The warrior had been nick-named Kitris' shadow by the apprentices. And she still couldn't remember his name.

"No. But we can't detect a demon, and we weren't looking for the chief of detectives," the warrior said.

Max pressed her lips together to hold in an unfavourable comment. The warriors of the Order were the military might that supported the magicians, but all too often - in Max's view - the magicians didn't give the warriors due credit for their skills. It was entirely typical of the Order that the warriors had been set to watching a place with no magicians put amongst them. So the warriors would not necessarily be able to tell if or when magic was being used. Or if a full demon had appeared, for example. Unless the magic or the demon was used to attack them. And then the warriors were ill-equipped to counter that. Doubtless Kitris, or whoever had given the order to keep watch on the docks, had decided that it wasn't worth the magicians' time. A mistake, in Max's view. This was the same piece of territory that had housed a Darsin not that long ago. She would have hoped that Kitris would have been more cautious after that. It seemed not.

"We need to go in," Faddei said grimly.

"This isn't your concern," Kitris said, lip curling. He seemed very sure of that, making Max uneasy. She could not imagine that Kitris or anyone else in the Order would stand by and let the demon and Evan just have the Raghavan territory, but she also didn't see any sign that Kitris planned to do anything about the Syndicate's occupation of the docks.

"It is the concern of everyone in this city. A full demon and one of the dark lord's progeny? Not just that, but they are in possession of a dangerous dark magic artefact," Faddei said. "I agree that it's primarily the Order's business, but it's a concern for us, too."

"There are no beasts there for you to tame," Kitris said, lip still curled.

"You're forgetting that this Syndicate has targeted the city's law enforcement agencies," Faddei countered. "One police cadet is dead. Several others are injured. There had been direct threats made against my people."

"I'd like to see if I can get more information about this book," Max said before Kitris could respond, breaking into what looked like it could be a protracted and ugly argument. There was one person she could ask, however reluctant she was to make the request.

"The only person in the city who might know something is Lord Kolbyr," Kitris said, turning his sneer on her even as he unknowingly echoed her thoughts. "And he's not going to talk to you."

"I have his personal number," Max said, straightening her back.

"Lord Kolbyr likes her," Ruutti said. She was settled next to Malik, apparently relaxed, but Max recognised the mischief in her face. "If anyone can get information from him, it's Max."

"If you'll excuse me, I'll give him a call." She didn't wait for permission, getting up from the table and heading out into the daylight, breathing more easily away from the tension around the table. Even with Malik's calming influence, there was violence bubbling under the surface.

Chapter Twenty

Outside, the daylight was beginning to fade in the late afternoon and Max found more warriors of the Order stationed in the parking lot, all of them armed and bristling with wariness. She hadn't wanted to make the necessary phone call with the audience inside the Hunter's Tooth, but realised that she wouldn't get much privacy for her call. Still, it was good to be outside again after the close confines of the Vault. And she was away from Kitris for a few moments, at least. Cas and Pol had followed her out, and pressed their big, warm bodies to her legs as she leant against the building and fished a heavy piece of card out from one of her pockets along with the phone Faddei had provided. She paused, staring at the black, typewritten numbers before she could bring herself to dial. She had never thought she would actually use the number.

The phone was answered on the second ring.

"Who are you, and how did you get this number?" The voice was male, but not Kolbyr.

"This is Marshal Max Ortis. Lord Kolbyr gave me his number some time ago. Is he available to speak with?" Max asked, forcing herself to a calm, polite tone. Ancient vampires like Kolbyr were very prickly about manners. And vampire hearing was extraordinarily good. The one who had answered the phone might be able to hear her rapid heartbeat.

There was a moment's silence, then a different voice. "My dear Marshal. I had heard rumours that you were gone from the city. I am delighted that is not the case."

"Lord Kolbyr. I was indeed gone," Max said. "There was an incursion into the Vault and I was drawn into it."

"How wonderfully unusual," he said. It was difficult to tell through the phone line, but she thought he sounded intrigued.

"The intruders in the Vault were looking for and then removed a particular item which held dark magic. I wondered if you might be willing to share your expertise on the matter?"

"This is sounding more and more interesting. Where are you?"

"I'm currently at the Hunter's Tooth. The head of the Order and the head of the Marshals are both here, too."

"I will join you all in a few minutes," Kolbyr said. The line cut off.

Max drew a breath, weary to her very bones. She tipped her head back against the wall. She didn't want to deal with Kolbyr as well as Kitris and Orshiasa, but it seemed she didn't have a choice. At least Faddei was here, and they were in Malik's bar. She was as safe as she possibly could be.

"Max, are you ok?" a female voice asked. One of the warriors. Khari. Her deep brown skin was glowing with health, black hair wrapped in a muted red headscarf.

Max couldn't help smiling. She liked Khari. Looking past the warrior, she saw two more familiar faces. Khari's husband, Joshua, who was a contrast to his wife with pale skin and bright red hair, and Osvaldo, a dark-skinned older warrior with grey threaded through his black hair. Along with Bryce, they seemed like a close-knit team and had not complained once about Max's slow speed as they trekked through the jungle of the Wild.

"It's good to see you all," Max said. "I'll be fine. Just a bit worn out. Oh, and Lord Kolbyr is on his way."

"Not the person you want to deal with on little sleep," Khari said, sympathy in her voice and face. "How's Bryce doing? We heard he was here, but we haven't seen him."

"He's in one piece," Max confirmed. "Probably even more tired than I am. He kept us alive."

"He's good at that," Khari agreed. "We'll send Lord Kolbyr in when he gets here," she promised.

"Thanks," Max said. She bent to give her dogs a pat and then, with no more excuses, went back into the Hunter's Tooth, the battered door opening to the sounds of an argument.

She walked across the floor, not meeting anyone's eyes, and picked up her plate, taking it to another table and sitting there. Her stomach was hollow and she needed to eat something before Kolbyr arrived.

While she shovelled food in, barely tasting it, she listened to the disagreement. It wasn't between the Order and Marshals, to her surprise. Rather, Kitris and Orshiasa were disagreeing on what to do next. No one else was talking to them. Faddei was conferring in low voices with Vanko and Zoya. Malik and Ruutti were still settled at the table, hands linked. Max wondered just how much energy Malik was having to use to keep the atmosphere in the bar on the right side of civil. She normally couldn't sense his power at all, as it was usually extremely subtle and gentle, threaded through the air of the Tooth. Today, though, she could feel the ragged edges of Malik's power brushing up against Kitris' and Orshiasa's tempers. If she had had more energy, she might have paid more attention to the argument. It was rare for one of the Guardians to so openly disagree with Kitris, and particularly in a public space. But the two were definitely in opposition.

She managed half of what Malik had put on her plate before the door opened again and a trail of cool, dark magic slid through the air. She didn't need to look up to know that Lord Kolbyr had arrived.

She stood up to greet him, and was surprised when everyone else stood as well.

Turning, she saw that it wasn't just Lord Kolbyr who had come into the room. There was a woman with him. Or, rather, not with him, but who had arrived at the same time. A tall, dark-haired woman in the plain grey robes of one of the Lady's Priestesses. Except that this was no ordinary Priestess. The subtle additional stitching on her robe would let anyone who didn't recognise her know that this was the High Priestess. Emmeline. A familiar sense of inadequacy washed over Max at the High Priestess' presence. She had never been able to please the stern woman, no matter how hard she had tried.

Max remembered the odd phone call she had received, what felt like half a lifetime ago, summoning her to a meeting with the High Priestess. Remembered, too, her flat refusal. She wondered who the High Priestess was here to see now. She couldn't imagine anyone else refusing a summons. She had her own reasons for not wanting to deal with Emmeline.

"Gracious Lady," Kitris said, sounding as close to humble as Max thought he could manage. He even bowed. "You honour us with your presence. How may we serve?"

"Kitris. Always a pleasure to see you. And you, Orshiasa. I'm sorry, I don't think I know many other people here," the High Priestess said, looking around the room. Something in her slightly chilly manner suggested that she didn't want introductions, and no one made a move to make themselves known.

Movement behind Emmeline alerted Max to the fact that she had brought another pair of priestesses with her, and another pair of Order warriors had come into the bar, perhaps to offer protection for the High Priestess. Max wasn't sure who they thought she needed protection from. The Marshals might not be formally affiliated with the Lady, but they would not harm one of Her servants.

"All are welcome here," Malik said, managing a smile.

"I came to speak to Miscellandreax," the High Priestess said, not looking at Max. "You will excuse us," she said to the others. She raised a hand and beckoned to Max, still without turning to her. "Come."

Conscious of all eyes on her, and unable to refuse the order with such a large audience, Max put down the napkin she was still holding and followed the High Priestess across the bar to a far corner. The woman took a seat at the outer edge of one of the rounded booths and flicked her fingers to the other side of the booth.

"See that we are not disturbed," the High Priestess said to the two Priestesses she had brought with her. The pair bowed and took a few steps away, magic rising in the air around them. Some kind of concealment spell, Max guessed, which would hide any conversation from the sharp ears of other people in the room.

Max took a seat, resolving to stay calm and patient. It had been several years since she had spoken with the High Priestess. None of their later conversations had gone particularly well, and she could not imagine why Emmeline was seeking her out now.

"You refused the invitation to come and see me," the High Priestess said, her voice cool. She was looking at a point just beside Max's shoulder. Max resisted the urge to look around and see if there was anything there.

"It wasn't phrased as an invitation," Max said. So much for her resolution to be calm and patient. She twisted her fingers together on her lap, out of sight under the table. "What do you want?" she asked. It was as close to polite as she could manage.

"You are much favoured by the Lady," the High Priestess said, briefly looking directly into Max's face.

Shock coursed through Max. That had sounded almost like a compliment from the older woman, but Max had never had a single bit of praise from her in all the years they had known each other. Max was far more accustomed to criticism and being told that she must try harder. Emmeline had never believed - not once - that Max had made her best effort at anything. Anger spiked and Max lifted her chin, staring back at the High Priestess. "Then the Lady has peculiar ways of showing Her favour," she answered. It was the first thing that occurred to her. It was the truth. "And I do not seek or ask for Her favour. I simply wish to be left alone."

"Oh, Miscellandreax, that was never possible. You were touched by the Lady's grace from your birth," the High Priestess said, sounding almost sad.

Max was almost too astonished to reply. "This is the first time I've heard this," she said, more bluntly than she had intended. "It doesn't matter," she said, the words out before she could tell if she meant them or not. She tried to push down her anger. "Tell me what you want," she demanded, more forcefully than before. "I've got work to do, and no time for more of your games."

The High Priestess stared back at her, face tight with displeasure, a spot of colour in each cheek. "Games?" she hissed. "You think that the Lady's service is merely a game?"

"I think it is the way you do it," Max answered, refusing to be intimidated. She was so tired. Her body was heavy, her eyes gritty with lack of sleep, her mind sluggish. She didn't have the energy for the push-and-pull conversation she normally had with this woman. She had no patience left, either. "I think that no one gets to be High Priestess without playing politics."

The colour in the woman's face had spread and her eyes glittered with temper. Max was familiar with that temper. The city's Gracious Lady might manage to appear to be a humble servant of the Lady and a properly devout member of the Lady's temple when out in public. In private, or perhaps just when she was with Max, she saw no reason to keep up the disguise.

"You are so ungrateful for the life you have been given and the advantages you have," the High Priestess bit out, voice shaking with fury.

"Ungrateful?" Max's brows lifted. "Hardly. I always did what was asked of me. Right up until I was called a liar," she said, holding the woman's glittering, furious eyes. "But I am sure you did not come here to argue. I am exhausted and have more to do before I can rest. So, tell me what you want."

The woman sat back, the fury fading from her face, replaced by something that might have been regret. The expression was gone so quickly that Max wasn't sure she had read it properly. "You did what was asked? That is not what Kitris said," the woman said softly, almost as if she was speaking to herself.

"I'm not interested in what Kitris thinks," Max answered, voice tight. She had always recognised that Kitris had his own way of looking at things. When she had been younger, before he had sent her on an impossible mission, she had assumed that it was because of his position as head of the Order. She had assumed that he must know things, and see things, that she could not imagine, and that was why so much of what he said and did was inexplicable. When she had come back from her mission and faced him, she had seen him with new eyes and realised just how wrong she had been. Kitris saw the world as he wanted to.

Emmeline stared back at her, face tight. Max waited for another one of her lectures, or a theatrical sigh and expression of disappointment at how difficult or obtuse Max was being. She got neither. Instead, the woman dipped her chin, as if acknowledging Max had a point, and changed the subject. "You have used the Lady's light. More than once," the High Priestess said, voice flat.

Max stared back at her, keeping quiet while her sluggish mind turned that over. It was true that she had called on her magic and produced light more than once in the past weeks. That particular skill was becoming a little easier with practice. Certainly easier than any of the elaborate mathematical formulas of magic that the Order had taught her. She couldn't tell what the woman's purpose was, though, in bringing it up.

When the silence had stretched on long enough that Max's skin was beginning to itch with discomfort, Emmeline made an impatient noise, her frustration clear. "You will come back to the Order and to the Lady's service. We have need of you."

"No," Max said, the word exploding out of her before she could stop it. The rejection rose from her toes all the way through her heart to the top of her head. "You sent me to the Order. The Order dismissed me. Neither you nor they have any claim on me," she said, the words clipped, her own anger rising up in a clean, burning wave that chased some of her exhaustion away. "I have done my duty to you and to the Order. Now leave me alone," she said.

She got up from the table and stalked away, past the silent Priestesses, who shot her sharp, sideways glances. She didn't care. Fury made her steps quick, hurt blooming in her chest. She didn't know why she was surprised. The temple and the Order had always seen her as something to be used. Not anymore. As she had told the High Priestess, she had a job to do.

Chapter Twenty-One

The others were settled around the tables, pretending not to be paying attention to the conversation she had been having with the High Priestess. Someone, probably Malik, had found Lord Kolbyr a chair and had set a drink in front of him. The vampire was settled opposite Malik, as comfortable in the bar as Max imagined he would be in his own home.

Kolbyr was looking around with every appearance of keen interest, taking in the faces and doubtless also the invisible lines of tension that Max could almost see around the table. Kitris and Orshiasa were carefully not looking at each other and she couldn't help wondering just how deep that particular division went. Amongst the Order - Guardians, apprentices and warriors alike - the public position was that Kitris was the leader and had to be obeyed. Any disagreements with him were almost all conducted privately. Until today, she couldn't remember seeing so many obvious signs of differences between him and one of the Guardians.

Bryce had moved from the table to stand next to the senior warrior and Max couldn't help wondering if he had chosen to do that, or if Kitris or Orshiasa had asked him to move.

Malik looked tired, despite Ruutti still sitting next to him, and Max felt a stab of worry, wondering whether she should have found a different venue to hold this awkward gathering.

Faddei, Vanko and Zoya had been busy drawing what looked like a crude map on one of Malik's napkins. Warmth bloomed in Max's chest as she took her seat between Faddei and Zoya again. Trust the Marshals to be planning their next move without waiting for everyone else to catch up. The napkin held a simple map of the docks, with a few entrances marked.

The back of Max's neck prickled. The High Priestess and her companions hadn't left yet. They were still somewhere behind her. Max didn't like having people at her back, but refused to give Emmeline the satisfaction of turning around and revealing how unsettled she was by the conversation they had had.

"I am most curious," Kolbyr said, before anyone else could speak. "What did you wish to consult me on?" he asked Max.

"Thank you for coming so quickly," Max said first, not just to buy some time to separate herself from the fury of her conversation with the High Priestess, but also to give the ancient vampire the respect which he would consider his due. "I mentioned that an artefact was removed from the Vault. One steeped in dark magic. It was a book. About this big." She measured with her hands. "The demon Queran and Evan Yarwood were hunting for it in the Vault. They removed it." She clasped her hands together in her lap as she remembered the awful sensation of the magic crawling over her skin. "It had an extremely strong aura. Very dark magic."

"Describe the cover and binding to me," Kolbyr asked. He had gone unnaturally still, his cold aura sliding out around him, reminding Max just how powerful and dangerous he was.

Max frowned, trying to recall the exact details. "I didn't get a close look, as I was a bit of a distance away. It was dark. Almost black. It looked like leather, with leather ties holding it together. There was a symbol of some kind on the cover. I can try to draw it, but I didn't recognise it, so I'm not sure I can replicate it exactly," Max said, looking for a spare napkin and a pen. Faddei handed her both. She sketched out what she thought she had seen and held it up. "Bryce, does that look right?"

"Yes," he said.

Kolbyr hissed, his human face slipping, his aura growing. In his human form, he was an attractive enough man, but vampires in their true form possessed an otherworldly beauty that drew people to them. Kolbyr's mask slipped just enough for some of that beauty to show through. Max could feel its pull even as she resisted it. "You are quite sure?" the vampire asked.

"This is what I remember seeing, yes," Max said, still holding the napkin up. "Do you know what it is?"

"Where is this book now?" Kolbyr asked, a sharp edge to his voice.

"Evan and Queran put it into a nullification pouch and took it with them when they left the Vault." Max hesitated, then went on, "It's possible they may have returned to the docks here. The Syndicate seems to have set up there, in what was Raghavan territory."

"We must get it back," Kolbyr said, leaning towards her, urgency in his voice.

"What is it?" Max asked.

"From your description, I believe it is the Arkus Codex," Kolbyr said, and paused as if letting them all absorb a momentous piece of information.

No one else gasped or reacted to the information, so Max assumed they were all as clueless as she was. She frowned. "Alright. Anything which has the dark lord's name isn't good, but what is the Codex?"

"Don't they teach anything useful in schools these days?" Kolbyr didn't wait for an answer, his control and his human appearance reasserting themselves. "The Codex is rumoured to be a map of the spells and barriers between this world and the dark lord's kingdom. It holds the keys to opening the Grey Gates and bringing the dark lord into this realm."

Now there were shocked expressions and a gasp or two around the table.

"That does not sound good," Faddei said. An understatement, if Max had ever heard one.

"It's nonsense," Kitris said, voice sharp. "The Codex is a myth. It's been rumoured to exist for hundreds of years. The more gullible of the dark lord's followers keep hunting for it, but no one has ever seen it."

"The Vault has been in operation for well over three hundred years," Max said, her face numb. "It's possible that the Codex was stored there all this time."

"Someone would have found it before now," Kitris said, waving a hand in dismissal.

"How?" Max asked, wrinkling her brow in genuine puzzlement. "The central principle of the Vault is that each magician's space is their own. Not even the Wardens or the Armourer go inside without good cause. And then only three times in the Vault's operation. So no one apart from the original Vault holder would have known it was there."

"Didn't you say that Evan Yarwood is one of His descendants?" Orshiasa asked, startling Max. After her previous answer to him, she hadn't expected him to speak to her again, or put in such a pointed question.

"I did," Max confirmed. "And he also told me he'd been planning the raid for a long time," she added, a sick feeling growing in her stomach.

"Then it is entirely possible that rumours of this Codex have been passed down through his family line," Orshiasa said, not looking at Kitris. "We know many of the more powerful followers of the dark lord do pass their rituals and beliefs from one generation to the next." He briefly met Kolbyr's eyes. "Although you would know that better than most, my lord."

"That is quite right," Kolbyr said, tilting his head in a gesture of respect to the Guardian. Max could not help wondering just how many times the two of them might have met over the spans of their long lives, and just how many times they had found themselves in complete opposition, in stark contrast to the meeting now, when they were on the same side. Or so she hoped.

"That makes sense," Max said, feeling she should say something. "It took a lot of planning and a great deal of power to set up the intrusion into the Vault. And despite the fact they had searched almost every individual Vault, they kept going. They knew what they were looking for, just not precisely where it was."

"And what do you propose now?" Kitris asked, with a sharp edge to his voice. "We burst into Raghavan territory on the off-chance that a mythical Codex has been discovered, and attempt to take it?"

Max stared back at the head of the Order. He had addressed the question pointedly to her, as if it would be her decision alone, and no one else had a say in the matter. And she could not work him out. The very foundation and purpose of the Order was to combat dark magic, and to stand as the Lady's representative against Her brother's works. The idea that Kitris would not want to act when there was powerful dark magic loose in the world was almost as shocking to her as the day he had accused her of lying and removed her from the Order. Of all the things she had believed him capable of, shirking the Order's duty was not one of them.

It seemed she was not the only one taken aback. Lord Kolbyr's normally impassive expression had changed to one of faint surprise.

"I cannot instruct you in what you should do, naturally," Kolbyr said, "but I would strongly suggest that urgent action is required. If this is the Codex, and it is in the hands of people who know how to use it, it could be catastrophic for this world." The vampire paused. "And even if it is not the Codex, the book which the Marshal and warrior described contained powerful dark magic and should not be left in the hands of a full demon and one of Arkus' descendants."

Max wondered if she was the only one who had noticed Kolbyr's reluctance to see their world destroyed. It was supposedly the aim of all dark magic practitioners to bring the dark lord into this realm, where their efforts would apparently be rewarded. Or so the naive and gullible ones would protest. But Kolbyr was neither naive nor gullible and, as Max had thought before, he would be reluctant to see his status and power overtaken by the actual presence of Arkus in this world. As it was, Kolbyr enjoyed not only the power and wealth accumulated over his long life as a vampire, but also the weight of authority that came with being one of the foremost experts on dark magic.

She kept quiet, not adding anything to his words. If he said that it was urgent to recover the Codex, then nothing she could say could possibly add any force to that statement. She sensed Faddei also holding words back. Her boss was many things, including a consummate politician when he wanted to be.

There was a slight sense of movement behind her and she turned to find that the High Priestess was still there, listening to the conversation that had taken place.

"I am in complete agreement with Lord Kolbyr. If there is even a chance that the Arkus Codex is in the world, and in the hands of not only a demon but a descendant of Him, then you must investigate this," the High Priestess said. Her words were directed over Max's head, along the table to where Kitris sat. "And I will make that clear to the Five Families if need be," she added. It was a bold command, but it was also backed by an equally powerful statement of support. The word of the High Priestess, who spoke for all the Lady's servants and temples across the city, would not be ignored. The Gracious Lady rarely openly intervened in the city's politics, but when she did, matters fell the way she wanted.

Caught between the urging of the ancient vampire and the prompting of the Lady's highest representative in this world, Kitris inclined his head, his expression hard to read. "I am always willing to be guided by you, Gracious Lady," he said. "Very well. We will have two groups. The Marshals and the warriors. The Marshals will begin at the landward side, the warriors at the seaward side." Max was quite sure she wasn't the only one who noticed that while Kitris appeared to accept the High Priestess' suggestion, he was doing things his own way. Keeping the Marshals and warriors separate. It was predictable.

"All the buildings need to be checked," Faddei said, in a calm voice. He would have noticed the separation of warriors and Marshals, too, but if he was bothered by Kitris' casual organisation, he didn't show it.

Kitris inclined his head in silent agreement, then spoke over his shoulder. "Samuel, get the warriors ready."

"At once," the senior warrior said. Samuel. Max wasn't sure why she could never remember his name, but it was already threatening to slip away. The warrior headed for the door, pulling a phone out of his pocket. Bryce stayed where he was, a slight frown on his face which Max couldn't read. Perhaps he was as disturbed by Kitris' evident reluctance to get involved as she was.

"I'll take my leave of you all. The Lady's blessing be upon you," the High Priestess said.

"And on you." Those settled around the table replied with the rote phrase. Even Lord Kolbyr, Max noted with inner amusement.

As the High Priestess left the bar, Faddei turned to Max. "We could use your help, you and your dogs. But you look worn out," he said.

"Marshal Ortis and the warrior Bryce are essential to this endeavour," Kolbyr said, before anyone else could speak, even leaning forward in his chair to emphasise the point. "They are the only ones here who have seen the book."

From the pinched expression on Kitris' face, he was none too happy about having her declared essential to anything.

"And will you give us some guidance on how to neutralise this Codex if we find it?" Faddei asked, his tone one of polite enquiry.

"I will accompany you," Kolbyr announced, eyes gleaming. His lips curved in a humourless smile. "I very much look forward to meeting Queran and Evan Yarwood again."

Max's mind gave her a full colour image of the last time Kolbyr, Queran, and Evan had been in one place together. Queran had set a pack of the Huntsman clan on the vampire, and Max. Kolbyr had torn his way through the clan members despite bullets hitting him. There hadn't been much blood left in the clan members once the vampire had had his fill, but the scene had been more than gory enough without that detail. Max shivered, and remembered another more recent dead body. "Queran admitted that he'd been the one to kill Ivor Costen," she told Kolbyr.

"Ah. The ritual that had aged the man," Kolbyr said, nodding. "Another reason why he needs to be stopped."

"What is this?" Kitris demanded. "A dark magic ritual? When was this? Why wasn't I informed?"

"Audhilde would have called your office to inform you," Max said, exhaustion weighing on her. She remembered Audhilde - among others - commenting on how absent Kitris had been.

"I don't remember any such thing," Kitris said. He sounded almost petulant. Max frowned at him, concern seeping into her irritation. One of the things she had always respected about him was how hard he had worked, and the interest he took in all workings of the Order. He'd always known who everyone was, what they were doing, and what issues there were around the city that should concern them. The fact he didn't seem to remember Audhilde's call was concerning.

"I was called to the body," Kolbyr said. "I can confirm that dark magic was used. I suspected the demon Queran, and Marshal Ortis has confirmed it. It's a matter of concern, but not the most important thing right now."

Max silently agreed, and turned to Faddei. "I am worn out," she acknowledged, "but if you have a keep-awake spell, I should manage a bit longer."

Faddei looked back at her, expression serious. The Marshals did not normally use keep-awake spells, as they were of relatively short duration and then usually knocked the user out for twelve hours straight afterwards. But she was quite confident that she wouldn't make it to the docks, let alone be useful when they got there, without some kind of support, and even Malik's coffee would not do the job.

"Allow me," Orshiasa said unexpectedly. "And for Bryce, too." The Guardian pulled two plain strips of paper out from under his robes and laid them side by side on the table, frowning down at them. Max felt his power stir and had to stop herself from leaning forward. Orshiasa's power was the clear, cool flow of a mountain stream with pure water full of the Lady's light. And he was an absolute master at using it. She had never tired of watching him work, even as she struggled to complete the most basic of the tasks he set for her. After a moment, his power dimmed and he lifted the paper, holding the first out to Max across the table, then turning to hold the other one out to Bryce. "Put it around your left wrists, and it will activate," he told them. "It should keep you going for at least another twelve hours, but you will then need to rest."

"Thank you," Max said. Twelve hours should be enough to get to the docks, find out where the book was, and get it back. Or so she hoped. She could always sleep in her vehicle if she couldn't make it home. Cas and Pol would be happy to keep her company, and keep watch.

"Go and get your assignment from Samuel," Kitris ordered Bryce, without looking around.

Bryce looked like he wanted to argue, but said nothing, heading out of the bar, the paper already around his wrist.

Max slid the paper around her own wrist and hissed in a breath as Orshiasa's spell uncurled, seeping in through her skin, sending a fresh and welcome wave of energy across her body. It wasn't the full onslaught of a normal keep-awake spell, but she could sense the depth of this spell and knew it would last.

"Zoya, go with Max," Faddei said. "Vanko and I will follow you and make arrangements on the way. Max, do you need more ammunition?"

"I've got some in my pick-up," Max said, shaking her head. She hadn't expended that many rounds in the Vault, and she had re-supplied her pick-up the day before she had been drawn away.

"Alright. Head here," Faddei said, pointing to a spot on the map he, Vanko and Zoya had been consulting over. It was at the landward side of the docks, so it seemed that Faddei had accepted Kitris' casual ordering of the groups. The head Marshal glanced across at Kitris, but the head of the Order said nothing, so Faddei turned back to his people. "We'll gather the Marshals there."

"I will follow Marshal Ortis," Kolbyr said, getting to his feet and straightening his sleeves.

"Do you want me to see if special ops can lend a hand?" Ruutti asked. She was still sitting with Malik, the pair of them looking as worn out as Max had been feeling. Malik had been using his energy to keep the bar calm, and Max guessed that Ruutti had been helping him. A stab of guilt worked through her. She should have chosen somewhere else to meet Faddei. But then, matters might have ended in an argument rather than a reluctant agreement from Kitris to explore the docks.

"No," Faddei said, shaking his head. "I don't want to risk more people."

"They would just get in our way," Kitris added, getting to his feet. "We have already adjusted our strategy to work around the Marshals."

Max could not help rolling her eyes. Kitris hadn't wanted to get involved, but now that he was committed to it, he was insulting people who might be able to help.

"Good hunting," Malik said.

With that encouragement ringing in her ears, Max left the bar with Zoya. Cas and Pol bounded ahead, out into the parking lot and straight to the back of her pick-up, apparently looking forward to a grand adventure. Max wished she shared their enthusiasm.

Chapter Twenty-Two

Four hours later, it was night on the docks, the ever-present mist in the air freezing against her skin as she and her fellow Marshals came out of another building, Cas and Pol ahead of her and the rest of the group behind her. While they had been searching that building, rain had started falling. Not gentle rain, either, but a heavy downpour that further restricted visibility. Max turned up her jacket collar and saw a few other Marshals doing the same, trying to add a little bit of protection against the prospect of cold water seeping into their clothes. It was small comfort to know that the Order warriors and Guardians would be under the same rain, and the thicker fog, at the seaward end of the docks.

Faddei took a few steps sideways, staying in the comparative shelter of the building, and pulled his phone out, the screen bright in the darkness, hitting keys to send a text. Probably to the senior warrior of the Order, letting them know they had cleared another building, as Faddei had done after every building they had cleared.

The Marshals had followed Kitris' plan for them to start at the landward end and work their way forward, while the Order and its warriors would begin at the seaward side. Max strongly suspected that Kitris believed that Evan was most likely towards the seaward side, and wanted to find him first and whatever it was that he had taken from the Vault. Kitris hadn't even offered to send a Guardian or senior apprentice with the Marshals, to deal with any magic they might encounter, probably wanting to keep all the power for himself in the expectation he and his people would be the ones dealing with the potential threat. And if she had come to that conclusion, Max guessed that Faddei had, too. He was far better at playing politics than she was. But Faddei had not objected to the Marshals' assignment, merely saying out loud that all the buildings did need to be checked.

Once the Marshals had made their way past the giant docking cranes and warehouses that sat nearest the dockside, they had come into the vast warren of mostly inter-connected buildings that had served as offices and living quarters and storage for smaller items along with a series of what looked like commercial garages set up to make repairs on the equipment and vehicles that had been used at the docks.

There was enough light from the torches the Marshals carried and the muted lights on the outside of the buildings for her to see Faddei's face tighten at whatever reply he received. Doubtless, Samuel was urging them to move faster. The warrior had already suggested that the Marshals would move more quickly if they divided into two groups. But a pair of Seacast monkeys had been spotted in the city and Faddei had already needed to send some of the Marshals to deal with them. They couldn't allow the destructive, powerful Seacast monkeys to roam unchecked, so he had sent a half dozen of the available Marshals to deal with the creatures, the remaining Marshals continuing on to the docks. He had told the warrior in no uncertain terms that he wasn't prepared to break up his team any further. Max hadn't been able to hear Samuel's response, but from the way Faddei had immediately ended the call, she suspected the warrior had not been pleased. He didn't know Faddei very well, clearly. If he had, he wouldn't have tried to make the argument in the first place. The head Marshal looked after his people, even if that meant proceeding slowly and carefully. He wanted all of them to go home at the end of their shifts. It was one reason why all the Marshals trusted him.

So the Marshals were searching in one group. There were eight of them, including Max and Faddei, all with their handguns out and ready. If they were hunting supernatural creatures, they would be wielding shotguns full of tranquilliser rounds. But they were after a different prey tonight, and so Faddei had ordered them all to carry their lethal weapons. They all had their shotguns as well, just in case. It was always wise to be prepared, in Max's experience.

The search so far had reminded Max in unexpected ways of her time in the Vault. The buildings they had been through had been multiple storeys high, a warren of hallways and metal walkways and rooms. Despite the extra energy from Orshiasa's spell, her legs were aching again from the many stairs she had climbed, and she had the constant sensation that she was being watched.

That could, of course, be because she was, in fact, being watched. They had three vampires for company. Lord Kolbyr had brought two as yet unnamed vampires with him. He hadn't bothered with introductions or any explanation as to why the other vampires were there. The pair were staying close by him in a manner Max had seen before with bodyguards, although the idea of Lord Kolbyr needing a bodyguard was almost laughable, particularly from these vampires. The pair were almost invisible to Max's senses next to Kolbyr's powerful aura and age. She was still keeping an eye on them, though. Even a weak vampire could be a threat to a human.

The unnamed vampires were returning the favour, openly staring at her when she was nearby, for reasons she could not work out. Luckily, they hadn't been close for most of the search so far. Lord Kolbyr had not done anything as mundane as search the buildings with them. Naturally. Instead, he had waited at the main entrance, ready to be summoned if they found anything. So the Marshals had been left to search in peace, which Max was grateful for.

As she ducked her head against the rain, and tried to ignore the vampires, she saw Cas and Pol sniffing around the edge of the building they had just cleared. Five stories of offices and storage rooms full of nothing more dangerous than dust and cobwebs from normal-sized spiders.

"What have you got there, boys?" she asked, flicking on her torch and moving towards them. She had lost all sense of where they were in the overall scheme of the docks. The buildings they had been in so far had been different shapes and sizes, and a few of them built with different materials, suggesting that they had been constructed as and when needed and not according to some overall grand plan. It would be a confusing enough place to be in during daylight, let alone at night and in the rain.

Cas took a step back as she joined her dogs, Pol still standing with his nose pointing down. They had found something worthy of attention. Max just hoped it wasn't a rat or some other kind of small creature. Her dogs might have insisted on being fed steak and chicken while they had been staying with Malik and Ruutti, but they were also fond of hunting when they got the chance.

There was no sign of life in the area that had caught her dogs' attention. Instead, there was a metal hatch in the ground, large enough to have been split down the middle with a great bar of what looked like metal holding the doors closed. It had been hidden by the shadows of the building.

"Faddei, do these buildings have basements?" she asked.

"I didn't think so," he said, joining her and frowning down at the metal doors. "But no one has a decent map or plan of the docks."

"Cas and Pol think there's something down there," she told him.

All around her, she could sense her weary colleagues sharpening their focus and attention. They had all worked with shadow-hounds long enough to know that when the dogs alerted, there was usually something there.

Vanko was kneeling at one side of the doors, trying to shift the large metal bar that had been laid over them. He grunted with effort. "This thing is solid," he complained. "Yev, give me a hand."

"Sure," Yevhen said, handing his gun and torch to his wife, Pavla.

"Do allow me," Kolbyr said, in his usual cool manner. He was somehow standing at Max's shoulder. He flicked his hand and his two vampires flowed forward, lifting the great metal bar with apparent ease. They set it to one side and then took hold of the handles, one to each door, and pulled.

Yevhen moved back to Pavla's side and took back his gun and torch, Vanko standing with them, the other Marshals joining them so that they were in a line, all their torches focused on the doors, weapons ready.

There was a grinding, creaking noise of rusty hinges as the doors opened. There was no light underground, the Marshals' torches showing what looked like rusting metal stairs leading down into pitch black.

"Yev, Pavla, send some light in," Faddei ordered. "Max, take the lead with your dogs."

Max nodded and took a step forward, nose wrinkling as the smell of unwashed bodies and rot curled up through the air towards her. "Oh, yuck. There's definitely something down there," she said, trying not to gag.

Soft, diffuse light moved past her, circling around her ankles and then disappearing into the dark below, letting her see that the steps led down about one storey from the ground level to what looked like a concrete floor. Before she could give the order, Cas and Pol were making their way down the steps, their claws clacking on the metal surface. Max followed with caution. The rain was now hitting the steps, and she didn't want to risk falling, particularly not while she didn't know what was in the basement.

She found herself in a large, square room with a few broken crates piled to one side, and another pair of doors ahead of her. These ones were wooden, sealed with a heavy bar of wood this time, and the smell was stronger as she moved closer.

"There's another pair of doors," she called back up. "I'll need a hand to get them open."

Almost before she had finished speaking, the two vampires had landed on the concrete surface, not bothering to take the stairs. Their eyes glittered with power in the poor light and she fought the urge to train her gun on them as they moved past her and to the door, lifting the wooden bar with ease and setting it aside. They then took hold of the doors and glanced back at her. Seeking her permission to open the doors. She nodded, gun and torch levelled at the doors, Cas and Pol to either side.

The vampires pulled the doors open, releasing another waft of smells that made her eyes water. She held her ground, the light that Pavla and Yevhen had created sliding past the doors into the room along with the narrower, brighter light of her torch.

Movement met her eyes and she tensed, finger ready on the trigger. But Cas and Pol were still beside her, alert but not worried, and she held still, waiting for more light to spill in. She panned her torch around and her jaw dropped.

People. There were people in the room. Too many of them for the crowded space, and all of them looking hollowed-out, a few with old injuries and bloodied bandages. They flung up their hands against the bright light of her torch, and cowed back, crowding together.

"Faddei!" Max called. She lowered her torch and gun. The people here were no threat. As she lowered the light, she realised that all the people in the space were wearing a uniform that she recognised. One of the men took a step forward, raising his hands as if showing he was unarmed. "Wait. I know you. You were one of the Raghavan soldiers," she said, a chill creeping over her as she looked around the crowd. "You are all Raghavan soldiers," she realised.

"We are," the man said, his voice hoarse. "Please. We don't want to hurt you. Please let us go."

"Of course," Max said, and put her gun away. Faddei was beside her, taking in the scene with a grim expression.

"How long have you been down here?" Faddei asked.

"I don't know," the soldier said. He took a step forward, movements stiff as if he was weak or hurting, or both. "Shivangi and Hemang left. After a couple of days, men came. With weapons. Put us down here."

Max exchanged glances with Faddei. "Did they wear black?" Max asked.

"Yes, that's right. Do you know them?" the soldier asked.

"Unfortunately, yes," Max said. She looked around the room, tracing the effects of their captivity on the people in the room. They'd been locked up in awful conditions, but she couldn't help wonder why the Syndicate had left them alive. The Syndicate members she had encountered so far seemed to have no difficulty in killing anyone who stood in their way. So, why not these former Raghavan soldiers?

"We had some food and water for the first few days, but then nothing. There's a water pipe in the ceiling that we managed to get to. It's kept us alive." The soldier's voice was matter-of-fact.

By then, the rest of the Marshals were down the steps, looking as horrified as Faddei.

"Get these people to the surface. There was a large room in the building, to the right, which should house them all. I'm going to call for help for them," Faddei said. "And if you've got any water or food you can spare, share them out."

The Marshals nodded, all of them putting their guns away and lending a hand in getting the weakened soldiers up the steps and outside. Most of the Marshals had extensive experience of dealing with shocked people, and used those lessons to gently shepherd the weakened soldiers out of the stench of the basement and up into cleaner air. The room Faddei had mentioned was some kind of a large, unused office space, Max remembered. It probably had enough chairs for them all, at least.

The soldier who had spoken stayed still, watching his colleagues be led past, his eyes filling with unshed tears as he looked back into the room. "Two of us didn't make it," he said, voice cracking. "Will you-"

"I'll see that they are taken care of and treated with respect," Faddei promised.

"We tried," the soldier said. "We all gave up strips of cloth, water, food. But it wasn't enough."

In his voice, and the visible trembling of his body, Max could hear grief and fear. The slow, grinding fear of being trapped underground with no light and no food. No one knowing where they were.

"Go on," she said, voice hoarse. "If Faddei says that your people will be looked after, then they will."

"You're the one who killed the Darsin," the soldier said, blinking at her. "The Darsin is gone. Why are you here?"

"The armed men stole something very dangerous," Max said, "we're looking for it." She hesitated. The soldier had been helpful before. "Do you know if there's a place that the twins might have used for a ritual?"

"There's an old temple. At the end of the next building. You can't miss it. It looks very different from everything else," the soldier said, standing a little straighter. "I can show you."

"You have done more than enough. Go and be with your people," Max said softly. "Help is on the way. We'll find the temple."

Chapter Twenty-Three

The Marshals left all of their supplies of food and water with the soldiers, along with more of the diffuse, magical light provided by Yevhen and Pavla, so that at least the soldiers would not be sitting in the dark waiting for more help to arrive. Faddei promised them that the Marshals' medical team was on the way, along with a team from the clinic and police officers to take statements.

To Max's surprise, Kolbyr had also instructed the two vampires with him to remain with the soldiers. It seemed an oddly kind gesture for him, but the vampires had taken the command without protest, taking up positions where they could watch for any approaching threats.

With Kolbyr's vampires in place, Faddei tried calling the Order, to update them and call for back-up, but his call hadn't connected. Max had overheard him leaving a tense message, and wondered if Kitris or his second-in-command were out of reach, inside a building, or just ignoring Faddei's call. Faddei put his phone away, a grim expression on his face.

"We can't wait. We need to go on," Faddei said.

Max agreed. Even so, Max was sure she wasn't the only one feeling guilty as they left the soldiers and headed back out into the dark and the rain. She wished there was more she could do, skin crawling as she thought about what the Raghavan's soldiers had endured. Kept in the dark, crowded into a single storage room with the bodies of two of their number slowly decaying in the corner. Evan and Queran needed to be stopped for that alone.

As they headed out of the shelter of the building, she realised that she, like everyone else, had picked up their pace, walking with purpose. They walked past the entrance to the next building without stopping, looking for the temple.

"We'll check the temple first," Faddei was saying as they reached the end of the building and a gust of wind threw more rain in their faces. "If it's empty, we'll come back and search here, then go on."

Whatever else he might have said was lost as a wave of familiar, cold magic slipped through the air, tucking itself under Max's collar, sending trails of ice along her skin.

"What is that?" one of the other Marshals asked.

They had all stopped, their guns and torches raised, gathering into a loose group back-to-back so that they were facing outwards, united against a potential threat.

Max had kept walking, Cas and Pol with her. She had a too-tight grip on her own gun, mouth dry. Every instinct she had was telling her to move away from the awful magic. But she knew she couldn't. Evan and Queran needed to be stopped. And if the book had been exposed, there was no time to waste.

"That's the book," Max said, setting her jaw against the awful feel of the magic on her skin. "Lord Kolbyr, is that what you expected?"

The vampire was abruptly by her side, apparently not affected by the rain or the wind, although he did look grim when she glanced across at him.

"If I had to imagine what the Arkus Codex would feel like, it's that," Kolbyr said. He returned her look, power showing in his eyes, his own aura spiralling free, sending more dark magic into the air. "You said it was in a nullification pouch?"

"Yes. Although Queran said that the pouch would not contain it for long," Max added. The rest of the Marshals had joined them, all of them looking tense. They were all, like her, far more used to dealing with creatures than with books steeped in dark magic.

"It seems not. Or they may have taken it out of the pouch," Kolbyr said. To Max's ears, he sounded more strained than eager to press forward and see the Codex for himself. "Do we have any nullification pouches?" he asked.

Max glanced at Faddei, who shook his head. "None big enough to contain the book," the head Marshal answered.

"Bryce has the one we took from the Vault," Max said, "and I'm sure that one of the intruders said they had others."

"Ah. Good," Kolbyr said. "I will prepare a spell just in case, but a pouch would be far more effective."

"The magic seems to be coming from over here," Vanko said.

Max wiped the rain off her face so she could see better. There was an old building made of large blocks of sandstone set apart from everything else in its own little space, with a ring of plants around it. It was an approximation of one of the Lady's temples, with pillars at the front and decoration around the edges of its pitched roof. It also looked completely out of place amid the square, functional buildings of the docks.

"One of the Lady's temples?" Faddei asked. He was speaking softly, almost to himself. Max understood the shock in his voice. It was one thing to believe that Queran and Evan might have brought the Arkus Codex to the docks. Quite another to learn that they had brought it into one of the Lady's Houses. It felt wrong, the sense of violation running through Max all the way to her bones. The Lady and Her dark brother were opposites. They should not exist in each other's Houses.

"The source is definitely in that building," Kolbyr said, and strode forward. Max hurried to keep up with him, Cas and Pol with her. Her dogs were in their attack forms, eyes gleaming in response to the foul magic. Shadow-hounds were more sensitive than most humans to magic, so she could only imagine how uncomfortable the sensation was for them. She wanted to crawl out of her own skin to escape it.

There was no one in sight as the Marshals followed the vampire across the gap to the entrance to the temple. There was no one standing between or behind the pillars at the entrance, which made Max more and more uneasy with every step forward, her body tense, listening for all she was worth for the slightest sound that might betray an attack. Even though she and Bryce had encountered a large number of the Syndicate in the Vault, and left a lot of dead behind them, she could not believe that was all of them. Particularly not if the Syndicate had managed to recruit from the Huntsman clan.

The feeling of icy trails of spider feet crawling across her skin was stronger now, as they moved closer to the building, and she could see a few Marshals twitching, as if trying to shed it from their skin. She didn't blame them.

She was going to suggest that they pause and form a plan, but Kolbyr was still moving, heading between the pillars towards the open doorway of the temple.

In normal circumstances, the sight of the city's most renowned expert on dark magic going into one of the Lady's temples would have been enough to stop Max in her tracks. The Lady's temples famously welcomed everyone, and yet somehow dark magic practitioners rarely found their way inside. Tonight, she just hurried to keep up with him.

The inside of the temple was shadowed, a series of highly decorated pillars surrounding the centre space, the ceiling overhead arched, flecks of paint visible here and there in the gloom. Max automatically checked for other entrances or exits and saw only one at the back of the temple, which was standard.

The only source of light was a ring of candles in the middle of the stone floor. There was no altar, and none of the Lady's magic in the space that Max could sense. If this had once been the Lady's House, it wasn't any longer. Instead, dark magic filled the air, sending more spider-web trails across her skin, chilling the air so that her breath clouded in front of her.

In the middle of the ring of candles was a heavy wooden pedestal, on top of which was a rectangular, pitch-black shape. The book Max had last seen in the Vault. There were a few people gathered in the light, their attention apparently on the book and not on the vampire and Marshals moving towards them across the temple floor. Queran, Oliver and Evan. They were all dressed in dark robes that Max recognised from the ritual in the Wild, their hoods back, leaving their heads bare.

Then she realised that they weren't standing around the book, but around a long, low bench that had been placed next to the book. There was a person lying on the bench, unmoving. Max's breath caught in her throat as she recognised him. Hemang. He, too, had managed to escape the Wild, probably alongside Evan and Queran. The remaining head of the Raghavan Family seemed uninjured, lying on his back on the bench, hands folded across his middle. He wasn't moving, though. She wondered if she was mistaken and he was, in fact, dead, and then wondered what purpose Queran and Evan could have for bringing his body here, and decided she didn't want to find out.

"Such drama," Kolbyr said, his voice carrying clearly through the space. "There's no need for all these theatrics."

The vampire had stopped just outside the circle of candles. Max flicked off her torch, putting it away, then holding her gun with both hands. She didn't like shooting people, but she would make an exception for Evan and Oliver. Queran was another matter. Bullets wouldn't work on him, and she just hoped that the Order and their Guardians would get Faddei's message and get here in time to deal with the demon.

"You're one to talk," Evan snapped back, lip curling. "Your whole life is one big performance."

Max's brows lifted. Whatever respect Evan might once have held for the vampire had clearly gone. And even though she had some sympathy with what he had said, she didn't fully agree with Evan. Kolbyr might play for his audience, but he had the substance to back up his self-assurance.

"How did you know where to find it?" Kolbyr asked. The question sounded genuine in Max's ears.

Evan seemed to think so, too, as a small smile pulled his mouth. Not a nice smile. "It pays to have relatives who liked family history," he said. "Annoyed I got there first?"

"No," Kolbyr said, the contradiction flat and unhesitating. "You have no idea what that book holds, or what it could unleash."

"Still think you know better," Evan said in response, frown gathering on his face. "Or are you afraid to face our master? I doubt He will be pleased at your interference again."

"Foolish child," Kolbyr said, his voice low and filled with a cold hatred that raised the hair on Max's neck. She had a feeling that they were seeing the true nature of the vampire just now. The sophisticated mask he wore had been stripped back to raw emotion, his aura curling out through the air. His presence was very nearly as powerful as the book's, and Max could almost trace the fault lines between Kolbyr and the Codex in the air. "You have no idea what you are doing."

"And you do? Hiding in the shadows, meddling from time to time, spending your days in study and research?" The last was said with such open contempt that Max blinked.

"Knowledge is always valuable," Kolbyr replied. He was moving, slowly, around the outside the ring of candles. "Something you would know, if you had ever bothered to acquire it."

Even as she took a step to follow Kolbyr, not sure what he was planning, Max sensed movement behind her. She glanced over her shoulder and saw the bulk of automatic weapons among the handguns held by the Marshals. For a moment, she assumed that members of the Syndicate had arrived, but then recognised the newcomers. Bryce, along with Khari, Joshua and Osvaldo. They spread out among the Marshals, weapons raised, trained on the group in the centre of the room.

Max could not help wondering where the rest of the Order's warriors were, and the Guardians, always assuming they had got Faddei's message. No one in this room right now, not even Lord Kolbyr, was equipped to deal with the Codex, Evan, Queran and Oliver all together. There was no time to ask or to worry more about that right now. She turned back to the trio in the middle of the candles, wanting to keep her attention focused on the threat.

Evan didn't seem to have noticed the warriors, but Queran had. He made a gesture to Oliver, and Max felt more magic stirring and gathering in the air. Without the Guardians, neither the Marshals nor the warriors had any protection against dark magic.

"So, what's your plan?" Max asked, cutting through whatever power struggle was going on between Evan and Kolbyr, trying to draw attention and halt whatever Queran and Oliver were up to, or at least buy some time. "Use the book to open another portal? Summon Arkus to this realm? Haven't you already tried, and failed, to do that?"

"Marshal Ortis," Evan said, lip curling in a sneer. "And I see you've brought friends as well." He had noticed the warriors, Max realised. He just didn't see them as a threat.

"You are in violation of at least a dozen city laws," Faddei said, his voice firm and calm despite the circumstances. He had stayed with the group of Marshals and warriors, gathered between a pair of pillars a few paces away from the candles. "Surrender now, and your cooperation will be taken into account."

Evan laughed. "Are you really trying to arrest me? Your laws don't apply to me, you idiot. I'm one of His heirs."

"This is not the dark lord's realm," Faddei answered. "This is the daylight world."

"Not for long," Evan said. He turned and reached for the book. He was wearing gloves again, Max saw. Heavy duty fabric that covered not just his hands but his forearms as well. Perhaps he was not quite as confident in his heritage as he was pretending.

As he reached for the book, a single shot rang out from somewhere among the Marshals and warriors. Evan spun back, hand going to his shoulder, and stumbled into the candles. Flames licked up the hem of his robes.

There was more movement in the shadows of the temple, from the exit at the back. Armed men and women wearing black. All of them with their weapons raised. The Syndicate had arrived. And Max had been right in her suspicions - there were a lot more of them than she and Bryce had encountered in the Vault.

"Retreat to the doors!" Faddei ordered, and took his own advice, backing away.

Max ducked behind the nearest pillar, not wanting to leave Kolbyr on his own, or leave while Evan was distracted. She wasn't sure what she could do, but something needed to be done.

Gunfire rattled through the old stone building and she huddled down behind her pillar. The Syndicate had spread out, splitting up to go around the centre of the room, she realised. Not wanting to accidentally shoot Evan, Queran or Oliver, she guessed. Or maybe showing some semblance of common sense and not wanting to get any closer to the Codex than they had to.

Evan was muttering curses under his breath as he swatted at the hems of his robes, trying to put out the flames. He had been clumsy in the robes the last time he had worn them, too, Max remembered.

She was moving before she knew what she was planning, charging forward, using her momentum and body weight to knock Evan out of the circle. As she passed over the ring of candles, searing heat flashed through her, making her cry out in pain. Then she was across the edge of the circle, Evan in her grasp, both of them hitting the ground with a thump that jarred her from head to toe. He kicked out at her, landing a blow in her midriff that sent all the air out of her and had her sliding back across the floor. He was far more powerful than any human.

She had kept hold of her gun, and scrambled to her knees, raising it and aiming at him. His robes were still smouldering around him, although the fire seemed to be out. He grinned and raised a hand, making an apparently careless gesture.

Magic slammed into her, flinging her all the way into the temple wall, her skull cracking on the stone before she slid down to the ground. She was seeing double, her ears ringing, the taste of blood in her mouth. She struggled to get her feet under her, using the wall to support her as she got up, gun still in her hand. Except she wasn't sure which one of the Evans in front of her she should be shooting at.

Low, vicious snarls in front of her alerted her to Cas and Pol, setting themselves between her and Evan. She wanted to protest. Even her formidable hounds were no match for a descendant of Arkus. But she wasn't sure which of the four shadow-hounds she should be giving the orders to.

She shook her head, hoping to clear her sight, but it only made things worse as she now had multiple versions of the scene in front of her. She was dimly aware of gunfire and shouting in the temple. Impossible to tell who might be winning that fight.

Ice-cold magic slammed into her, pinning her back against the wall, wrapping around her throat, cutting off her air. The blackest of dark magic, it sapped energy and life from her body. There was no point in fighting. Arkus and His followers were too strong. They would break Him free of the underworld and He would reign in this world. There was nothing she could do. Nothing anyone could do. She might as well just give in. After all, she had never been worth much. And nothing had changed.

She sagged against the wall, held up by the dark magic around her throat, and felt hot tears on her face. She didn't need anyone else telling her she was worthless. She had spent much of her childhood listening to that. She had even believed it from time to time.

And then the High Priestess had told her that she was favoured by the Lady.

In the despair, a tiny, white-hot spark of pure anger lit inside her. For years, she had done what was asked of her. She had studied, and done her best to learn the lessons that were being taught to her. And the reward for her hard work was being given an impossible task. Which she had done. She had closed the Grey Gates. Her. On her own. No one else had helped. And her reward for that was to be dismissed, to be called a liar.

The white fire of fury grew. She was not worthless. She was not a liar. She had survived the Grey Gates. She had her own life. And she could use magic. Maybe not in the way Kitris had wanted her to. But that wasn't the only way. He didn't know everything.

Light filled her, pushing aside the dark depression, loosening the grip on her neck so she could breathe again. She slumped against the wall, using it to hold herself upright, sucking in great, heaving gasps of air.

There was only one Evan now. And a pair of shadow-hounds steadfastly guarding her, facing him.

She raised her gun, light coursing along her skin, along the surface of her gun.

"You should not be able to do that," Evan said, white around his face. "What are you?" The echo of Queran's question rang around her head. This time, she had an answer.

"I am Max," she answered, and shot him.

A blur passed between them before her bullet hit home, another body tearing Evan out of the way so that Max's light-coated bullet soared through the empty space across the line of candles and into Oliver Forster's chest as he stood, hands raised in some spell or other.

Oliver stumbled, falling to his knees, shocked expression on his face as if he could not comprehend what had just happened. As if being shot in a room full of armed people was something quite unbelievable. He put a hand to his chest, staring at the blood on his palm, and then slumped forward, across Hemang's too-still body.

Max had no more time for Oliver. Evan had been pulled out of the way by Queran, the demon glaring back at Max as he stood beside his master.

"She's not human," Evan hissed.

"Don't be ridiculous," Max said. She was tempted to fire at him again. There were still trails of vivid white light across her skin and the gun. But Queran could apparently move faster than a bullet, and the Marshals and warriors were behind him. If she missed Evan, she might hit a friend.

"No, he's right," Queran said, lips peeling back from his teeth. "Imagine. All these years I thought you were nothing more than an irritating assignment. A punishment. Boring, boring, boring."

"What are you talking about?" Max asked.

"She doesn't know," Queran said to Evan, sounding delighted. Max was quite sure that anything that Queran was pleased about was a very bad thing.

"What?" she demanded.

"We've got work to do," Evan told Queran.

"As you say," Queran agreed, inclining his head in what looked like a gesture of respect. Max's eyes narrowed. Even though the demon had saved the supposed human, she had a strong sense that it had not been out of care or affection. No, it had been because it was to Queran's advantage to keep Evan alive. And Max couldn't figure out why. Not yet, at least.

"Make sure we are not interrupted," Evan ordered Queran, and turned away from Max, heading for the centre of the room.

Queran gathered power, the currents of magic shifting against Max's skin. She tried to move position so she could get a clear shot at him, without endangering anyone else, but her legs weren't working properly and she stumbled, having to hold herself up against the wall. Cas and Pol stuck with her, both of them growling.

Magic sped away from Queran, heading for the front of the building. Not to kill, as Max had feared. Instead, the demon used his magic to pull stones out of the floor and thrust them into the opening, blocking the doorway. All the Marshals were out there, Max realised. All but her. Along with the warriors.

She was alone. Locked in the temple with an ancient and powerful vampire, the Syndicate, Evan, Oliver and Queran for company. The Syndicate members turned towards her, weapons raised. She had no defence against bullets. None. Once they started firing, she and her dogs would be dead in moments. Still, she didn't need to just accept that. She braced her back against the wall, raising her gun. She would take out as many of them as possible.

Before she could fire, rapid automatic gunfire sounded from behind one of the pillars. The Syndicate members began falling. Max almost sobbed in relief. She wasn't alone. Someone else was here with her. On her side.

She forced her body to move, away from the open space on the wall, towards the nearest pillar. It would provide some protection, at least. As she stumbled her way across the floor, her body still not working properly, she saw who was firing. Bryce. Relief made her light-headed for a heartbeat, a spark of warmth blooming in her chest. Of course it was him. He hadn't left with the others.

She leant against the thick stone pillar and breathed. Pain radiated across her back from where she had hit the wall and, although her sight had cleared, there were sharp lines of pain across her skull. She probably needed medical attention, she realised dimly. There was no time for that now. She scrabbled in a pocket and found a painkiller patch, slapping it on the exposed skin of her neck. It helped a bit, the magic stinging as it went to work.

Bryce's gun fell silent. Max looked around. Each one of the Syndicate members was dead or dying on the ground.

"Do you think there are more?" Max asked, words ringing oddly in her skull.

"I'm sure of it," Bryce said. He switched the magazine on his gun and sent her a sharp look. "Are you alright?"

"I don't think so, but there's no time to stop," Max said. She peered around the pillar. Evan was back in the middle of the circle, his robes still smouldering at the ends where they had caught fire. Queran was standing watch nearby, his eyes unerringly meeting Max's across the short distance. He was keeping an eye on her, Max realised. He thought she might cause problems. She almost laughed. Despite the painkiller, she ached from head to toe and wasn't sure she could walk more than a few steps without falling. The idea that she might cause a demon or part-demon problems was ridiculous.

But there was someone else here who might. Kolbyr. She looked around the space, trying to work out where the dark magic master had got to, and saw him standing in the shelter of the pillar next to hers. He was staring into the circle, his eyes seemingly fixed on the Codex.

"Can you nullify it?" Max asked.

"I've tried," Kolbyr answered simply. "There's magic built into the circle that's interfering with my spells."

"Can you get closer?" Max asked. It seemed the next logical step.

He wasn't looking at her, but she saw his expression change and saw the stiffness of his body. He didn't want to move, she realised. He wasn't sure he could actually get across the circle and nullify the Codex.

Max looked down at the gun she held in her hand, and the sparks of light still cascading over her skin and the metal weapon. She was fairly certain that if Kolbyr didn't think he would succeed, her efforts weren't likely to help, either. But she had to try. Evan was opening the Codex with his gloved hands and the stench of putrid rot and smoke spilled out of the book into the air, the rush of it causing the candles to dance.

She knew that smoke. The grey, formless smoke that seemed to get everywhere in the underworld. It hid creatures of magic and rage that she had no name for and the sight of it made her want to turn and run. Run and run and run. She could still feel the tears of the creatures at her skin, trying to drag her down into the smoke.

A sob lodged in her throat and she turned it into a cough. This was not the underworld. This was the daylight world. Arkus did not rule here. And if she had her way, He never would.

Max waved for her dogs to stand back and took a step away from the pillar, lifting her gun. She started firing into the circle.

Queran had done something to the magic, though. Her bullets slowed as they reached the candles, until they were barely moving at all when they reached the edge of the circle. Nearby, Bryce fired as well, his bullets meeting the same fate.

Max spat a curse, reloaded her gun and took a shaky step forward. The fury was gathering inside her again, white hot and powerful, light cascading over her skin.

She reached the circle of candles and took a step over them. The heat seared her skin. Along with the grey smoke it was an echo of the underworld and the horrors within it. She paused, wanting to pull back, wanting to run away. Let someone else deal with the dark magic for once. But there wasn't anyone else. The only other person who might have been able to deal with Evan was still standing by the pillar, his eyes intent as he watched her.

Pain rang through her, and she couldn't help but cry out as she pushed through the ring of candles, surprised that she didn't immediately catch fire.

Oliver stared at her in astonishment. He was sitting on the floor next to the bench with Hemang on it, a hand pressed to the wound in his chest. She must have missed his heart. But then, she hadn't actually been trying to kill him.

"You-" he said, pink froth at his mouth.

"Aren't you just full of surprises?" Queran asked. He was moving across the circle to her, a hard expression on his face.

Max lifted her gun and fired. Inside the circle, her bullets worked normally, at least half a dozen of them thudding into Queran's torso. He stopped, expression changing to one of astonishment to equal Oliver's. He stared down at his chest and then looked back up at her. "You-" he began, then grimaced, pulling on the robe hard enough to tear the fabric. He shrugged out of the cloth and threw it to one side, revealing his normal business suit. Except there were holes in this one, and a bloom of red on his torso where Max's bullets had struck home. He put a hand over the wound and turned it over, staring at his bloodied palm in astonishment. "You should not be able to do that," Queran said, tilting his head down to look at the blood seeping out of his clothing.

"Oh, really?" Max asked, holding her gun with both hands. The bright white hot fury was still burning in her, cascading over her skin and the metal of her weapon. She had hurt him. Finally. She fired again. The demon staggered back, reaching out on instinct to stop himself from falling. His blood-covered hand landed on the open pages of the Codex and he screamed. A cascade of light emerged from him, travelling over the Codex.

Evan, standing by the book, yelled in outrage as Queran's blood smeared the pages, the demon falling heavily to the ground beside the pedestal. He reached out and tried to wipe the blood away with his gloved hand.

"Now look what you've done. Idiot," Evan muttered.

"Stop what you're doing," Max ordered. "Close the book and step away. Now."

Evan turned to her, face tight with anger. "You've lived long enough," he said, and raised his hand, dark magic gathered in his palm. He threw the magic at her.

She didn't have time to duck, firing back at him instead, seeing and hearing her light-covered bullets hitting home.

Then the dark magic struck her like a wall falling on her. She crumpled to the ground, overrun by darkness, hearing and feeling something snap in her wrist as she fell, badly. Everything was black around her. The faint sparks of light across her skin gone. As she transferred her gun to her other hand, she realised that it wasn't just the dark magic. She couldn't see a thing. She was blind. Panic closed her throat. She couldn't see where her enemies were. Her hearing stayed sharp, though, and she heard low grunts of what sounded like pain. Her bullets had hurt Evan. Good.

She was still surrounded by dark magic, crawling over her skin, but outside that she could sense more magic gathering. Clean, familiar magic. Then Queran's voice: "I can sense Guardians. We need to go. Now." Queran was still alive. She had hurt him, but not enough.

"The book," Evan said, protesting.

"Leave it. You're injured. We can retrieve it another time." Queran's voice was sharp, commanding. More dark magic surged overhead. Queran's magic. Max held up her gun, but didn't fire, not sure where to aim. Worried about hitting a friend, she didn't pull the trigger, trying to track Evan and Queran by sound, hearing nothing.

The sensation of Queran's magic faded, leaving her aching and alone and sightless.

Chapter Twenty-Four

Rapid footsteps sounded on stone, along with more gunfire. Bryce, if Max had to guess. She wasn't alone, she remembered. There was Bryce. And Kolbyr. Somewhere. She blinked, shaking her head, trying to clear her sight. The absolute black had gone, but everything was shades of grey and odd shapes.

Nearby, she could sense magic stirring. Unclean and twisted, it scraped against her skin. The Codex. It felt far more active than it had been. Before Queran smeared blood over its pages.

"Bryce, do you have the nullification pouch from the Vault?" she asked.

"Yes," he said. He was far closer than she realised. Right next to her, in fact.

"How did you get through the candles?" Max asked, astonished. Even with the foul magic of the Codex next to her, she could still sense the ring of power that the candles were marking out.

"It was uncomfortable," he conceded. She heard the sound of cloth against cloth and then felt the bliss of the dark magic disappearing from her senses. She tried to sit up, relief washing over her, her body protesting the effort. She reached out for some support, her hand landing on the smooth wooden surface that must be the pedestal holding the book. She shifted over, biting back a cry of pain, and put her back against the pedestal. She couldn't sense the book at all now. Her face was wet with tears of combined relief and pain. Now that the fight was over, all the hits she had taken were making themselves felt across her body. And she still couldn't see a thing.

"It's done," she said, relief making her voice high and shaky. "The Codex is contained. We stopped Evan and Queran." She wasn't sure she quite believed it. Not yet.

"Well done, indeed." Kolbyr's voice was too close as well. "I've cancelled out the protective circle," he added, and Max realised that she could no longer sense any magic, not even Kolbyr's. "Are you blind, my dear?" he asked.

"Mostly, yes," Max said. The grey shapes were gradually forming into more solid objects.

There was a rush of movement, two large, blurred forms approaching her. Even without her sight, she had no difficulty in recognising Cas and Pol. Her dogs settled to either side of her, very careful not to lean against her, as if they could sense just how much she hurt. She wished she could see them or move to pet them, but just sitting still and breathing was taking most of her energy.

"Using too much magic will do that. Your sight should return soon," Kolbyr said. Without being able to see his face, Max couldn't be sure, but he sounded back to his normal self.

"I didn't think I used that much," Max said, fumbling to put away her gun. The wrist of her dominant hand was full of heat and pain. She remembered the snap she had heard and felt and could only hope it was something that could be repaired. She needed that hand for work.

"How remarkable," Kolbyr said. He was still too close. It sounded as if he was right in front of her, perhaps kneeling. She wished she could see him. It made her uncomfortable to have him so close, to not be able to see his expression. She didn't understand what he meant, and without being able to see him, didn't want to ask him about it.

"Evan and Queran got away," she said, changing the subject.

"For now, yes," Kolbyr said, "but that pair won't be able to stay hidden for long."

A muffled explosion sounded, making her jump and bite back a cry as pain stabbed across her rib cage and spiked in her head. Clean magic poured into the space along with the sounds of footsteps. Many footsteps.

"Oh, good, the Guardians and their warriors have arrived to save the day," Kolbyr murmured, his voice pitched low to carry to her ears alone. She choked on an unexpected laugh at the sarcastic bite to his words, then had to gasp as more pain gripped her. The painkiller patch had definitely worn off.

"Where's the book?" The voice, loud and demanding, sounded like Kitris.

"It's here, sir." Bryce answered from somewhere close to Max. "In a nullification pouch."

"Is that Oliver Forster?" Kitris asked, his voice coming closer. "Is he dead?"

"I think so," Bryce said. "Marshal Ortis shot him."

"I was aiming for Evan, but Queran pulled him out of the way," Max added, feeling that was important. And having a vague idea that she might get into trouble if the people around her had thought she had deliberately shot one of the city's most prominent and powerful magicians.

"And I see Hemang Raghavan, too," Faddei said. "Also dead. What's he doing here?"

"I speculate that he was there for whatever ritual the demon and descendant had planned," Kolbyr said, his voice sounding unnaturally calm. Max didn't trust that calmness. Not one bit.

"Do you know what the ritual was?" Faddei asked. It seemed he didn't trust the vampire, either.

"I did not get a look at the open pages before the Codex was closed," Kolbyr answered.

That wasn't an answer, Max knew, but she couldn't seem to formulate an appropriate question for the vampire. While she was still trying to put words together, a solid grey shape came closer to her and she could almost make out Faddei's familiar face.

"Max, are you alright?" he asked.

"A bit sore. Can't see very well right now," Max admitted, all at once feeling vulnerable and small. "Might need some medical attention." The only time she had been in more pain than this had been when she was in the underworld, through the Grey Gates. There, she had screamed until her voice was gone. Now, she did her best to keep her breathing shallow and maintain awareness of what was going on around her.

"It's on the way," Faddei said. "Evan and Queran?" he asked.

"Got away," Max said, hearing her own frustration as clearly as she felt it. "I shot both of them. Evan was injured, I think." She wasn't sure about Queran. He had seemed hurt, but he had still managed to get Evan out of the building.

"Well done," Faddei said. "That should slow him down a bit. Is that the Codex?" he asked, his voice moving away. Max tracked his shape as he got to his feet and took a step sideways. As she was propped up against the pedestal the book was sitting on, he didn't have to move far to get a better look. He was still within reach. Still between her and Kitris, which she appreciated. And Cas and Pol were still on either side of her. She might not be able to see their expressions, but she knew her dogs would be watching everything that was going on, ready to react if she was threatened. She wished she had the strength to pat them, and mentally promised them plenty of treats when she was healed enough.

"It is," Kolbyr confirmed. "Be very careful with it. The warrior Bryce managed to get it into the nullification pouch, but there's blood on it."

"We know how to handle dangerous magic," Kitris said, the sneer in his voice evident. Max's brows lifted at the tone. For someone who hadn't believed that the Codex even existed, he was being very dismissive of the one person in the city who might be able to help him understand what he had.

"I'm sure you do," Kolbyr murmured. It was hard to tell, but she thought he was being sarcastic again.

"It's Queran's blood," Max said, thinking that was important. Not just human blood, but demon blood.

"That's good to know. I can feel another nullification spell in place, as well as the pouch. Yours, Lord Kolbyr?" Orshiasa asked, his tone far more polite than Kitris' had been.

"Indeed. I had one prepared and it seemed prudent," Kolbyr answered.

"It is fine work. The Codex is contained for the moment," Orshiasa said. He sounded calm, as level-headed as normal, and Max felt her shoulders relaxing in response. Kitris might snap and snarl at everyone around him, but Orshiasa would know what needed to be done.

"We'll take it from here," Kitris said, and the tension came back to Max's shoulders. She still couldn't see properly, so couldn't be sure who he was speaking to, but she suspected he was directing his words at the Marshals. Trying to assert his authority and take charge. Which was ridiculous. He was the head of the Order. Dark magic was his jurisdiction. There was no need for the aggression she could hear in his voice.

"What, exactly, does that mean?" Faddei asked.

Her sight cleared enough to see a little further. Faddei was standing a couple of paces away, facing Kitris. She couldn't make out the detail of their expressions, but they both looked tense.

"It means we'll deal with this. Get your people out," Kitris said.

"I'm not moving Max until she's been seen by one of the paramedics," Faddei said, his voice fading as he turned away. "And here they are," he said. Max heard the relief in his voice and wondered just how bad she looked.

Her sight had cleared enough that she could see the bright uniforms of the medical team approaching, their forms misshapen with the large packs they carried, a stretcher between them. She tried to sit up, to protest that she didn't need a stretcher, and the world slipped sideways, the little bit of vision she had recovered sliding into black and she slumped on the floor, losing consciousness.

Chapter Twenty-Five

Max woke to a now-familiar sound of beeping machines and the smell of hospital. She wrinkled her nose in disgust. This was getting to be something of a habit. She opened her eyes and found, to her relief, that she could see. The walls were a muted shade of blue, the window showing a dull grey sky outside, and there was a dark-clad figure sitting in a chair nearby. He met her eyes as she looked across at him and smiled. Half-awake, she found herself remembering their all-too-brief kiss in the Vault, wondering when they might get a chance to repeat it.

"I'm glad to see you awake," Bryce said. The ordinary words cut across her memories and she blushed.

Before she could answer, two shadows moved from the floor and came to the side of her bed, ears lifted and dark eyes staring at her. "Cas, Pol," she said, and lifted a hand, giving them each a pat in turn. "I'm surprised you're on the floor," she added. The last time she had woken up in a hospital bed, they had been in the bed with her.

"They weren't on the floor when I came in," Bryce said, "but I asked them to get down. It didn't look comfortable."

Max blinked, startled. "They don't normally listen to other people. Unless there's food involved," she added. "Oh, and thank you," she said belatedly, heat rising in her face. He had cared enough to get the dogs off her bed. And he was right. It wasn't comfortable sharing a bed with the hounds, particularly not a hospital bed designed for just one person. She moved her hand away from her dogs and tried to sit up, muttering a curse as her other wrist pinged with pain. She fell back on the pillows and lifted her arm, looking at the honeycomb lattice that covered her arm from her elbow to her knuckles.

"Apparently, your wrist was broken in three places. You Marshals really do have good healthcare. The healing magician was here most of yesterday. The bones are back together, but need some more time to heal fully," Bryce told her.

"Thank you," she said again, blinking in surprise. He seemed to have been paying close attention to her treatment. "Any other updates?"

"You had several cracked ribs and a concussion. The healing magician took care of those, too, but said you'll still be sore and have bruises for a while. You've been unconscious for about three days," Bryce said.

"Oh. Alright. Anything else?" Max asked. Now that Bryce had mentioned it, she could feel the various bruises across her body. Injuries too minor for the magician's attention, she assumed. She was used to bruises and soreness, though. The really dangerous pain had gone, and that was the main thing.

His mouth twitched in a smile. "Are you sure you want to know?"

"Yes," she said, without hesitation. She found the button that would lift the back of the bed and pressed it. It felt much better to be sitting up and able to look at him without twisting her neck. Cas and Pol were still next to her and she stroked their ears. First she had disappeared for two days, and then she had been injured badly enough to need a hospital stay. It had not been a good week for her hounds.

"Kitris is claiming that the Order stopped whatever was happening at the docks," Bryce said, the humour fading. He shook his head.

"Of course he is," Max said. Whatever the medical staff and magician had done to her in the three days she'd been here, her mind was surprisingly sharp and she had no difficulty in picturing Kitris saying exactly what Bryce had reported. "Doubtless he's also saying that he led the charge. Did he perhaps rescue some kittens while he was there, too?"

Bryce laughed. It was a rich, warm sound and Max liked it. Then he sobered. "Don't you care?"

"About him taking credit? Not really."

"But you were there. You saved us," Bryce said, frowning.

"Did I?" Max asked, nose wrinkling. "I'm not sure anyone was saved. Evan and Queran are still out there. And they will try something again, as long as they are alive."

"A lot of people are alive because you stopped them. Even just for now."

"And I'm alive because you were there," Max said softly. She closed her eyes for a moment, remembering the shadowed temple, the cold sensation of dark magic on her skin, the sounds of gunfire in her ears, filling the space. It had been Bryce, her dogs and her. Oh, and one powerful vampire. "What about Kolbyr?" she asked, opening her eyes.

"He sent you roses," Bryce said, tilting his head to a vase near her bed. "He was surprisingly calm when Kitris took the Codex away from him."

"Yes," Max said, eyes lingering on the roses. Now that Bryce had drawn her attention to them, she could smell the heady, decadent scent through the room over the chemical smells. "For a dark magic expert, he's not that keen on the dark lord getting out of His realm," she commented.

"I noticed," Bryce said, mouth twitching.

There was another flower arrangement next to the roses. This one was full of white, elegant flowers that Max had no name for.

"Those came from the temple," Bryce said. He got up, moving to the flowers and picked up two small envelopes from the flat surface, bringing them across to Max. "No one has read the cards, but there's a lot of curiosity," he told her, unexpected mischief in his face. He handed her the cards and went back to his seat.

Forced to work one-handed, Max fumbled with opening the first envelope, recognising the heavy paper and bold lettering from the first flowers Kolbyr had sent her.

When you find the watcher again, call me. I have a score to settle. K.

Max read the message twice, trying to find a hidden meaning to it, but she couldn't see one. She set that aside and opened the second envelope. There was another, equally short, note in lighter handwriting.

Your place is with the Order. I have told Kitris to expect you.

There was no signature, but Max didn't need one. The High Priestess was once more trying to interfere in her life and tell her what to do and where to go. Max tucked the card back into the envelope and looked across the room at Bryce. When she had first woken up, she had assumed that he was off duty, although she had been surprised to see him here. But now she wondered. Would Kitris have sent him to bring her back to the Order?

He met her eyes across the room and she remembered seeing the little sparks of brilliance in them before, even if she couldn't remember right now exactly what colour they were. His expression softened to one she'd never seen on his face before.

"I'm glad you're going to be alright," he said, voice low and warm.

Heat rose up her face and all thoughts of trying to ask him if Kitris had sent him here faded into nothing. "I'm glad I'm going to be alright, too," she said. "You still owe me a drink."

"I do," he agreed, a smile crinkling the corners of his eyes. She had not seen him smile enough, she realised.

Before she could ask him anything else, the door opened and Faddei came into the room. He grinned when he saw Max awake, and nodded a greeting to Bryce.

"About time you woke up," Faddei said, and put a hand on her shoulder.

"It's good to see you, too," Max answered. "Although I hope it's a very long time before I'm back here."

"Me, too," Faddei said cheerfully. He took a seat on the other chair in the room, next to Bryce. "I've just been to see Ellie. She's in the room about two doors down."

"How is she?" Max asked at once.

"Itching to get out of here," Faddei said, the easy tone and smile reassuring Max more than his words did. "She's making a very good recovery and should be back on duty in a few weeks."

"That's good to know," Max said, relief coursing through her. She did not envy Ellie Randall's superior officers trying to keep the formidable woman away from her job, but she hoped Ellie would listen to the medical advice. As Max had learned - the hard way - when medical professionals told you to rest, you should listen to them.

"So, what do you remember?" Faddei asked.

"Most of it, I think. Up until I passed out," Max said, wrinkling her nose again. That was also getting to be a bad habit.

"We didn't realise how badly injured you were until the paramedics got there," Faddei said, serious for a moment. "It's a good thing they were already on site for the Raghavan soldiers."

"How are they?" Max asked.

"All the ones we found alive are still alive," Faddei said. "It turns out their captain is next in line as head of the Raghavan Family. I'm not sure who was more surprised when he was told about it."

"At least he won't be performing any dark magic rituals down at the docks," Max commented. She might have met the man at the wrong end of a gun, but she had formed a good impression of him overall. He certainly didn't seem as self-centred or careless of others as the twins had been.

"No. He's invited the Order in to make sure there are no more spells or hidden magic traps," Faddei said, and glanced at Bryce, mischief in his face. "I'm not sure how Kitris feels at being relegated to a janitor."

Bryce grinned. "I'm sure he's about as pleased as you think he is," the warrior said, surprising Max. He was loyal to his core, and although he might not have much love for Kitris, she had not expected him to speak so openly against him. "I haven't seen him for a couple of days." Bryce sobered, and sighed. "He seems to think I should have somehow got hold of the Codex myself and brought it back to the Order without the need for all the trouble."

Faddei's brows lifted. "And did he also think you should fight your way past Lord Kolbyr to get the Codex?"

"Almost certainly," Bryce said, that glimmer of mischief back.

"I think if you'd asked nicely, Kolbyr might have given you the Codex," Max said. "Although, he'd want to know where it was going to be stored."

Bryce and Faddei exchanged glances. Max's attention sharpened. "What?" she asked.

"Kitris is refusing to discuss the Codex with anyone, and won't even confirm to the council that it exists," Faddei said. He looked tired, Max realised. "He's now refusing to answer the council's messages, or speak to them."

"What is going on with him?" Max asked, more forcefully than she had intended.

"I can't be sure," Bryce said. "I've been given a few days off," he explained. Which explained his lack of obvious weaponry, Max thought, but not what he was doing spending his time off here, in her hospital room. "But I've heard from a few of the other warriors. There have been rumours around the Order of Portents surfacing. None of the Guardians will confirm it, but it's being widely gossiped about."

Max drew in a sharp breath. Portents were bad news. They were the evidence in the daylight world of the dark lord making an effort to escape from the underworld. What the Portents actually were, and how many were needed to be worrying, were closely guarded secrets known only to the Guardians and Kitris. But if there were Portents in the world, then that would explain some of Kitris' behaviour. Max didn't think it explained everything. Not in the least. Kitris had lived through previous Portents and attempts to open the Grey Gates. He had never shied away from the Order's duties before.

"And Hemang Raghavan and Oliver Forster's bodies have disappeared from the city mortuary," Faddei said.

"What?" Max asked, astonished. "I bet Audhilde is furious."

"Last I heard, she had summoned every single person who had ever even walked past the mortuary in the past week, let alone worked inside it, and was subjecting them to some powerful interrogations," Faddei said. He was perfectly serious. "She hasn't been able to explain what happened yet, but I think it's only a matter of time."

Despite the light blankets covering her and the temperature of the room - which she could see on the wall thermometer - Max felt cold wash over her. Evan Yarwood had somehow gathered together highly skilled people into the Syndicate in less time than it took the city council to decide on new furniture for their meeting room. He might have been defeated for now, but she was confident that she hadn't seen the last of Evan or Queran. The Huntsman clan had been killing people across the city. The Order was preoccupied with Portents. Bodies had disappeared from the city morgue. One of the most powerful dark magic users in the city had sent her flowers again. And the High Priestess was trying to summon her back to the Order.

All told, it was enough to make her want to huddle down, pull the blankets over her head and stay there. Let someone else fight it out. She wanted no part of the politics or the power plays.

Cas put his head over the side of the bed, dark eyes soft as he looked at her. Pol joined him. She stroked her good hand across her dogs' heads and ears, feeling their warmth and the silky soft fur under her fingers. If she did try to hide, Cas and Pol would follow her. She knew that. But they had never turned from a fight in their lives. And she knew, even as the temptation settled in her mind, that she was not going to hide. This was her city. Her home. As well as her dogs, there were people here she cared about. And people who didn't deserve to get caught up in whatever awful scheme Evan and Queran had in mind.

And she was not powerless. She might not be able to wield magic the way that the Order had taught her, but she had called light magic more than once and could feel the hot spark of it burning inside her even now. It was a good weapon against the dark.

So she could not hide. She wouldn't. She lifted her chin and looked across the room to Faddei and Bryce. Two very different men, with very different places in her life. But she trusted them both.

"We need to track down Evan and Queran. Any idea where we start?" she asked them.

THANK YOU

Thank you very much for reading *Hunted*, The Grey Gates - Book 3. I hope that you've enjoyed continuing Max's story and learning a bit more about the world of The Grey Gates.

It would be great, if you have five minutes, if you could leave an honest review at the store you got it from. Reviews are really helpful for other readers to decide whether the book is for them, and also help me get visibility for my books - thank you.

Max's story will continue in *Forged*, The Grey Gates - Book 4, which I expect to be released in early October 2023. It's currently available to pre-order at Amazon.

Meantime, if you want to be kept up to date with what I'm working on, and get exclusive bonus content, you can sign up for my newsletter at the website: www.taellaneth.com.

CHARACTER LIST

(Note: to avoid spoilers, some names may have been missed, and some details changed)

Alexey T'Or Radrean - human, male, twin to Sandrine and apprentice to Radrean
Alonso Ortis - human, male, married to Elicia
Arkus - dark lord, lord of the underworld
Audhilde (Hilda) - vampire, medical examiner
Aurora - human, female, shadow-hound trainer and handler, married to Ben
Ben - human, male, shadow-hound trainer and handler, married to Aurora
Bethell - lady of light
Bryce - partly human, male, one of the warriors of the Order
Cas - one of Max's dogs
Cira Caballero - female, Armourer at the Vault
Connor Declan Walsh - human, male, head of one of the city's most powerful families
Constance Farmer (deceased) - female magician who owned a Vault
Damayanti Raghavan (deceased) - human, female, matriarch of Raghavan Family
David Prosser - human, male, councilman for one of the city districts

Ellie Randall - human, female, senior police officer in the city
Elicia Ortis - human, female, married to Alonso
Evan Yarwood - human, male, chief of detectives in the city
Faddei Lobanov - human, male, head of Marshal's service
Forster - family name of one of the powerful families in the city
Gemma - human, female, one of the warriors of the Order
Glenda Martins - human, female, nurse at the city clinic the Marshals use
Grandma Parras - human, female, Leonda's grandmother
Grayson Forster - human, male, owns the Sorcerer's Mistress, member of Forster family
Harvey James - human, male, deputy chief of police
Hemang Raghavan - human, male, Shivangi's brother
Hop - partly human, male, one of the warriors of the Order
Huntsman clan - one of the Five Families
Inigo Fernandez - male, one of the Vault Wardens
Ivor Costen - male, member of Huntsman clan
Joshua - male, one of the warriors of the Order, married to Khari
Killan - partly human, male, one of the warriors of the Order
Kitris - male, magician, head of the Order of the Lady of the Light
Khari - female, one of the warriors of the Order, married to Joshua
Kolbyr - vampire, male, master of dark magic
Leonda Parras - human, female, chief armourer for the Marshals
Lukas - vampire, male, part of Audhilde's household
Malik - male, owns the Hunter's Tooth
Max Ortis - female, Marshal
Nati - human, female, Elicia and Alonso's daughter
Nico - human, male, magic user
Noah Willard - human, male, police sergeant
Oliver Forster - male, magician, member of the Forster Family
Orshiasa - human, male, Guardian in the Order
Osip Smolar - human, male, Marshal
Osvaldo Martinez - male, one of the warriors of the Order
Pavla Bilak - human, female, one of the Marshals, married to Yevhen

Pol - one of Max's dogs

Queran - outwardly a human male

Radrean - human, male, Guardian in the Order

Raymund Robart - human, male, lead researcher and scientist for the Marshals

Ruutti Passila - female, detective

Sandrine T'Or Radrean - human, female, Alexey's twin and apprentice to Radrean

Sean Williams - human, male, police Sergeant

Shivangi Raghavan - human, female, Hemang's sister

Simmons - human, male, member of police specialist unit

Sirius - human, male, shadow-hound handler

Sofiya Pavelko - human, female, Marshal

Therese - human, female, dispatcher for the Marshals' service

Vanko Tokar - human, male, one of the Marshals

Walsh - family name of one of the powerful families in the city

Yevhen Bilak - human, male, one of the Marshals, married to Pavla

Ynes - human, female, Nati's daughter, Alonso and Elicia's granddaughter

Zoya Lipka - human, female, one of the Marshals

ALSO BY THE AUTHOR

(as at February 2024)

The Grey Gates (complete)
Outcast, Book 1
Called, Book 2
Hunted, Book 3
Forged, Book 4
Chosen, Book 5

Fractured Conclave
A Usual Suspect, Book 1 – expected to release early May 2024

Ageless Mysteries (complete)
Deadly Night, Book 1
False Dawn, Book 2
Morning Trap, Book 3
Assassin's Noon, Book 4
Flightless Afternoon, Book 5
Ascension Day, Book 6

The Hundred series (complete)
The Gathering, Book 1
The Sundering, Book 2

The Reckoning, Book 3
The Rending, Book 4
The Searching, Book 5
The Rising, Book 6

The Taellaneth series (complete)
Concealed, Book 1
Revealed, Book 2
Betrayed, Book 3
Tainted, Book 4
Cloaked, Book 5

Taellaneth Box Set (all five books in one e-book)
Taellaneth Complete Series (Books 1–5)

ABOUT THE AUTHOR

Vanessa Nelson is a fantasy author who lives in Scotland, United Kingdom and spends her days juggling the demands of two spoiled cats, two giant dogs and her fictional characters.

As far as the cats are concerned, they should always come first. The older dog lets her know when he isn't getting enough attention by chewing up the house. The younger dog's favourite method of getting her attention is a gentle nudge with his head. At least, he would say it's gentle.

You can find out more information online at the following places:

Website: www.taellaneth.com

Facebook: www.facebook.com/taellaneth

Printed in Great Britain
by Amazon